T.

South Lanarkshire Libraries

This book is to be returned on or before the last date stamped below or may be renewed by telephone or online.

…olves around two …ucial struggles …

…ation—that of the nation of Finland after centuries of …eign rule, and that of Finnish women."

Publishers Weekly, **Starred Review**

"In the strange, enclosed world of 1950s Lapland, when detective Mauzer arrives to investigate the case of a missing grandfather… it will take all her nascent feminist courage to right the wrongs she uncovers."

Sunday Times, **Crime Club pick**

"A captivating first novel… 'My dear girl,' her patronizing boss instructs, 'justice in a cold climate is not a natural phenomenon.' But the stubborn and resourceful Sgt. Hella Mauzer seems just the police officer to deliver it."

Wall Street Journal

"Welcome to the most stubborn of cops, righting wrongs in cold Lapland, a memorable character with just the right disdain for authority and its amoral attitudes to justice and women."

Maxim Jakubowski, author of *The Louisiana Republic*

"One of the finest books to be released this season. The true joy is Ivar's ability to blend Cold War politics, sexual politics, geopolitics, and personal tragedy in Hella's pursuit for justice."

Mystery Scene Magazine

"Cold-war Lapland is a glitteringly fresh setting and the protagonist is an unexpected character who I'd love to meet again."

Morning Star

Katja Ivar grew up in Russia and the US. She travelled the world extensively, from Almaty to Ushuaia, from Karelia to Kyushu, before finally settling in Paris, where she lives with her husband and three children. She received a BA in Linguistics and a master's degree in Contemporary History from Sorbonne University. *Deep as Death* follows on from the success of *Evil Things,* her debut novel.

DEEP AS DEATH

Katja Ivar

BITTER LEMON PRESS
LONDON

BITTER LEMON PRESS

First published in the United Kingdom in 2020 by
Bitter Lemon Press, 47 Wilmington Square, London WC1X 0ET
www.bitterlemonpress.com

Extract from T. S. Eliot's poem "The Hollow Men" included
with kind permission of Faber and Faber Limited

A CIP record for this book is available from the British Library

ISBN 978–1–912242–30-6
eBook ISBN 978–1–912242–31-3

Typeset by Tetragon
Printed and bound by the CPI Group (UK) Ltd, Croydon, CR0 4YY

To my grandmother, Klaudia, born in 1929
A medic, a wife, a mother
Her stories illuminated my childhood.

And to my tiny angel Marguerite, as always.

Between the idea
And the reality
Between the motion
And the act
Falls the shadow.

T. S. ELIOT
"The Hollow Men"

PROLOGUE

1935

She didn't know what scared her the most: the man, or the lake.

Both looked dull and familiar, but she knew dark shadows lurked underneath. She had known it all along, without ever admitting it to herself; she had just gone about her day, steering clear of both. She had thought that would be enough, but she was wrong. When the man threw open the door of the barn, where she sat huddled with the boy, she took a sharp breath as a cold wave of panic washed over her body.

"*Temptress*," he called her, spitting out the word as if it tasted bitter. "Whore." He said it like he meant it, and then he took a step towards her, a cattle whip in his hand, his eyes narrowed. She pushed the boy aside and lunged for a corner of the barn, squeezing her body through the opening she had used to get inside. Black windowless walls surrounded her; the only way out was over the lake. If the man stayed where he was, she could slip past the house, keeping close to the shore, and get away.

She stifled a sob. Maybe he wouldn't come after her. Maybe he'd just whip the boy, who wouldn't mind so much – he was used to it. Her mind was wiped blank by fear. Not even for a fleeting moment did she consider going back to explain herself; in her panic, she couldn't think of a way to make him understand she had only meant well.

The sharp crack behind her meant the man wasn't going to stay inside. He was hacking at the wood with an axe, widening the opening.

She decided she stood a better chance with the lake.

It was late spring, but only the calendar knew this. It was snowing heavily, fat, damp snowflakes clinging to her hair and dress, muffling every sound. No one would be out in this weather. No one would help her. The frozen lake stretched white and peaceful as far as her eye could see, but she knew better. Towards the north shore, where a stream fed into the lake, patches of white gave way to heavy grey slush. That was where the man drove her.

She looked over her shoulder as she ran, slipping on the ice. The boy on the shore would not help; he was paralysed with fear. All he could do was stand there, his eyes wild and pleading, and watch the man chase her.

"You're dead, Lara," the man said, not even out of breath. His voice was quiet, not menacing. He was stating a fact. She headed straight towards the north shore, where the ice wouldn't hold his tall frame. He realized that and stopped. She stopped as well, panting, facing the man across five yards of thin, treacherous ice. Her crimson dress was like a drop of blood, trickling onto a white shroud. She was lighter than the man, but not light enough. The ice would give way at some point. Viewed from up close, it seemed illuminated from within, by some mythical creature, by a sea monster coiled below. The man sat down slowly, stretching his legs out in front of him, thrusting his hands into his pockets. He'd wait her out. He had all the time in the world.

She sat on the ice, too, and looked at the shore, its ragged skyline of tall dark trees and windowless walls, black on black. She refused to look at the man. She still hoped that if she waited long enough, he'd get tired and leave. Then she had an idea. A prayer! A prayer to her guardian angel. The words came easily to her, but she only got to the end of the first sentence when, with a gentle shush, the ice beneath her started to cave in. She gasped. She had stayed still for too long. The water was so cold it stopped time. It bit at her ankles, worked its way into her boots. Her heart jammed somewhere in her throat, but her mind was miraculously clear. She could still escape. This was bad, but not as bad as the man waiting for her. And she knew what to do – everyone who grew up in this country did. No brisk movements. She spreadeagled her body on the ice and started to glide forward, making herself light. Like a bird. She inched her way forward until she managed to drag her lower body out of the water. Now she could crawl. Her feet were frozen, but she couldn't afford to stop.

Then she remembered: the man. He was still waiting for her, and he was smiling. For an instant, his clear blue eyes locked on hers. There was nothing in them at all.

It doesn't matter if I lose some toes, she thought. Doesn't matter at all. I'll just stay here like this until morning comes. There will be people then. Ice fishermen. Children sent to replenish water reserves. The man will have to leave. Until then, I can't move.

Her veins were full of ice, and her thoughts slowed. Would her mother come looking for her? Would the boy on the shore call for help? The snow before her eyes was the colour of dead fish.

"You look like a fallen angel, Lara," the man said. "And that snow on your hair – like a tiara. Do you remember those garlands you made, last summer? Do *you* remember?" The last question was for the boy, who was approaching them with small cautious steps, his eyes shiny with tears.

The man shook his head in disgust and thrust a hand into his coat pocket.

"Goodbye, Lara," he said again, and opened his hand. He was holding a rock the size of her fist. He aimed carefully.

As the stone left his hand and flew towards her, she realized what he was doing.

The boy screamed. One piercing note, mouth wide open, eyes screwed shut.

The rock shattered the ice right in front of her face, and she could just glimpse the inky water beneath before it swallowed her whole.

PART I

Beware

1

Hella

26 February 1953, Helsinki

The judge was old and irritated. He peered at me over the wire-rimmed glasses that sat on the tip of his nose.

"Anything to add, Miss?"

My lawyer fluttered nervously by my side. He was fresh out of law school, and much too impressed by the grand mahogany-panelled hall we were in to add anything of value. Still, he cleared his throat, pulling at his too-short jacket sleeves. His wrists were as thin as a boy's. "Your Honour, in my closing argument —"

The judge waved an impatient hand. "I have already heard your closing argument. What I want to know is what the defendant has to say." He pointed at me. "You! Why did you attack that man?"

There was whispering from the bench to my right where my victim was sitting, his one remaining eye glaring at me.

"Your Honour," I said. "I am afraid you misunderstood —" My lawyer drew a sharp breath. That was about the only thing he had told me before the proceedings started: never contradict the judge. Never. And that was exactly what I was doing now. "The accuser was the one who attacked me. I was merely defending myself."

"With a rusty nail?" The judge's voice was carefully neutral, sympathetic even.

"It was the only thing I had on hand."

"Is that right?" the judge said, his beady eyes never leaving mine. "You were in a logging camp in Lapland, which is to say in the middle of nowhere. You ventured into a place inhabited by men, where no respectable woman would ever expect to set foot. Worse, you were in that gentleman's bedroom. Did he drag you there?"

"No."

"Then you came to his sleeping quarters of your own accord?"

"I did, Your Honour. That is not an invitation to be raped."

Next to me, my lawyer buried his face in his hands. Even in his limited experience, I was a crackpot.

"Hmm," the judge said. "Let me get this straight. You expect that you can walk into a man's bedroom, flirt with him, then get away unscathed?"

"That's what I said, Your Honour. As a police officer, I had reasons to go to that logging camp, and into that room, and those reasons had nothing to do with romance or seduction."

The judge stared at me for a long time, wondering perhaps if I'd explain my reasons further, but I kept quiet. What had happened to me was nobody's business, and I was ready to suffer the consequences. To the judge, I was a former police officer from Ivalo, Lapland, discharged from the force for disobeying my supervisors' direct orders and now being sued by a man who claimed I had damaged his leg when I attacked him.

"Well," the judge said at last. "Perhaps that is the truth. Still, the accuser has provided a medical certificate which states that the wound you inflicted prevents him from exercising his profession. You are a truck driver, are you not?" he asked my self-proclaimed victim, who almost jumped from the bench, nodding.

"Yes, Your Honour."

"A very valuable profession. Especially at a time when our country, having finished paying war reparations to the Soviet Union, is undergoing a massive reconstruction. We need working men. We need truck drivers." The judge turned back to me. "You are not married, are you? So what do *you* do for a living?"

He knew already, of course. He just wanted to hear me say it.

"I am a private investigator, Your Honour."

The judge chuckled. "What do you investigate? Missing cats?"

"I specialize in murder cases, Your Honour."

Now the spectators in the courtroom were laughing too. Even my lawyer leaned forward to hide a smile.

"Murder?" the judge said. "Murder investigations pay well, last I heard. The court finds you guilty of assault on the person of Seppo Kukoyakka and sentences you to pay damages to the amount of…" He paused, his eyes assessing the value of my cheap wool jacket and tired leather pumps, noting the absence of jewellery. "One hundred thousand markka."

Six months of police sergeant's wages. Not that I was employed any more.

My lawyer gasped. He sprang to his feet as the judge's gavel hit the desk in front of him. "Your Honour, a hundred thousand markka is an extraordinary sum and the defendant —"

"Case closed," the judge said, not looking at him. "People like Miss Mauzer are a danger to society. You will have the chance to appeal, if you so wish. Next!"

The lawyer threw me a dejected look. "You shouldn't have been so provocative," he said. "It would have been better to say you got scared, changed your mind. The judge would have been easier on you. Now, what are you going to —"

I got to my feet. They were already bringing the next defendant into the courtroom, a vagabond who smelled of urine. The show was over, the public shuffling towards the exit, grinning.

"Don't you worry," I said to the lawyer. "How much time do I have to pay the sum?"

"Two months."

"Then I'll find a way to pay it."

He stared at me, his Adam's apple working up and down his thin neck. "I'm sorry, Miss Mauzer," he said at last. "I should have prepared you better." He leaned over to pick up his briefcase. "Good luck. You're going to need it."

Five minutes later, I stood on the steps of the courthouse, the frozen expanse of the Baltic Sea stretching ahead of me. The guidebooks called Helsinki the White City of the North, except that there was nothing white about it. To me, this was a city of softened greys and sunless mornings, of blurry shadows and damp drizzle. Its sky was ancient and low, its air charged with salt. A city of seafarers, merchants and soldiers. This was a place I was determined to once again call home. Luck or no luck.

2

Hella

The snow globe sat on my desk, on top of a sheet of wrapping paper. There was a figurine of a child inside it. It looked like Eva: painfully thin, almost translucent, with a great mane of red-gold hair that reached down to her waist. The hair didn't move as I turned the globe upside down – only the synthetic snow did. It swirled inside the glass sphere, the plastic child caught in a snowstorm. With the tips of my fingers, I caressed the smooth cool surface, thinking of all the little phrases I had stashed away in preparation for the big day: *We don't have to be friends – I just want us to get to know each other a little. I'm not trying to replace anyone, Eva. Your dad and I never meant for it to happen, but sometimes life is like this. It sweeps you off your feet.*

"No no no no no," Steve said, restlessly pacing in my tiny, cluttered office. Three steps to the left took him to the window and the view of the patched-up roofs that stretched all the way to the green-and-gold dome of Uspenski Cathedral. One step to the right, and he was in front of the door that opened on what the landlord insisted on calling a reception area – in reality, a room little larger than a cupboard, furnished with two mismatched chairs and an umbrella stand crammed between them. "You're kind, and generous, and selfless. And tough," Steve added, once he shot a glance at the reception area and confirmed that it was empty. "You're not asking this of me. You're not that kind of person."

Rising up from my chair, I turned to face him. "I am, trust me."

Steve rubbed his face with both hands. He looked tired, his tall frame slumping forward a little, his blue eyes blood-shot. "You're the kind of person who blackmails the father of a fragile child?"

"Yes," I said, after a glance at the snow globe. I hadn't got round to wrapping my gift, and now I probably never would. "That's me exactly. So is it a yes or a no?"

I'd never meant to have this conversation in the first place. The day had already been awful enough as it was; first the courthouse, then a food stamp office where I'd had to queue for an hour before being told by a bored employee that they'd just run out of coupons and I had better come back the following day. And now this.

It had started innocently enough, with Steve dropping by to tell me he was awfully sorry but he wouldn't be able to see me tonight after all. He had forgotten that Eva was performing in a school play. *Playing Ophelia, can you imagine?* He had to go to the play. Of course he did.

"Lovely," I replied. I had been planning on spending my evening at home with Steve, but the theatre was even better. Even when played by fourteen-year-olds, Shakespeare has the power to make one realize how insignificant our problems are in the grand scheme of things.

Steve paused. He had been wearing his coat when he came in, but when we had started talking he had taken it off and slung it over the back of the visitors' chair, the only comfortable one in the room.

"Hella," he said. "I know it's not a good time…"

I should have stopped him there. I should have shrugged it off, told him it didn't matter. But some angry force inside me, looking for a fight and more reasons to cry, decided that it was time to finally clarify the terms of our relationship.

"Didn't you say that Elsbeth and Eva both know we're living together? Didn't you" – here I paused because I found it difficult to control my voice – "didn't you tell me that Eva was looking forward to meeting me?" I looked at the globe; I wanted to smash it against the wall. How happy I had been when I found it in a little store on Kirkkokatu. I had been looking for the perfect gift, and that was the one: not too personal, but thoughtful nonetheless.

Steve threw his hands up in the air. "True," he said. "All true. But now's not a good time. Eva is worried about the performance. She's afraid she'll forget her lines, afraid she'll look ridiculous in front of her classmates. You know how it is with teenage girls."

"But she doesn't have to see me," I said. "I'll stay put in my seat, you don't even have to tell her I'm there. I don't know much about teenage girls, but from what I hear they're pretty self-obsessed. She probably won't even notice the woman sitting next to her father."

"Probably not," said Steve. "But Elsbeth will."

"And is she nervous because her daughter's acting in a school play?"

"She," Steve said, frowning at me, "will be nervous because her own parents are coming and she hasn't told them about our separation yet."

"Oh. So you'll all go like a happy little family, and you'll see me tomorrow when you can?" My voice took on a sarcastic undertone, but Steve pretended not to notice.

"Not like a happy little family. Like a family. Why's that a problem? You're an adult, Hella. You should understand. A big girl like you."

He shouldn't have started on the big girl thing. I'd heard that one more than enough; no wonder I snapped. "I've been very understanding for the last four years. Maybe now it's time I start thinking about myself a little."

"Don't you always?" Steve was getting as angry as I was, his jaw set and unyielding, his eyes narrow. "No one forced you to embark on an affair with a married man."

The realization hit me like a slap in the face. "It's you," I said. "All this time I thought it was about Elsbeth, but it's you. You're still not ready to introduce your daughter to me. You're still not sure that you and I are a couple."

All those evenings I had spent waiting for him, all his claims that his marriage was over, that he was only staying for the sake of his child, that his sickly wife couldn't manage on her own – it all came back and crushed me like a tidal wave. When I emerged, there was only one thing that mattered. I needed to know where I stood.

I took a deep breath. Then, in a voice as loud and clear as I could muster, I asked him to choose. Either it was me, in which case I was going to see the damned play, or it was them. And if it was them, I wanted him out of my life.

"Is that what you really want?" Steve said. He was standing in front of me, one hand on top of the filing cabinet, the other balled into a fist.

"Yes," I said, forcing the tremor out of my voice. "It's simple really."

At this, Steve looked out of the window with a puzzled expression on his face. It was snowing again, another dreadful winter's day, the sun hovering just above the line of the horizon, almost erased by blurry white streaks of snow. In an hour, the sun would set. So this is it, I thought. The last straw. Could it really be that simple? A child's school play, for Christ's sake, we'd been through worse. He loved me. I knew he did. He would do the right thing.

His glance left the window and stopped on me.

"Then," he said, "we're over." He picked up his coat from the chair, started to pull it on as he turned for the door. "You can put my things in a suitcase and leave it on the landing. I doubt anyone would want to steal my stuff."

With his hand on the doorknob, Steve paused as if he wanted to say something, then thought better of it. He shrugged and walked out, leaving me behind. Like a fish just out of water, my mouth gaping open, my mind blank.

3

Hella

The realization of what had just happened dawned on me after the sound of Steve's footsteps died away on the stairs. I had put too many expectations on that first meeting with Eva. I couldn't be light-hearted about it any longer; I couldn't put things into perspective. And of course, with the weight of my pathetic hope crushing all rational thought, I had blown it.

Uninvited images flooded my mind: the cold nights to come, the empty apartment above the language school, dinners for one eaten straight out of a pan because what did it matter now?

My first instinct was to go home, open a bottle of vodka and drink myself into oblivion. Erase all coherent thought, erase the longing.

Wallow in self-pity.

Sob my heart out.

It seemed like a good idea; the only thing that stopped me was the woman waiting across the street. I saw her as I was leaving the building. She had been looking up at my windows, but when she spotted me on the doorstep she turned away quickly and pretended to busy herself with her watch. This made me pause. Even though the woman's face was partly hidden by a sable hat, it was not Elsbeth, of that I was certain. Elsbeth was tall, blonde and pretty as a picture. Most people I knew looked surprised when they saw her, and I knew why: they wondered why Steve, Helsinki's most popular – and only – American DJ and radio presenter, had left her for me. This woman was short, buxom and blonde. A peroxide blonde, not a natural one. There was something jarring about her, but I only realized what it was when I retraced my steps and dived back into the building. The woman's face looked cheap, there was too much make-up – the lips were too red, the eyebrows non-existent. But her clothes were expensive: a sable coat, soft leather gloves and the sort of shoes you only saw on the feet of people who never had to walk anywhere.

The woman was here to see me, but she was hesitating. I considered my options. The vodka binge was still tempting, but could I afford it? What I had told the judge that very morning had been wishful thinking: I did advertise my murder-solving capabilities, but no murder investigations had come my way yet, and they probably never would. The only people who came to see me were, ironically enough, wives who suspected their husbands of cheating. And money was always tight. In all the cases I'd had, the husband had been the only breadwinner in the family. The wives paid me with whatever they could put aside from their grocery shopping budget, and that wasn't much. So that woman on the street, with her fancy clothes… Even if it was the usual philandering spouse story, I had to take it. Unless I wanted to be penalized further for not paying the court.

I climbed the stairs back to my third-floor office and waited, forcing myself to recite the *Kalevala* to avoid thinking

about Steve. I was on *Beauteous Daughter of the Ether, her exist-*
ence sad and hopeless / Thus alone to live for ages when I heard
a tentative knock on the door.

"Miss Mauzer?"

Up close, the woman looked older than I'd first thought,
closer to fifty than forty. Her name, Klara Nylund, told me
nothing.

I pointed at the visitors' chair. "How can I help you, Mrs
Nylund?"

"It's Miss," the woman corrected, pulling off her gloves.
Her nails were painted the exact same shade as her lipstick:
ruby red. "It's about one of my girls."

It was only then that I understood. My potential client
was nobody's wife. She ran a brothel. There were a number
of them around – Helsinki was a port city, after all, and with
all the refugees flooding the streets, lots of girls were on the
market. Although, given the woman's clothing, this brothel
was probably at the upper end of the market. I flipped my
notepad open. "What happened to the girl?"

"She drowned," the woman said matter-of-factly. "Last
month. Nellie went down on the ice in West Harbour. The
ice gave way."

"And?"

"And the police seem to think it was an accident."

"But you don't believe that," I said. Immediately, my
inner voice screamed: *Bravo, Sherlock! If you go on like this,*
your visitor will get up and leave.

The woman must have been thinking along the same
lines because she squinted at me. "How long have you been
doing this job, Miss Mauzer?"

"I was a police officer," I told her, with more confidence
than I really felt. "In Helsinki, I was the first woman ever to
be part of the homicide squad. After that, I worked in Ivalo."

"And now you're here," the woman added, scanning the room. She didn't need to add anything. The threadbare rug on the floor, the chipped desk, the icy chill of my office, they all screamed failure. "He assured me you were OK," the woman said doubtfully to her folded hands. "How much do you charge?"

"It's five hundred markka a day, or we can agree on a flat fee. Did someone recommend me?" I tried to keep the hopeful note out of my voice. No one ever did. Aside from the cuckolded wives, of course, but I doubted very much that any of them would be speaking to a madam.

The woman nodded, fumbling in her bag. "Him." She pulled out a business card. Cream vellum, elegantly formed letters. CHIEF INSPECTOR JOKELA, HEAD, HELSINKI HOMICIDE SQUAD.

"You know him, right?" the woman asked. She was having second thoughts.

"Jokela and I go back a long way," I said. What I didn't say was that there was no love lost between us, and never had been. And that I couldn't imagine any reason for him to recommend me, except if he was convinced that the girl's death had indeed been an accident and police time would be wasted on it.

There was a silence. I kept my eyes on the card, wondering whether the woman would get up and leave, and if that was the case, whether I was still going for the vodka bottle. Just as I was about to suggest to Miss Nylund that she come back once she had made up her mind, she pulled an envelope out of her bag and slapped it on my desk.

"Good," she said. "I hope you're good. Because Nellie – she was one of the better ones. I want you to find who did this to her, and I want that person to pay for what he did."

4

Chief Inspector Mustonen

"My dear boy," boomed Jokela's voice, "come over here." Those who were still at the office at that hour watched as I shot a desperate glance at the wall clock – it was a quarter past five already and I had promised Sofia I'd be home early. I picked up a folder at random and trudged towards Jokela's office. I knew why my boss was asking to see me: it was time for one of our increasingly frequent drinking sessions. Just the two of us and a bottle of expensive whisky, the provenance of which I preferred to ignore.

Work sessions, Jokela called them. Some days, he gave the impression of actually believing in that excuse. He would make me open a file and ask me irrelevant questions while he poured the whisky. The work part of the sessions usually lasted for the first glass or two. After that, we would invariably slip into a discussion that had nothing to do with the case and everything to do with the way the world at large was treating Jon Jokela.

"Here," my boss said, pushing a chair towards me. "Have a seat." Jokela was wearing the new open-collared uniform that had been created in preparation for the Olympic Games the previous year. The uniform was supposed to give the police a modern, less military appearance. I rarely wore it: for what I had to do, plain clothes were better.

"So, my boy, what have you been working on?"

"Roof signs for police cars. This way, the public will be aware of our presence. I'm certain it will reduce traffic offences."

Jokela pulled a face. "Haven't heard of such a thing. More likely than not folks will get scared and drive into ditches. Do they put roof signs on police cars in America?"

"No. We'd be the first. And here's another idea. Why don't we establish a dedicated traffic police? All those farmers we hired in the run-up to the Olympics would be perfect for the job."

My boss pulled an immaculate handkerchief out of his trouser pocket and wiped his forehead. His office was stiflingly hot. The windows, sealed for the winter, were steamed up with fog; a gas fire hissed in a corner. There was talk of the homicide squad moving into another, more modern building, but dinosaurs like Jokela were resisting. He loved being there, loved the moose antlers fixed to the walls, the bulbous office furniture, the view across the square to the neoclassical facade of Helsinki Cathedral. To him, that office represented some sort of gentlemen's club. But Jokela didn't have a family, he didn't have a life outside of the office. I did.

"Well, I don't know," Jokela said. "Maybe there's something in your idea. I'll think about it. And what about the rest of the boys? What are they doing?"

"The Goldberg assault file is ready to go."

"Good job."

"Not mine," I smiled. "Pinchus was the one working on it, and he's been very diligent as usual. A valuable member of the team." I paused. There was a pink business card on Jokela's desk.

Jokela glanced up at me. "What is it?"

"I saw you talking to a woman, earlier this afternoon. I was wondering if it was the drowned girl's madam?"

"That was her."

"Oh." Now I was hesitating. If the madam had come to ask how the investigation was progressing, why hadn't Jokela told her to go and see me directly? Because he had doubts over the way I was running the case all by myself? Or was I just being paranoid? Aloud, I said: "I was surprised she managed to get an appointment with you."

"That's because I know her." Jokela winked. "You're too serious, my boy. You should get out more, have a fun night with me. That wife of yours is lovely and all, but a man needs variety."

"I love Sofia," I answered, smiling to soften my rebuttal. "What did the madam want?"

"To know where we were with the investigation." Jokela pulled the bottle of whisky towards him, poured me a glass, refreshed his own. "I owe her a small favour."

Of course he did. Everyone who was anyone in Helsinki had been to Klara Nylund's club at least once.

"I'm still working on it," I said. "Though I didn't really get very far. I don't even know whether we're dealing with a murder or an accident or suicide. The forensic pathologist thinks he may have spotted something, but he's not sure. I sent a query to Interpol, asked them if they'd had similar cases in other port cities." I took a sip of my whisky. It tasted like cough syrup.

Jokela's small eyes were on me. "Relax," he said. "This sort of investigation is a drag. You'll never find the killer – if there even *is* one. The girl fell into the water. Big deal! This city is built on water. There are – I don't know – dozens of islands!"

"Three hundred and fifteen, to be exact."

"You see! That's why they call this city the Daughter of the Baltic. The girl must have been hurrying somewhere, the ice gave way... You do that too, right, you take shortcuts through the bay?"

"Everyone does."

"Exactly! And I prefer my people to focus on more important jobs than a drowned prostitute. Klara Nylund kept insisting, so I told her to contact a PI."

I frowned. "Which one?"

"Mauzer." Jokela hooted with laughter, sending drops of whisky flying in all directions.

"Great idea. She's perfectly competent."

Something in the way I said it made my boss squint at me. "You're hiding something."

I laughed it off. "Everyone does. And anyway, it's good of you to give Hella a chance. As I said, she's perfectly competent."

Jokela patted me on the arm. "Of course she is. Of course. That's what I thought too, let's help out poor Hella. After all, I knew her father. I heard she's not doing so well."

"No," I confirmed, "she's not. From what I've heard."

"Then we'll drink to her success." Jokela filled his glass again. "To Hella!"

I raised my glass reluctantly. I didn't expect to lose control of the investigation but I knew Mauzer, the way she operated. Maybe it was for the best. "To Hella!" I said. "To her success!"

5

Hella

Helsinki is a city for walking fast. The bitter wind constantly blowing off the sea is there to make a point: no leisurely strolls here. No loitering. As soon as Klara Nylund was gone, I wrapped my coat tight and hurried home, past the neoclassical splendour of Senate Square and down Unioninkatu, the cobblestones slippery under the soles of my shoes.

As I walked, I wondered whether my day could possibly get any worse. It was a rhetorical question, not a challenge to the gods. What I needed was a warm bath and a little something to eat before I sat down with the notes Klara Nylund had left me. One thing I *didn't* need was an unexpected guest.

So when, at half past five, I mounted the creaky stairs of my apartment building and spotted a bulging pigskin suitcase and a pair of shapely legs in a too-short skirt standing next to it, my first instinct was to run back to my office and wait until the legs were gone. I had a pretty good idea who they belonged to, and no desire at all to see their owner.

This split second of indecision, while I was hovering on the stairs, sealed my fate.

"Hel-*la*!" cried the sugary voice and Anita flew down the stairs, throwing her arms round my neck as if we were the best of friends. "So happy to see you! How *are* you?"

She took a step back, looked at me critically and frowned. "You're even thinner than before. I didn't think it was possible. *And* you've got a ladder in your stocking."

"Thank you," I muttered, making my way upstairs and fumbling in my pocket for the key. "I know."

My lawyer had insisted I wear "nice ladylike clothes" to court, and I had complied. I had coiled my wild mane into a bun that resembled a cowpat, put on my only skirt suit, and even invested in a new pair of stockings. Which hadn't even lasted a day. Somehow this minor disappointment crystallized all that was wrong with my life.

"What's this about?" I asked Anita, my hand on the doorknob. I had rather hoped never again to see hide or hair of anyone from the police station in Ivalo. So did I really have to invite our former receptionist, who I'd never been close to, into my apartment for a cup of coffee and a chit-chat? And why did she have that suitcase with her?

Anita smiled: bright lipstick, perfect teeth, dimples. "It's a long story. Can I come in?"

"Sorry." I shrugged. "Sure. It's been a rough day."

My unexpected visitor picked up her suitcase and fluttered into my apartment. "Oh," she said. "I love this place. It's so … uncluttered. All those bare walls."

"Yeah." I dumped my bag on a chair and, leaving Anita to admire my sweet spartan home, went to the kitchen and put the kettle on. The coffee jar was almost empty, but I still managed to prepare two fairly decent cupfuls. I put them on a tray, together with a sugar bowl, and carried it into the living room.

Where I almost dropped the tray.

"What are you *doing*?"

Anita flashed a smile at me. "Surprise!"

I put the tray on the table, my hands shaking. "What do you mean, 'surprise'? You're hanging your clothes in my wardrobe. I thought you were just visiting?"

"Well, actually," Anita said, deftly slipping a silk blouse onto a wire hanger, "I'm in Helsinki for good. I decided to follow in your footsteps, to try and be a hero like you."

I stared at her. The girl was mad. For the three years I'd known her back in Ivalo, the only detective work that had ever interested Anita was finding a lipstick to match her nail polish. "You mean you want to be a cop?"

"Homicide detective, like you," Anita beamed. "I've been thinking about it for a while, how I'd look in a uniform, and I decided that was it. This is what I want to be!"

"In case it escaped your notice, that's all in the past. I'm not part of the police force any more."

"Doesn't matter. Everyone in Lapland knows your name. I applied to the training programme the day after you resigned. Actually, I started two months ago."

I pulled a chair towards me and sat down heavily. Call me slow, but the situation was still unclear to me. "Where did you live?" I asked her. "Until now?"

Anita extracted a pair of crimson suede pumps from the suitcase and set them carefully in the back of the wardrobe. "With my cousin."

"Ranta? Is he in Helsinki too?"

"Yep," Anita smiled. "He always said he'd live and die as a police officer in Ivalo, but he transferred two months ago to work in the archives. Didn't want to leave me alone in the big city. I was surprised he did, at his age – we celebrated his fifty-sixth birthday last week – but here we are." She peered critically into my wardrobe. It was already full, but her suitcase wasn't empty yet. "Do you know where I can put the rest of my stuff?"

"What happened with Ranta, then? Did you have a fight?"

Anita was already dragging her suitcase towards my bedroom. "I won't stay long," she assured me. "Maybe a couple of months. You'll see, we'll have fun together. Ranta was impossible, you know how he is, you've worked with him. Always snooping around, going through my things. Violent too, sometimes. I couldn't take it any longer. There. Oh, goodness gracious!" I heard something smashing on the floor. A moment later Anita emerged, a piece of broken glass in her manicured hand. "That bed looks like two people have been sleeping in it. Are you seeing someone?" Her voice held an incredulous tone.

I stared at her, wondering if I had heard her correctly. Was it me who just two hours ago had been afraid of solitude? There were worse things. And Anita was one of them.

I wanted to start working on the case as soon as we finished our coffee, but Anita's mind was set on having what she called a girls' evening. That seemed to involve putting curlers in each other's hair, painting our nails and eating pancakes. And drinking sparkling wine.

"I don't have any," I said.

"I noticed." Anita wrinkled her nose prettily. "Your kitchen is empty, except for all those pickle jars." The implication *no wonder your boyfriend ran away* hung between us like a cloud.

"There's some pressed caviar left in the icebox outside the window. Also a bottle of vodka. Help yourself. You can't get Prosecco with coupons in any case."

"I don't drink vodka," Anita said, in a helpless, dying-to-a-whisper sort of voice that must usually obtain the desired effect. "And pressed caviar is for the poor."

"As you wish."

I pulled Klara Nylund's notes out of my bag and started to read. According to the madam, Nellie had announced she was going solo on 15 February. She had still been alive on 17 February, when she had dropped by her friend's place to borrow a curling iron. On the morning of 18 February, when the friend, Maria, came to Nellie's to get her iron back, the girl was gone. Her body was found several days later, floating in the harbour.

"Are you really going to work all evening?" Anita asked.

"That's my intention, yes."

"You don't even have a TV. There's this show I love, it's called —"

"Anita." I pointed at the file. "Do you mind? I'm trying to focus here."

"*I Love Lucy.*" Anita slumped on the sofa, but a second later she was up on her feet again and wrapping a blanket around herself. "This place is freezing," she said. "I never realized you were one of those superwomen who never feel the cold."

I clamped my hands around my ears and tried to focus on the file, but it was no good.

"Six foot tall," Anita was saying, her face hidden behind a magazine she'd pulled out of her bag. "Size eleven shoes. Maybe even president. What?"

"Nothing."

"You were muttering to yourself!"

"I was wondering about the six-foot-tall size eleven president."

Anita flew off the sofa and slammed the magazine on top of the file. "Associated Press," she said. "It's about the women of the future. What they'll look like in the year 2000, if the Soviets don't blow us up before then." I stared at the illustration. On it, a massive Amazon towered above two curvaceous beauties. "Is that what they think? That the woman of the future will look like the steel kolkhoz maiden, but without her male companion and her pedestal?"

"Yes!" Anita's voice was breathless with excitement. "Women will know how to wrestle, and they'll be dressed in special synthetic suits, and, and … they'll have pills instead of food. And, Hella, we might even have a female president."

"That could be useful," I said, pushing the magazine aside. "The pills, I mean. No cooking. Now can I continue reading?"

Anita puffed up her cheeks and blew out a long, discontented breath. Then she leaned over my shoulder and started to read my file.

According to Klara Nylund, there was no boyfriend, no promise of marriage, no man Nellie would want to present to her family. But she also noted that she probably wouldn't have known even if there had been someone: she had close to twenty girls, she couldn't keep an eye on everything. The address of Nellie's best friend, Maria, was scribbled in the margin. I decided to start with her.

"Couldn't Nellie have drowned accidentally?" Anita asked. "This sort of thing happens all the time."

"Sure. And the police are probably right. It's the fact that Nellie suddenly quit her job that made Klara Nylund wonder. Apparently she wasn't the independent type."

"Wait a second…" Anita, finally tired of her stooping position, pulled up a chair and sat next to me. "Does the madam think Nellie got involved with a man who got rid of her?"

I nodded, my eyes on a studio portrait of a beautiful girl dressed in a high-necked white blouse, her blonde hair tied in a bun. This photograph had been supplied by Nellie's family; in it, she looked like an office worker, not an escort.

I had asked Klara Nylund about this, and the madam had shrugged it off. Lots of the girls lied to their families about their occupation, she said. There was another photograph where the girl wore a low-cut gown and earrings, and had her hair loose, but the madam had given that one to the police.

"There's something I don't get," Anita said. "If Klara Nylund told the cops all of this already, why would she want a PI as well?"

"She went to see Chief Inspector Jokela in the homicide squad to see how the investigation was progressing, and he told her the file wasn't a priority for them because they're not even certain a crime was committed. The pathologist's conclusion seems to be that Nellie slipped on the ice and fell into the water. Cause of death: drowning. And Klara Nylund couldn't really insist – she's not related to the girl. Officially, her business establishment doesn't even exist."

"It doesn't?"

"No. Prostitution is illegal. According to Jokela, if Nellie's parents insisted, the police would look into it more closely, but otherwise…"

Anita's eyes widened. "Let me guess. Nellie's parents told all their neighbours that their daughter had a respectable occupation, and they're afraid the truth will come out if there's a proper investigation?"

"Exactly. So Jokela told Klara Nylund that Inspector Mustonen has been working on the case but he's got no results so far, and it was time for him to move on to something more important. Because the madam kept insisting, he gave her my address and told her a PI might be a better option."

"Nice guy, Mustonen," Anita said dreamily. "He makes me think of that actor, what's his name?"

"Errol Flynn?"

Anita brightened: "Yes. Too bad he's married to that horse-headed creature who keeps bossing him around. He loves her, too. I ran into him at the jewellers once, he was looking to buy her a gift."

I sat up sharply. "Do you know him?"

"Uh-huh. The training programme alternates between theoretical courses and fieldwork. Ranta got me a place on Mustonen's team. I do nothing of course, apart from wear flattering dresses, serve coffee and generally provide a nice contrast to all the manly detectives, but I can see the way they operate. Mustonen is one of the nicer ones. Hasn't ever tried to grab my bum in the corridors yet."

"I guess he's a decent guy," I said, feeling silly. "He never tried with me either."

Anita burst out laughing. "That, honey, is not really all that surprising."

I dreamed of the dead girl. In my dreams, Nellie was much younger; she looked about ten. She floated on her back in the murky waters of the port, her hair spread out like tentacles, her lips frozen, blue. A tall man was standing on the embankment, hands thrust into his pockets, a felt hat pulled low over his face. Waiting for something. My heart was beating too fast. I glided up to him in the darkness, stopping maybe a yard short. The man, who must have heard the sound of my steps, turned towards me. He didn't have a face, but I knew who he was, and I knew why he was grabbing hold of my wrists and pushing me gently into the icy water. *Don't act surprised,* he told me. *You're a big girl now. You've got to understand. I have a family to protect.*

I woke up screaming, disoriented, and for a while I couldn't figure out who the other person sharing my bed was. It was only when I switched the night lamp on that I could make out Anita's flaxen hair and her small hands clutching the pillow. The air in the room was cold and damp. Shivering, I picked up a cardigan, threw it over my shoulders and felt my way into the kitchen. I could never go back to sleep after that dream. Awake, I didn't believe for a minute that Steve could have had anything to do with the dead girl. Asleep, I wasn't so sure. And I wasn't taking any chances.

Instead, I wrapped the cardigan tighter around me, gulped down the remainder of the cold coffee from Anita's cup and settled on the living-room sofa with the file. Young and radiant, Nellie gazed at me from the photograph supplied by Klara Nylund.

And once again I thought of the *Kalevala*, that most Finnish of all poems:

> And the waves are white with fervour,
> To and fro they toss the maiden,
> Storm-encircled, hapless maiden,
> With her sport the rolling billows,
> With her play the storm-wind forces...

6

Chief Inspector Mustonen

Even with a lifetime of training behind me, the coldness of the water took my breath away. I dived quickly, emerged quicker still. Didn't stay my usual five minutes. Maybe it was because of all I'd had to drink the previous night. I wondered if I could use it as an excuse to put an end to my drinking sessions with Jokela. Probably not. My boss would just tell me to stop exercising.

Sofia was waiting next to the hole in the ice with the towel, like she always did. Smiling. The worst part was over, her morning sickness a distant memory. My wife's belly was round and she laughed a lot. She was certain this second baby would be a boy as well. She wanted to call him Janus, like the father-in-law she'd never met, but I had rejected it absolutely. Finally, Sofia seemed to have settled on Jonas.

"Thank you, darling." I blew her a kiss and she stepped back from the edge of the water, throwing me the towel. I wrapped it around my waist. At this early hour, we were alone on the shore; I didn't have to worry about anyone seeing me.

"Will you train Arne too, when he's old enough?" Sofia made a show of shuddering. "Ice-water dips so all the Mustonen men stay fit and healthy and handsome?"

"Of course I will! My father always said what doesn't kill you makes you stronger."

I swept my wife off her feet and ran up the slope with her. "Do you think I could manage this without the ice dips?" I panted.

She was laughing, protesting, but as we drew nearer to the house I stopped paying attention. Inside, the phone was ringing. Not many people had our number. It could be Sofia's father; it could be Jokela. If my boss was calling me at home, it meant there was a new case. Not a small one, either, or he wouldn't have bothered. No, it must be something big.

7

Hella

My father always said Helsinki was a city of lost souls. A place forever caught between East and West, the onion-shaped domes and the neoclassical facades. A paler copy of St Petersburg, now revolutionary Leningrad. A city whose golden age had been before the First World War. A city scarred by shrapnel and painted in pastel colours. A city of broken dreams, none of these more broken than those of the girl who had written the pathetic little letter I was reading.

> *Dear Mother,*
>
> *I hope you are in good health and that the weather is not too cold. Here in Helsinki, the winter is mild, though it still snows a lot. It's a good thing I spend my days in the office. In your last letter, you asked me about the other girls, if they were nice. They are, for the most part, but our supervisor says we talk too much.*

"So this was Nellie's white lie?" I said, folding away the letter Klara Nylund had provided with the file. "An office job?" The effects of my bad night were kicking in and I needed coffee badly, but Maria, Nellie's best friend and our only witness, hadn't offered me any. I had woken her, I think. Unable to sleep, I'd showed up at the address Klara Nylund had given me – a run-down building in Punavuori – at eight in the morning, and then had spent the next ten minutes with my finger pressed on the doorbell.

Maria shrugged, studying her nails. Her face was too white, as if she'd never seen the light of day. "A stupid girl daydreaming," she said. "Nellie couldn't very well tell her mother the truth, could she? So she said she worked at the radio station, as a secretary. Not that it fooled anyone, if you want my opinion, though it wasn't in their interest to say otherwise. She was her family's only source of revenue. The fact that she was unhappy – that wasn't their business. They didn't want to know."

The tiny apartment was overheated and cramped, with clothes all over the floor, but it offered a nice view of the sea. I strolled towards the window. "All right," I said. "So Nellie, who was supporting her widowed mother and four-year-old son, lied to her family and told them she held an office job. Then one day she tells Klara Nylund she's going solo, and several days later she turns up dead. Is it reasonable to think she might have stopped working for Klara Nylund because she'd met someone?"

"I don't know," Maria said. She pulled a strand of hair out of her ponytail and started twisting it around her finger. "Are you really a former policewoman? Klara told me you were a friend of the inspectors in the homicide squad."

"I used to work with Inspectors Jokela and Mustonen, but now I'm on my own."

"Why? Did you quarrel with them?"

"Not at all." I hoped I was convincing enough. "My relationship with the police is great – they recommended me."

"Yes," Maria said. "That's what I've heard."

This interview was not going the way I had expected. "Maria," I said. "I don't mean to frighten you, but it's in your best interest to tell me if you know anything at all about the circumstances surrounding Nellie's disappearance."

The girl looked away. She knew something, but she wasn't going to tell me. She was too scared.

"Do you know what I think?" I said.

Maria looked up at me.

"I think your friend met someone she was serious about. At the time of her death, Nellie was three months pregnant, did you know that?"

The girl didn't answer.

"There are ways to get rid of unwanted pregnancies, and I would expect that someone in your profession would know all about them. So the question is: why didn't she? Did she think she had a future with the baby's father?"

"If Nellie believed she could don a frilly apron and pretend the past never happened, she was stupid. For women like us, getting married is about the worst thing that can happen: losing our independence and being prevented from using the only asset we've got? No thank you." Maria attempted a laugh. "Nellie knew what I thought about it. She wouldn't have confided in me. Besides, we weren't even that close."

"She came to you the day she disappeared, because her curling iron broke and she needed to borrow yours."

"That doesn't make us friends," Maria snorted.

That wasn't what Klara Nylund had told me. She said the two women had been inseparable. I wondered if my theory was correct. If there had been a man, Maria must have known something about him but been too afraid to tell. Why? Because she also knew that the man was dangerous? A thug? Would responsible Nellie have fallen for a man like that? Or it might have been someone powerful. Someone important.

A man who could offer a better future to Nellie, her son and her unborn child. A man who had killed her instead.

8

Chief Inspector Mustonen

For a man like Jokela, a clear conscience was a sign of a bad memory. I knew he'd forget this, too, as soon as our visitor walked out of the restaurant. The consequences would be mine to handle, while Jokela would reap the benefits.

Of course, as my boss liked to point out, it was not as straightforward as that. I would reap the benefits too – indirectly. The police chief, Dr Palmu, was on the verge of retirement, and Jokela was well positioned to replace him. And if Jokela climbed to the top of the career ladder, I could take his place as head of the homicide squad. The youngest ever, as Jokela reminded me every time we talked about it. *Just think of it, my boy: head of the homicide squad and you're not even thirty-five yet, not a wrinkle on you, not a grey hair. Think about how your father-in-law will see you once that happens. Some respect there, yes? He won't be embarrassed any longer that his only daughter married a farmer's son.*

With this in mind, the man facing us across the table was a godsend. Police Chief is a political nomination. You don't climb that high if you're not vetted by the ruling party. Jokela had their support but he wasn't the only one;

every sabre-toothed rat in the police ranks was vying for the position. Now that was about to change. Unless, of course, I refused to cooperate.

The man sitting across from us was small, wizened even. He looked like some sort of crooner, a Sinatra in miniature. But his name was typically Finnish: Alvar Virtanen.

"So, how about it?" Virtanen said, spreading his tiny hands on the table in a gesture meant to show that we were all good friends here. "I suppose we agree that Ahti is guilty of nothing more serious than being a high-spirited young man with natural appetites."

Jokela glanced at me sharply. "What do you say, my boy?" As usual, he was waiting for me to compromise myself before he even uttered a word.

"Let me see if I've got this straight," I said. "Your nineteen-year-old son, Ahti, was out on the town yesterday, and he had a bit too much to drink."

Ahti's father leaned back, frowning. "I see no problem with that. Ahti is of age."

"Naturally." I shifted in my chair. I needed to be careful about what I said next.

"Ahti was driving a car he borrowed from you, a red Chrysler Newport."

A tiny nod from the father.

"He lost control of his vehicle and smashed into the boulders just outside the West Harbour terminal."

"That's right."

"Ahti was unharmed, except for some minor cuts and bruises, and so was his passenger – who was she, by the way?"

"We know who she was," Jokela interrupted. "Her name's irrelevant."

"Not if I have to go and explain to her why she needs to keep her mouth shut."

Ahti's father and Jokela both winced.

"My dear boy," Jokela said, reproachful, "no one's asking you to cover up a crime."

"No," Virtanen added in haste. "Because there was no crime."

The man didn't like me, I could see that. Still, Virtanen was stuck with me, and if we were playing, it was on my own terms. I waited, thinking about my police career and the irony of this request. Somewhere, some evil god was clutching his side in a fit of hysterical laughter.

"Her name is Elena," Ahti's father said at last.

"Is she of age, too?"

"She's eighteen. Her aunt is a very diligent woman, she examines the girls' papers before she hires them."

"Right," I said. "I'll take your word for that. What about the car?"

"Ruined." Virtanen shrugged. "But it was insured, and the ice on the road is the municipality's fault, not my son's."

There was silence. They were pussyfooting around the real issue. But once it was said out loud, it couldn't be undone. I chose a different approach.

"What does Ahti do? Is he a student?"

"My son is reading law."

"And I trust he intends to follow in his father's footsteps?"

The father nodded cautiously. "Ahti has a passion for civil service. It would be a pity to ruin the boy's future career over one unfortunate accident."

"Of course," Jokela said. "Of course. Chief Inspector Mustonen will make sure that doesn't happen." He stomped on my foot under the table to drive his point home. *Bastard.*

A doe-eyed waitress came up to our table offering a coffee refill, but Jokela sent her away. "What is your problem, Mustonen?" he hissed. "The matter is pretty straightforward.

The young woman was drunk, she was incoherent. Even the witness recognizes that. The fact that she insisted on going to the police … she probably regrets it as we speak, but what's done is done."

"Forgive me if I'm wrong," I said to Virtanen, ignoring my boss. "From what I understand, the young woman is claiming that your Ahti was holding her against her will, and that his idea of a fun night was a *bain de minuit* in Helsinki Port." Virtanen closed his eyes briefly, a picture of human suffering, a man misunderstood. I pressed on: "And when the witness rushed over to help the passengers out of the car, he saw that the girl's hands were tied?"

Virtanen's eyes flew open; his fist landed on the table. "They were just messing around, for Christ's sake! I recognize that the idea of tying up the girl was unfortunate, and that the midnight ice dip, with or without the girl, was plain stupid. But young men make mistakes. That doesn't mean they – and their families – should have to pay for that with their careers."

There we were, at last. "Well," I said, keeping my eyes on the father, "as long as we all recognize how important that is for the careers of all the parties involved. I'll interview the girl and the witness and see what I can do. You're probably right and the girl just panicked because she heard the stories going around. Let's hope it was just that. In the meantime, I recommend that you keep Ahti home for a while, make sure there are no other unfortunate accidents. It could draw unwanted attention to what happened yesterday night. Are we clear on the terms?"

"Yes," the father said. "We are." He was looking at me when he said that. Not at Jokela.

9

Hella

I didn't know what I was expecting. Crimson silk, certainly, and velvet and lace. Tall champagne glasses and sensual girls in negligees. But during the daytime, at least, Klara Nylund's establishment looked like any other house: freshly painted woodwork on the outside, the smell of cooking on the inside. Roast lamb. My stomach growled.

The girl managing reception heard it and smiled, the gold tooth in her mouth gleaming in the morning light. "Can I help you, Miss?"

She was wondering who I could be. I didn't look like a prospective employee. I didn't look like anybody's wife either.

"My name's Mauzer. I'm here to see Miss Nylund."

The girl nodded, interested now. So the news had got around.

"Up the stairs, second floor."

She didn't offer to accompany me, so I made my own way there. The stairs were covered in thick carpet, and there were photographs on the walls. Lots of pretty girls, most of them blonde, all of them young. One of the frames was empty: Nellie.

Klara Nylund was standing on the landing when I got there. Without a word, she escorted me into her office, motioning towards a high-backed chair.

"Any luck with Maria?" she asked once I had sat down.

I shrugged. "She knows something, but she's not telling. I'm guessing she was afraid. I need to know more about this place, when you started, who your clients are – that sort of thing. If you had other girls disappear in the past…"

The madam looked tired, dark circles under her eyes sinking deep into her skull. I caught my reflection in the splotchy glass behind her: I looked worse.

"Smoke?" The madam pulled a crumpled pack of unfiltered Chesterfields out of the pocket of her cardigan.

"No thank you."

"You must be the only girl in Helsinki who'd say no to a cigarette." She watched me with narrowed eyes. Her words, when she spoke again, came out drenched in smoke. "So, about this place. We first opened in December 1938. I inherited this house – I was already in the hospitality business, so I thought I'd open my own place. It was smaller then. Just me and two girls. And before you say anything, I know what women like you think about my trade. I'm not ashamed of who I am."

"I'm not judging you."

"You'd be the only one."

"Maybe."

Klara Nylund chuckled. "Anyway. We closed after a year."

"Because all the men had gone to fight in the Winter War?"

She answered with another question. "Do you know that syphilis rates spiked when the war started?"

"They doubled, right?"

"Make it times eight. And gonorrhoea, times three. I couldn't keep this place going. I spent the war years helping out at the Surgical Hospital in Ullanlinna."

I had been there too, with my mother and my older sister, Christina, who had spent her time flirting with the soldiers. I wondered if Klara and I had met back then. Not that it mattered.

"When did you reopen?"

"1946. There were lots of girls on the streets, the locals and the refugees. They'd come knocking, ask me to take them in. Most of them would stay a couple of years, then find something different. The idea they have when they come here is that they'll hook up with and marry one of the clients. It never happens, of course."

"Nellie definitely hooked up with someone. She was pregnant at the time of her death. Did Chief Inspector Jokela tell you that? It was in the medical report he gave you, but it's written in such a way that someone who's not used to the terminology would never guess." I showed her the report. "It's here. *Gravida*. That's Latin for pregnant."

The madam nodded slowly. "Nellie had been looking unwell recently. I remember asking her about it, but she shrugged it off, told me it was just a bug she'd caught." Klara Nylund frowned. "Do you think that could have been the reason?"

"That's why I need to know the names of Nellie's clients." I pulled my notepad out of my bag, unscrewed the top of my fountain pen. "You cater to a well-off clientele. Those men have a lot to lose."

Klara Nylund stood up. "That's exactly why they come to my place and not other establishments, and that's why there's no list. I'd be risking more than my business if I gave you the names of my clients. No, you'll have to do without."

"How?"

"I don't know. Interview people working in the port. This isn't someone she met through my place, and any regulars she had were not the type to kill anyone. We don't cater to homicidal maniacs here."

"You'd be surprised," I said.

"Nothing surprises me any more. Being surprised is *your* job."

Klara Nylund marched towards the door and opened it wide.

The interview was over.

10

Chief Inspector Mustonen

As my father-in-law was fond of saying, the only difference between a man and a boy was the price of their toys. I thought about that as I left the cafe through the back door and started walking down the busy street. Young Ahti had very expensive toys. They could spell trouble, not only for the Virtanen family but also for me now I was involved. I needed to tread carefully but act quickly. Assess the damage, see what could be done.

First, the car. No matter what Ahti's father said, I needed to make up my own mind. People lie, objects don't.

The Chrysler had been towed away to a garage on Ratakatu, where it sat awaiting assessment by the insurance company. I considered taking a cab there, but the morning traffic was already heavy, and besides, I wouldn't be able to claim expenses on that one. So I walked, my felt hat pulled low over my face, my mind racing. Had I just made a mistake? And what would happen if I changed my mind?

All around me, the street was teeming with people. Men hurrying to their offices, armed with briefcases, dowdy housewives returning home from the market with their bags full. A newspaper boy peddling *Helsingin Sanomat*. The cover story was on Julius and Ethel Rosenberg's campaign for clemency. I bought a copy. The boy barely looked at me. This was what I enjoyed the most about living in a big city – you could do your own thing and, as long as you looked respectable, no one took notice.

The garage was on a narrow street and I could hear banging – metal on metal – before I even turned the corner. There was no one in the reception area, so I strode right in, my warrant card in my pocket. Better to avoid showing it.

"What do you want?" A stocky guy in overalls glanced up from whatever he was doing on the carcass of a Ford. I pointed towards the cherry-red Chrysler in the yard.

"Assessment."

"Sure." Even as the mechanic answered, he was turning away, his mind already on other things. I looked the part: young, professional, wool coat, briefcase, hat. If the man in overalls had thought about it even for a moment, he would have realized that no lowly insurance expert could afford a coat like mine, but people like him don't think. Besides, I'd never said I was sent by the insurance company. If things went belly-up, I could claim I'd showed him my card but that the mechanic hadn't been paying attention.

The Chrysler was a beauty, with its swept-back roof, its curved rear windows. I walked around it, leaning close to the car in case the man was watching me. The car looked barely damaged. I'd been expecting worse. The right headlight was smashed, and there was a dent in the bumper. Probably a problem with the steering, too, given that the car had been towed here. I tried the doors, which opened easily. There was a jumble of clothes on the back seat: a stole, a tie, a woman's pointy shoe. I picked up the objects one by one in my gloved hand, wondering whether at some point they might prove useful to the investigation. I thought about that girl, Elena; if she realized how lucky she had been. Lucky to have had the car skid on the ice, lucky that a passer-by had rushed over to help. Lucky to be alive.

I needed to interview Elena, and I also needed to see young Ahti. The boy must have known that the body of a prostitute had been pulled out of the harbour recently, but he had still done what he did. So far, I had only two working hypotheses: either the boy was stupid, or he had a very weird sense of humour. I refused to consider the third possibility, that the boy was a good candidate for the role of mass murderer. It was too early for that. I needed to find more evidence first.

I was also wondering about Hella Mauzer. How long before she heard about last night's accident and sprang into action?

11

Hella

The pathologist looked like a Popeye who some prankster had managed to squeeze into green surgical scrubs three sizes too small. His huge bulging forearms ended in deft, sensitive hands. At that precise moment, those hands were pulling on a liver-spotted scalp with a scarlet rim running around its circumference. The skullcap, coming loose, made the same sucking sound as a pickle jar being prized open.

"Back off, young lady," the pathologist muttered without looking up. "This is not a place for a woman."

I took my hat off. "You have one on the table before you. Or do you mean this is not a place for a *live* woman?"

"Hey! My favourite sleuth!" Tom strode towards me with his arms outstretched, something viscous dripping from his gloved fingers. "Give me a hug! How's your lumberjack stallion?"

I glanced at the corpse he had left behind on the metal table. "Tom, this is the only coat I've got. Can we smack the air like the French?"

Tom blew me a kiss, sending droplets flying in all directions. "Find yourself a chair. I'm nearly done with this one."

He wiped his hands on his shirt, his blue eyes twinkling behind horn-rimmed glasses. "Do you know what Napoleon Bonaparte and Scarlett O'Hara had in common?"

"No." Tom's favourite game: asking medical riddles you stood no chance of solving.

"Then think," he said.

The body Tom was working on was that of a wrinkled old woman. In his huge hands, she looked like an air-dried child. "Does she have things in common with Napoleon and Scarlett too?" I asked.

"Oh yes."

All the chairs in the autopsy room had mountains of paper on them, so instead of sitting I leaned against a wall. "What did she do in life?"

"She was a seamstress. But her hobby was costume re-enactment."

He bent over the body again, humming to himself.

I didn't want to look, so I picked up one of the magazines lying on the chair and leafed through it. It was an issue on Finnish athletes – a national obsession since the Olympics. The article on pull-ups had the corner turned down. "Do you really need to do this much exercise?" I asked Tom. "Can't you be like other humans? Flabby and beer-bellied?"

"Are you giving up, Hella Mauzer?"

"Yes."

"All right, but only because it's you. Listen to what I've found here: sub-endocardial haemorrhage in the left ventricle, fatty yellow liver … like foie gras. Does that tell you anything?"

"Arsenic poisoning."

"Good," Tom said. "Very good." His deft fingers were prising open the dead woman's flesh, and I had to breathe deeper and concentrate on his voice, ignoring the rush of blood in my ears.

"I'll wait outside —" I started saying, but Tom spoke at the same time.

"The woman's daughter is accusing her brother's wife of doing the old girl in."

"And did she?"

Tom shook his head. "You really are slow today. Must be the constricted blood vessels caused by the extreme cold over in Lapland. That's why your voice sounds funny, too, as if you can't breathe. What did I tell you her hobby was?"

When I didn't say anything, Tom supplied the answer himself. "Costume re-enactment."

"Do you mean to say she dressed like Scarlett O'Hara?"

"That green curtain dress Scarlett wore," Tom said cheerfully, "was a *major* health hazard. Scarlett was a fictional character, she survived. This one wasn't so lucky. Add to that the emerald-green wallpaper in her room, and there you have it. Arsenic poisoning. In that sense, the old girl shares the tragic fate of Napoleon."

"I thought the English poisoned him?"

"Oh no," Tom said. He started stitching, his head bent low, frowning with concentration. "Some people pretend that's what got him on St Helena. Not the Brits. The wallpaper. The brilliant green one is laced with arsenic. Napoleon happened to love that colour."

I looked at the old woman's body. "Was that really enough to kill her? A dress and some wallpaper?"

"That and Dr Campbell's complexion wafers." Tom looked at me sternly. "Never buy those things."

"I won't." I peeled myself off the wall. "Steve left me, Tom. Again. My complexion doesn't interest anyone any more. But that's not why I'm here."

"It's not because you wanted to see an old friend?"

I pulled Nellie's photograph out of my bag. "Seen her?"

Tom squinted at the picture. "I have. She wasn't as beautiful when she got here, but yes, I've seen her. Poor thing."

"Can you tell me what you found?"

"Step aside," Tom said, as if he hadn't heard me. "You're in front of the supply cart."

He dropped his used gloves on a shelf, then turned towards the door. "Will you wait while I change? We'll discuss this over coffee. I don't know about you, but I'm starving."

Five minutes later, we were walking down the narrow corridor that led to the exit. The autopsy room was on the ground floor of the Surgical Hospital, but it could very well have been on a different planet. It smelled different, the sounds were muffled, the faces, lit by blinking fluorescent lights, took on a greenish hue. When strangers asked Tom what he did in life, he invariably answered: "I'm a thanatologist. I study death, and my abode is the underworld." Usually, this was where the conversation stopped while the hapless stranger drifted away, mumbling something about the need to replenish his glass.

"Do you remember telling Mustonen that Nellie was three months pregnant?" I asked. "It's in the file, but I wonder if you discussed it?"

"Yes, and he shrugged it off, said that it wasn't at all surprising if she was, given her profession."

"And you share his opinion?" My words came out sharper than I intended. "If she got to three months without doing anything about it, it must surely mean something."

Tom sighed. "You know there's no love lost between me and that pompous ass. But when he's right, he's right. The pregnancy doesn't mean a thing." He raised a hand. "Don't start bitching just yet. Hear me out."

"What?"

We were getting close to the exit and the hospital sounds and smells were seeping towards us: chlorine, boiled cabbage, an ambulance's wail.

I stopped and faced Tom. "Don't tell me you see prostitutes as second-rate citizens."

Tom glanced at me cautiously. "Well, not exactly. No, of course I don't think that. It's just that their profession – there's an inherent risk factor in it. But the problem with Nellie was not her pregnancy. It was something else. It's one of those cases where you suspect things but can't be sure. No conclusive evidence either way."

"Did you tell *that* to Mustonen?"

"I did. I said I wasn't sure, and he said he'd look into it. But let's face it, Hella. That guy is building a career. Investigating a prostitute's death, it's a lot of hassle for very little reward. Not the kind of case he's likely to spend a significant amount of time on." Tom held the door for me and we emerged into the daylight. "Which is probably the reason we're having this conversation right now."

12

Chief Inspector Mustonen

If you must lie, be brief. The story I had prepared for Elena the escort could be summed up in five short words: *no one will believe you.* As I climbed the steep stairs leading to her fourth-floor apartment, I rehearsed the speech in my mind. I planned to stay five minutes, no more. Deal with it, go back to the office. Try to wipe the encounter from my mind. Maybe even convince myself I did the right thing.

But when Elena finally opened her door a suspicious crack, she didn't look at all like I'd imagined. I had thought Russian; I had thought potato-faced blonde with big breasts. I had to give it to the ankle biter: the boy had taste.

The girl was slim and dark and exotic. She had huge violet eyes framed by the longest lashes I had ever seen. She looked like Scheherazade, like something out of a dream. I blinked, willing myself to remember the woman I loved: my wife. Fair-haired, modest and pure. And now, finally, getting some energy back for a bit of bedroom exercise.

"Are you here about my attacker?" Elena asked in a small voice.

I flipped my warrant card open and shut, too quickly for her to see anything, but the girl was no idiot. "Can I see it?"

"Yes," I said. "Certainly."

She studied the document, frowning. Her eyes flew to my face, back to the card. "Homicide squad? Chief Inspector? Do you mean to say that Ahti was the one who —"

Jesus, I thought. I wouldn't be able to pretend I'd never seen this one. She wasn't taking any chances. She'd remember me all right: what I said, how I looked, the colour of my damned shoes.

"May I come in?" I said. "It'll be easier to talk."

"Of course," the girl said, but she was still holding onto the door chain. "I have a friend with me in the apartment, do you mind if he stays?" And, before I could answer: "Vlad?"

Vlad looked Russian all right; he was also huge. He stared at me for a long time before finally nodding and releasing the chain. "Come in. I'll be watching."

"Maybe you don't need the police," I quipped, entering the room. It was furnished in Slavic style: striped cotton rugs on the floor, blue and white Gzhel cups next to a gleaming samovar. "You seem to have first-class security." Elena smiled back, though it was clear from her expression she didn't think that was funny. Vlad the gorilla growled something unintelligible.

"So," I said, pulling a chair towards me. "You're right about the fact that, normally, the homicide squad doesn't get involved with the sort of accident you had. But we like to be proactive." I smiled. "That didn't come out right, did it? What I mean is, we want to make sure people feel safe in this city. Not everyone is lucky enough to have a friend like yours." I nodded towards Vlad but got no reaction. "So basically, I came over here to tell you that the local police station has already transferred an account of the accident to me and it seems clear enough. We'll be conducting a background check on your supposed attacker —"

"Wait a minute —" Vlad started. I silenced him with a raised hand.

"— and if anything comes out that points to his involvement in other accidents, we'll get back to you."

Elena threw a helpless glance towards her chivalrous servant, who rose from his chair.

"Elena here," he said in a heavily accented voice, "she was tied up and held against her will. If they didn't get into a car accident, she would have been killed. You know who the guy was. Go arrest him."

"Vlad, is it?" I said, standing up as well. "Can you maybe give me your last name? And your residence permit? I trust you're not Finnish, given your accent. You too, Elena, please."

No one moved, but the temperature in the room dropped by several degrees. I folded my arms across my chest and waited. When I was certain no answer was forthcoming, I turned to leave. "You see," I said over my shoulder, "that's exactly the problem with you. You're illegal residents. In the eyes of the law, you don't even exist. So before you go around accusing upstanding Finnish citizens, you need to settle that little matter first."

Vlad and Elena exchanged a couple of words in Russian. I don't speak the language, but the meaning was clear.

I stopped at the door.

"As I said, we're going to look into it. We take our citizens' concerns very seriously." I put an emphasis on *citizens*, to drive the meaning home.

As I ran down the steps, I wondered if they had got the message. Vlad maybe not, he didn't look bright enough. But Elena... I wondered if I should turn back. I wondered if she'd notice the little card I had dropped in the hallway: no name on it, just an address in Fastholma. I also thought that I should have questioned her about the incident. I had no doubt it had happened. But had it just been a kid fooling around, or was there more to it? And was there any chance in hell of proving that young Ahti had been involved in the other girl's death? Might he make a good suspect?

But then I thought: *Nah.* He was too young. That boy, a mass murderer? Come on! No one would believe that.

13

Hella

The weather turned while I was in the autopsy room. The low dark skies opened up; when Tom and I emerged from the morgue, sleet was pounding the street, making it difficult to see anything beyond the warm glow of the cafe's windows. Once inside, Tom shook himself like a big, affectionate dog and grinned. He dropped his hat and briefcase onto the chair next to him and signalled to the waiter.

"Yes, sir?"

The waiter, who had floppy white hair and no lashes I could discern, stared at us with undisguised disapproval.

"It'll be the usual. No, wait." Tom glanced at me. "Make it two. This young woman here needs —"

"Oh no," I cut in. "Absolutely not." Tom had a habit of ordering weird foods and pretending to enjoy them. Last time we had eaten together, he'd kept going on about how healthy young deer blood was. Good for the complexion and everything. So no, I was not going to risk it.

"I'll just have a coffee, please," I said to the waiter. "And a cardamom *pulla* bread." I glanced at Tom. "I'd rather die slowly of clogged arteries than fall victim to another of your experiments."

"You're wrong."

"Maybe. Can we talk about Nellie?"

"Shh." Tom spread his hands on the table. "I need my drink before I can tackle the serious stuff. Tell me about Steve while we wait. What happened?"

I threw my hands up in the air. "Because my wretched love life isn't serious?"

"Not really. You'll get back together, as you always do. And even if you don't, you'll always have me."

"That's not exactly the same," I blurted out before I had time to think about it.

"Why? I'm as handsome on the inside as he is. There's just more of me."

"True." I drummed my fingers on the table. In the background, the waiter was grating some vegetable or other over a tall glass. "Anyway, Steve's gone, end of story."

"Because?"

"Because I made a scene."

"Not you." Tom grinned. "I'd never believe it."

"I was feeling down, all right? And please would you stop with your interrogation now? I'll be fine."

The waiter came over with my order and a strange concoction in a tall glass. It looked sort of milky.

"What is it? Yak's milk with herbs?"

Tom took a sip and smacked his lips. "Close. Goat's milk with honey, melted butter and horseradish. I've never felt better."

I smiled into my coffee. "Good for you. Can we get back to the dead girl?"

"Well," Tom said. "I suppose you know how people drown in ice-cold water? A so-called torso reflex, also known as cold shock response?"

"Not first-hand, no. Come to think of it, not second-hand either."

"Actually" – Tom smacked his lips again – "short of being hit by a bus or struck by lightning, cold shock is one of the most extreme things a human body can experience. It's potentially lethal." He stuck out his thumb. "First, your heart rate picks up because all the blood vessels constrict when they come into contact with the cold water. You gasp, and not just a little. A huge, heaving gasp that totally fills your lungs. If your head is under water at that moment, you drown instantly."

"OK," I said. "But if the person doesn't drown immediately? Can she swim to safety?"

Tom stuck out a second finger. "Not easy. After the gasps, hyperventilation sets in. Even a good swimmer will find it difficult to swim more than a few yards. Your best chance is to pull yourself up where you fell through the ice."

"But you can't do that if your attacker is standing right there, ready to push you back in," I said. "Is that what you think happened to Nellie?"

"The third stage is called hypocapnia," Tom continued, as if he hadn't heard. "It's a result of the hyperventilation. The symptoms are dizziness, cramps, numbing of the hands and feet, not that it matters any longer. You will also find it difficult to hold your breath – you'll feel like you're suffocating – and the pain will be intense if the water temperature is below forty degrees Fahrenheit, which it was in this case."

"Enough," I said. "I get it. If ever I fall through the ice, I'll just whisper a short prayer and let myself drown."

"Focus on your breathing. For a fit person like you, it does get better after about three minutes. If you don't pass out from the cold first. Or, better yet, don't go anywhere near the water."

"Thank you. I'll keep that in mind. Can we get back to our victim? Do you think someone pushed her through the ice?"

"Well," Tom said, "there were two things. First of all, she had a wound on one side of her head."

"Maybe she banged her head on the railings, stumbled into the water."

"Maybe." Tom didn't sound convinced.

"Could it have happened somewhere else and she just drifted?"

"No. I looked at the patterns of the currents and there's no way she could have been brought into the harbour if she drowned somewhere else."

"So someone hit her, then pushed her over the railings? Is that what you're saying? I stopped by the harbour on my way, and the ice is pretty thick there, so there must have been an impact."

Tom smiled modestly. "You didn't ask me about the other thing I noticed."

I waited. He was going to tell me anyway. He took his time though, first asking the waiter to bring him a second glass of goat's milk, then fussing with his scarf. I hated it when he did that, but there was nothing I could do, so I just sat there, sipping my coffee and gritting my teeth.

"Her earrings," he said at last. "They were torn from her ears. Mustonen told me *fish*. And maybe," Tom snorted, "*may*be earring-gobbling *fish* exist, but I've never heard of them. More likely, someone ripped the girl's earrings out of her earlobes. Before she drowned."

"So to you, it was a murder. It's just the evidence that's inconclusive."

Tom looked at me sternly. "This is your chance to prove to that bastard Mustonen that you're way more capable than he is. Just watch your back, will you? He might not like it."

14

Chief Inspector Mustonen

The card was still where I had left it the previous night after snatching it from Jokela's office: on my desk, propped against the silver-framed photograph of my family. Thick pink paper, the initials K. N. and a telephone number. Nothing else. I stared at it for a long moment, then scooped it up and dropped it into the wastepaper basket.

I had work to do. Serious work. Jokela had asked me to represent the Finnish police on the committee dedicated to cooperation with Interpol. There was talk of exchange of best practices, and the inclusion of local data in the cross-continental information system Interpol was trying to establish. A meeting was scheduled for the following day, and I had a sheaf of documents to read. In English, which was not easy for me, and next to impossible for Jokela. So I tried to concentrate on that, but it was no good. My mind was on the drowned girl. I decided that Jokela had made a mistake sending Klara Nylund away. I should have continued with the investigation, kept an eye on things.

Now it was probably too late. Jokela would have a fit if I told him I was having second thoughts. Already, when I had mentioned it might be useful for me to see young Ahti, Jokela had stared at me as if I was mad. *Absolutely out of the question*, my boss had said. *Don't even think about it.* All this because a politician's son was involved, and because Dr Palmu had been seen hyperventilating at the staff meeting earlier that week. Jokela thought his time had come, and maybe it was true. Maybe it was also true that I would follow in his footsteps and become the youngest ever head of the homicide squad. Right now, it made no difference. The death of Nellie Ritvanen should have been investigated by the police, not some hapless PI. I supposed my qualms could be interpreted as a case of bad conscience. Or professional pride. If there was an arrest on that case, I wanted to be the one who made it.

Even with my door closed, I could hear my boss telling elaborate war stories to a suitably spellbound audience in the break room. Jokela was laughing at his own jokes, to the sound of an obediently cackling chorus. How ironic that the man could remember his stories so well, but never the people he'd already told them to. Everyone present in the room would probably be able to recite Jokela's stories even if woken from a deep sleep.

The card was out of the wastepaper basket almost before I realized what I was doing. I pressed the telephone to my ear. One of the girls answered on the second ring.

"I need to talk to Ms Nylund."

She didn't ask me who I was, just put the receiver down and yelled, "Klara! For you!"

As I waited, I kept glancing at my closed door. If anyone came in, I'd just have to pretend I had dialled a wrong number. No way could I allow word to get around that I had been calling the madam.

"Who is this?" Klara Nylund came on the phone, breathing hard.

"Chief Inspector Mustonen."

"What's happened?"

"Nothing. I heard from my boss that he recommended you contact a PI, so I wanted to know if you went to see Miss Mauzer."

"I saw her yesterday afternoon." The woman paused. "Is that really why you're calling? Or are you trying to find out if she's uncovered something?"

"Did she?"

"She's working on it. I like her, she's got good ideas. She's been talking to Nellie's friend, Maria, she thinks the girl knows something."

I listened and my heart rate picked up. Jokela was wrong to underestimate the former *polissyster*: there was every chance that she'd get to the truth first. I had to act, and fast.

15

Hella

I had never realized it until then, but one of the main advantages of living in a big city was that you could pick your own friends. You didn't have to fit in. You could ignore your neighbours and choose your companions, not have them chosen for you. In villages, you had to socialize with people with whom you had nothing in common but your birthplace. But in big cities? You could do as you pleased. Life was smaller, more confined. At least mine had been until Anita came along.

If I'd been hoping she would spend her evenings elsewhere and only show up at my place for the night, I had just been proven wrong. Anita's cheerful warbling – "Vaya con Dios", a recent hit by Les Paul and Mary Ford – greeted me at the top of the stairs. Along with the smell of something burning.

I dumped my bag on the floor and shut the door behind me. "What are you cooking?"

"Well," Anita said, giggling, "it was supposed to be a Runeberg torte. Only it sort of stayed flat." She had Steve's old shirt thrown over her dress like an apron, and that was when I realized I'd forgotten to put his things outside the door the previous night. I looked around. His trench coat was gone from the hook and his boots were no longer by the door.

Anita had already disappeared back into the kitchen. "Did someone come round?" I called after her.

"Uh-huh." And then: "Oh, for heaven's sake!"

I peered in. I suppose a man would have said Anita looked adorable, standing there in a cloud of flour, her blonde hair in an elaborate coil on top of her head, her blue eyes twinkling. I could well imagine Steve thinking just that.

"Did my boyfriend come over here while I was away?"

"Your ex," clarified Anita, matter-of-fact.

I felt like knocking her off her feet and stuffing the torte down her throat. Instead, I hissed through gritted teeth, "Yes. My ex. Did he come, yes or no?"

Anita nodded.

"Did he leave me a message?"

"No. He just packed his things and left."

I faced her. "Is that all? He didn't ask…" I took a deep breath. "Did he say anything at all?"

Anita rinsed her hands and turned towards me. "He said this kitchen stinks. I noticed it, too, by the way."

"He did?"

"He also said you're a pain in the neck."

"He didn't!"

"He said you don't realize how beautiful you are."

"You're lying."

"Yep," Anita said. "He didn't say anything. Anyway, how long were you living with him?"

I wondered if I should lie. The truth – the brevity of our life together, the fact that Steve had run off so quickly – was almost more than I could bear. But Anita, who was no fool where this sort of thing was concerned, must have noticed the limited number of Steve's belongings and drawn her own conclusions.

"Just a week," I said.

"You're blushing."

"I'm not. I just stayed outside too long. Probably have a touch of frostbite. As to Steve and me, we were sort of trying to see if it would work, you know, before committing long-term. Obviously it didn't."

"Then," Anita shrugged, "you'd better forget about him. You know how the saying goes. Girls want a lot of things from one guy, but guys want only one thing from a lot of girls. And once they get it —"

"Steve's not like that."

"You poor thing," Anita said. "Are you hungry? We can eat the caviar."

Five minutes later, having sliced rye bread and spread sticky grey caviar on it, we settled on the sofa.

"Pity there's no butter," Anita said, biting into her sandwich. "The newspapers pretend that food rationing is likely to stop soon. Maybe even before the end of the year. Do you remember what it was like – going out shopping, buying what you wanted? Good butcher's sausages to make *lörtsy* pastries, egg butter, Christmas stars?"

"I guess I've got used to living with less. Maybe it's not so bad."

I carried the plates back into the kitchen. When I came back, Anita was curled up on the sofa, the crocheted blanket pulled over her legs.

"So," she said. "What did you do today?"

I started ticking off on my fingers. "I went to the apartment Nellie occupied before her death – it's already been rented out and her things shipped to her mother's house. I interviewed her neighbours, her milkman, the postman…"

"Anything interesting?"

"No. I also talked to the other girls she was friendly with. Caught them while they were dressing up for their evening. They all claim —"

"That's one of my fantasies," Anita said.

"What are you talking about?"

"I heard those girls have the most exquisite dresses."

I stared at Anita until she blushed and looked away. "Anyway," I continued, "it doesn't seem like these girls know anything useful. They all say that Nellie had never been threatened, and she didn't have any debts."

"She could have met someone outside" – Anita searched for the right word – "her workplace."

"Yes. She could have. That's what I was thinking too. Tomorrow morning I'll try Maria again. She knows something, but for some reason she's wary of me."

"Did you talk to the pathologist?"

I hesitated, not sure if I wanted Anita to know about my friendship with Tom. If it ever got back to Jokela, he probably wouldn't be happy about it. "What about you?" I said, changing the subject. "How was Jokela today?"

"His same old self."

"And Mustonen?"

"Preoccupied, but I don't know what with. I barely saw him."

"You haven't told him you're living here, have you?"

"I did, actually," Anita said. "Well, I didn't *tell* him, I told Tarja, our secretary, but he was nearby and he heard me. He sort of made a joke about it."

"What joke?"

"I don't remember." Anita busied herself with her bag.

Must have been something about my housekeeping skills, I thought. "He didn't ask about me working on this case, did he?"

"Nah," Anita said. "He probably thinks it's for the best."

I looked at her. She was bent low, filing her nails, so I couldn't catch her eye. I was not sure if what she said was true, even though she believed it herself. I knew Mustonen: unless he'd changed dramatically over the last few years, he wouldn't be happy if someone like me solved the case after he had dismissed it. Mustonen didn't like to lose. He wanted to be the best at what he did, and he wanted everyone to know it.

But before I had a chance to ask another question, I heard rushed footsteps outside, then a sharp knock on my door.

"Mauzer," my neighbour said, "a phone call for you. The woman said to hurry."

16

Hella

Even though the phone was located in a booth, the madam's screaming greeted me halfway down the stairs. I held the receiver away from my ear.

"It's Maria! She's been mugged!"

"Hold on," I said, when the madam finally paused for breath. "Is she hurt?" I didn't ask if the girl was alive; I hoped she was.

"Her face is ruined," Klara Nylund breathed out, suddenly quiet, as if someone had put a lid on her. "Her teeth are knocked out and —"

"I'm coming. Is she at her place?"

The phone was on the ground floor of my building, which was occupied by a language school. I paid them a small fee, they let me use the shared line. It didn't mean I could stay on it long.

Once Klara Nylund whispered a yes, I put the receiver down and climbed the stairs to my apartment. I needed to grab my bag and fend off Anita, who had been hovering by the door with puppyish enthusiasm, her coat and hat already on.

"I'm going with you!"

"Oh, no," I said. "No no no." I had been expecting that. Anita had that zeal of a new convert, she was itching to take part in a real investigation, but there was no way I was letting her. The girl was too young; she'd be a hindrance, not an asset. Besides, I'd never felt the need for a sidekick, or the urge to discuss my cases. I supposed that made me a loner. "You stay here," I said. "You need your nine hours of beauty sleep. I'll see you tomorrow morning."

Before she could answer, I was out of the door.

It was probably not as bad as it looked, though that was not a thing to say to a girl whose only card in life was her face.

Maria's tiny apartment was chock-full. There was the madam, in an evening dress and a mink stole, her crimson lipstick bleeding into the fine lines on her face. There were a couple of top-heavy guys with broken noses and cauliflower ears. Several girls in various states of undress. They had all rushed to Maria's rescue, alerted by a neighbour. Maria was lying on the sofa, an ice pack pressed to one side of her head. Her eyes were like slits in her swollen face.

I kneeled beside her. "Did you see your attacker?"

She shook her head no.

"How did it happen?"

Turned out, Maria had spent her day in the apartment, but had realized as dusk set in that she had run out of cigarettes. The tobacconist's was on the corner of her street. She was out for less than ten minutes, but when she approached her front door, someone had been waiting on the landing, concealed in the shadows. She felt a hand grabbing her neck, propelling her inside. That was when she got lucky: her foot caught on the leg of a side table, which came crashing down.

Maria glanced at her saviour, a matron in a flowered dress. "I heard it," the woman said. "The noise, I mean. I live on the other side of the landing, and I have keys to Maria's place, just as she has keys to mine, so she can water the plants when I'm away. I grabbed a poker and the keys, and went inside."

I couldn't help being impressed. "Did you see what he looked like?"

"No, he must have heard my keys turn in the door. He ran out onto the balcony and skidded from roof to roof. I didn't see him at all." The look on the woman's face suggested that if she had seen the attacker, Tom would have had his hands full tonight.

Maria moaned. We had forgotten about her. Klara Nylund perched herself on the arm of the sofa and started caressing the girl's hair.

"We need to send you away," she said. "Maybe your family —"

"No." Maria shook her head.

I had an idea where she could go, a place so far away that no one would ever find her, but I was not quite ready to mention it yet.

Instead, I said: "Maria. Listen to me. It's possible Nellie got involved with a gangster or a thug. Did you tell anyone – and I mean anyone at all – that you knew something about her death?"

The girl sat up suddenly and threw her ice pack to the floor. "How many times do I have to say it?" she hissed. "I don't have any information about Nellie's death. I don't. And I didn't mention it to anyone. There's a maniac going around, hunting Klara's girls. Did you hear about Elena? She used to work for Klara too."

I stared at her. "No, I didn't." Out of the corner of my eye I could see Klara Nylund looking as puzzled as I was.

Maria was sobbing again. "What good are you then? Everyone knows who the killer is! Everyone! But no one will stop him because his family is rich. Now get out of here!"

I hadn't seen that coming. I prided myself on having a decent network of informants, a legacy of my time on the homicide squad, but maybe I was fooling myself. I had seen two of my informants the day before, and neither of them had mentioned it. Maybe the only stories they told me now were public knowledge anyway.

The madam didn't say anything when she heard about the latest port attack. She didn't need to: I may be a lousy detective, but even I know when I've messed up. She just wrapped her scarf tighter around her neck and hurried back to her establishment. She had a business to run, after all. Although, going by the feeling in Maria's room, her girls would be quitting in droves before long.

I stood outside, thinking. It was late, but not too late. I could track down that Elena girl, question her, take it from there. That was the advantage of dealing with prostitutes: they were up all night. I could practically work this case around the clock.

At first, luck was on my side. My first contact – a black market operator nicknamed Egg who lived right next to Uspenski Cathedral – told me everything I wanted to know. Almost.

"Elena is a Soviet," he said as he shuffled back to his armchair after opening the door for me. "*Very* pretty. Lots of clients." He sat down heavily. Egg was in the business of trafficking American cigarettes and whisky. Only a few people knew he had started out selling egg powder from the Allied supplies on the market, which was where he'd got his nickname. The fact that, with all the good food he could afford, he had begun to resemble an egg himself, was just a happy coincidence.

"The story goes," Egg said when I took a seat across from him, "that lovely Elena deserted her native country the day she discovered the reason you can buy just one shape of pasta in the Soviet Union."

He was clearly waiting for me to ask the question, so I played along. "And what *is* the reason for all the pasta being the same shape?"

Egg cackled, delighted. "The Soviets make pasta on the same machines that they use to make bullets. Same calibre. So that when there's another war they can stop making pasta and produce ammo instead. Anyway, when Elena learns that, she flees to Helsinki. She settles in quite nicely, does a bit of freelancing. One day, she's messing around with a politician's son" – here Egg's voice took on a reverent under-tone – "and apparently the boy decides that what she needs most of all is an ice dip. The suggestion doesn't go down well with her – she starts wriggling, and the car goes into a tailspin." Egg threw his hands up in the air. "No harm done, not even a bruise. But our girl overreacts, starts screaming about abduction, and tries to drag the police into it."

"Who?"

"The local station at first, but then bigger fish got involved."

"Who?"

"Ah…" Egg laughed softly. "Your nemesis. The golden boy of Finnish policing."

"Mustonen."

"You two were quite the pair, did you know that? Both of you defying the names you were born with. I mean, seriously, Hella the Gentle, you don't really live up to your first name, do you? Always rushing about like a Fury. And partnered with a Mr Black, all blonde, blue-eyed and presentable. At least Mustonen's parents didn't have a choice – the dark in his name goes back generations." My informant chuckled and looked at his watch. "That will be two hundred markka."

"Wait. Give me Elena's address."

Egg gave me a look. "You'll need to double the price."

I winced. I was almost out of cash. Could Anita be relied upon to buy food over the next few days, giving time for me to get back on my feet? I counted out the money and Egg scribbled an address on a torn envelope. "Here you go." He pocketed the money, looked me in the eye. "Only don't waste your time. The girl's already left."

"How? When?"

I should have realized that Egg was about to con me. He never looked people in the eye unless he was lying to them. "Tell me that, at least," I urged him.

He threw a smooth glance at my wallet. I turned it over, letting the remaining five markka tumble to the floor.

"OK," he sighed, "but only because I haven't done my good deed of the day yet. No one knows why Elena left. But here's something that you might find interesting: your friend Inspector M went to see her this morning."

"And?"

Egg winked at me. "And just after that, she vanished."

17

Hella

There was not much I could do after Egg shut his door on me. The city around me was sleeping, blanketed in heavy snow. If I tried to see Elena's neighbours at this hour, they probably wouldn't even open up. Even when you came as the police, lots of people were tight-lipped; a PI, in the middle of the night, badgering them about some prostitute? No way anyone would bother.

I trudged back to my apartment, still reeling from the discovery that I had missed the mark. I hoped Anita was asleep already. But as I rounded the corner of my street, I saw the two windows on the fourth floor shining with electric light.

When I finally hauled myself up the stairs, the door to my apartment was wide open. There were voices coming from my bedroom. I couldn't hear what they were saying, but it sounded like an argument. I recognized Anita's angry chattering. The other voice – male – sounded familiar too.

"Anita?" I called out. "Is everything OK?"

The voices stopped at once. A moment later, Anita's tousled head peered out. "Hi! Thank God you're back."

She stepped out of the room, followed by our late-night guest. It was Ranta, Anita's cousin and my former colleague from the Ivalo police station. I owed him, so I stifled a curse and smiled instead, a strained smile that he didn't reciprocate. I was wondering what he had been doing in my bedroom, and if I'd find some of my things missing when he was gone. With Ranta, there usually were.

"I came to check up on the dumb blonde," he said, "see if she's doing OK, because you can't really trust her to make the right decisions. Young girls like her fall in with the wrong crowd, or get themselves pregnant, and good luck dealing with the consequences." For such a small, crooked, unprepossessing man, Ranta had an exceptionally beautiful opera-singer's voice. He strolled towards me, his hands in his pockets. As usual, he smelled like a garbage bin. Must be his rotting teeth, or the things he ate, or both. I held my breath as he got closer.

"So how are you, pariah?" he asked. "Bumbling along?"

Pariah was what Ranta had used to call me in Ivalo, because, deep down, that's what I was. Now it looked like the nickname had followed me to Helsinki.

"She's on a case," Anita told him, arms folded across her chest. "She's investigating a murder!"

Ranta sneered. "Good for you. Then I'd better leave you to your detective work, Mauzer. I only hope you aren't too busy to watch over *her*!" He almost stabbed Anita's forehead with a dirty finger. "Otherwise, she'd need to come back and stay with me."

"No way," Anita said, her voice rising. "You'll spend your time spying on me, threatening —"

I walked towards the front door. My intention was to indicate to Ranta that he was not welcome here. But when

I opened the door, I discovered the school caretaker's son standing on the landing, out of breath.

"A call for you, Ms Mauzer." He glanced at a slip of paper he was holding. "Mr Steve Collins. About a new case."

In the living room, Anita and Ranta were still screaming at each other. I stared at the boy, my heart beating too fast, then fumbled for some change before remembering I didn't have any. Steve had probably left something behind, I thought, before checking myself. No, that couldn't be it. Steve never called if it wasn't serious. He wouldn't have called about a forgotten sock.

"Ms Mauzer?" the boy said tentatively, dancing from foot to foot.

A call about a case was just an excuse, I decided. Steve wanted to come back. But I couldn't talk to him right then, I needed to think about it first, on what conditions I'd take him back, and it was impossible to focus with all the noise. Besides, it looked like Ranta was about to break something.

"I'll call Mr Collins back," I said to the boy, snapping my bag shut. "In ten minutes. Did he give you his number? I need to settle something here first."

The boy gave me the slip of paper with the number scribbled on it, then, after one last longing glance at my bag, ran down the stairs.

As soon as the door clicked shut, I screamed: "Stop it!"

"What?" Ranta was unfazed. "We're just talking." Still, he let go of the sobbing Anita and thrust his hands into his pockets.

"No," I said. "You were just leaving. Now!"

I threw the door open again.

"OK, OK, pariah!" Ranta mumbled. "I'm going." Slowly, he picked up his coat and hat. I was hoping to see the last of him but he paused on the doorstep. "I know what you're like when you follow a lead," he said. "No snowflake left unturned. But that case you're working on, you need to watch your step. Could be dangerous."

"Are you threatening me?"

His tiny eyes skipped over my shoulder and settled on Anita, their expression hard to read. "No. It's a warning." He turned and started down the steps, leaving me standing there, wondering.

"Ugh," Anita said. "He probably doesn't know anything, just wants to look important. Don't pay him any attention." She reached up and started pulling at the pins in her complicated hairdo, sending her blonde curls tumbling down her back. "Who was that at the door?"

I hesitated. If Steve wanted to come back, I needed to get rid of Anita first. No way was I bringing him home if she was around. Steve was a good guy and he loved me, I was sure of that, but that girl... He'd just sit around, goggling like a moron. "It was a phone call from a new client," I said at last. "They want me to find someone for them."

"Oh," Anita said. "I thought it might be Steve. You were blushing when you talked to that boy." She winked at me. "Are you going to call him back? Your new client?"

"I'm going to do it right now."

The telephone was downstairs, in a booth that the school caretaker locked for the night; I had to knock on the boy's window to get the key. He glared at me – I should have asked Anita for some spare change to pay him for his efforts – but gave it to me in the end. By that time, my heart was banging so loudly against my ribcage, I wondered if the boy could hear it.

I dialled Steve's number, twisting the cord around my finger while the phone rang. I thought I'd ask my friend Esteri if Anita could stay in her apartment for a while. I knew Esteri was going on a cruise with her granddaughter the following week, a tour of the Mediterranean, so her apartment was going to be empty for quite some time. And then —

Steve picked up on the third ring. "Hello, Mauzer."

I hesitated. Steve didn't sound lovestruck, but maybe he was playing it cool. I decided to match him. "Hello, yourself. What's up?"

There was a silence. Just as I started to wonder if I should invite him round, Steve said: "Actually, I'm sorry I bothered you. One of the guys I work with said he needed to hire a PI because he's being blackmailed, so I thought I'd recommend you. But he just told me he changed his mind."

"Oh." I didn't believe him for a second, but then, I didn't *want* to believe him. "And how's everything with you? Your daughter?"

"She's fine. Completely fine. We all are."

"Well, in that case, I'd better go."

"Yeah," Steve said. "Sorry if I woke you."

"That's OK. I wasn't sleeping." But he had already hung up.

I stayed in the telephone booth until the caretaker's son lost his patience. "Hey, Ms Mauzer," the boy called. "Are you done? I need to lock up."

"Yes."

The staircase was in darkness. My apartment, too. That was why I didn't see Anita until I was almost at the top of the stairs.

"It was him," I said. "My new client." My voice faltered.

"Sure."

She thrust a glass into my hands. Even without bringing it to my lips, I knew what it was. Vodka. Then Anita went into the bedroom and shut the door behind her.

I downed the glass and then poured myself another one, but I still couldn't sleep. Too many thoughts were running through my head, about the dead girl, and the fact that, at twenty-nine, I was officially older than the median age of the Finnish population. I also thought about my life back in Lapland, about Käärmelä and its log houses with their ornately carved windows, its ancient church, all of it now buried under three feet of snow. About my friends Irja and Timo and their adopted son Kalle, and my god-daughter Margarita, now two months old. How I longed to see them. I almost decided that I should move back to Lapland; the only thing stopping me was the realization I couldn't trust Mustonen to do the right thing.

At some point, I dozed off. When I opened my eyes again, grey shadows were dancing on the walls and my feet were frozen, but my mind was clear. I knew what I needed to do.

18

Chief Inspector Mustonen

"How did it go yesterday?"

Startled, I glanced at Jokela and then at the back of the man walking in front of us. Not someone I knew, but that didn't mean a thing. I had no intention of telling my story in front of anyone.

"Huh?" Jokela said again, who either didn't realize we were within earshot, or didn't care.

I shook my head. "Later."

It was nine in the morning. I had bumped into Jokela in the lobby of Headquarters, and we were striding together towards the stairs. I was carrying an umbrella dripping with melted snow. Jokela's hands were free and his coat dry: he had a car and a driver waiting for him every morning. I knew that I'd have a car too – I was going to ask for the white Studebaker – the moment I got Jokela's job, but some days it seemed like an impossible dream. More likely than not, I thought, I'd go down in flames while my boss continued to rise.

When we reached the third floor, I followed Jokela into his office, shutting the door behind us.

"No problems at all with the girl," I said. "She left Helsinki, by the way."

Jokela's eyebrows shot up.

"Oh? Did you" – he hesitated – "help her disappear in any way?"

There were a lot of things I could have said. That I didn't appreciate the insinuation. That I didn't enjoy doing the dirty work. That I had a family to support and that Jokela's shenanigans ran the risk of costing me my career. But, like it or not, Jokela was still my boss.

"She's gone," I said. "That's all you need to know. And the witness who saw the accident in the port has a bad case of amnesia."

Jokela brightened. "Good. Good job, old boy."

"There's still a problem," I said.

"What?" Jokela was taking off his coat. He stopped mid-movement.

"Mauzer. She's snooping around. You sent the madam to see her, remember? It's just a matter of time before she finds out about Ahti. If she hasn't already."

Jokela looked at me scornfully. "She's a woman, for Christ's sake. You're not afraid of a woman, are you?"

"She's good at what she does."

"Is she? Can't say I've noticed. Anyway, she'd be easy to stop."

"You don't expect me to threaten her, do you?" I said. "There are limits to what I would do to help your friends."

My boss frowned. He'd rather forget I was doing what I was doing at his request. "No," Jokela said slowly. "Of course not. But I happen to know that she has a court-imposed fine to pay." He shrugged. "There could be something in that. Think about it."

He reminded me of Sofia's father. A smug, cynical, unfeeling bastard. He made me sick. Out loud, I said: "Right. But there's another problem."

"Oh?"

"One of the madam's girls was attacked last night."

"Dead?"

"No, she was lucky. A neighbour intervened and saved her."

"She see her attacker?"

"She says no."

"So what makes you think —"

"Remember when we recommended that Virtanen keep his boy locked up at home for his own good? Do you think he complied?"

Jokela started rubbing his face. Even for him, this was getting to be a bit much.

"No," I said, when I realized Jokela wasn't going to answer. "He didn't. Your young protégé was spotted in Punavuori around the time of the attack. I don't like this, Jon. I really don't."

19

Hella

The morning was damp and cold – the thermometer indicated –10° Fahrenheit – and my sleep-deprived, hungover body spent it shivering uncontrollably. By noon, I knew as much as I was ever likely to find out. Maria's suspected attacker was a boy called Ahti Virtanen, and his father was a very big fish in the ruling party pond. Rumour had it that Ahti was responsible for the prostitutes' murders as well. The boy was young, just nineteen. Not that it wasn't possible – after all, the world's youngest multiple killer, Jesse Pomeroy, had been caught at fourteen. But I was not convinced yet.

There were no witnesses; Elena had vanished without a trace. As to the man who had seen the accident in the port, he was refusing to talk. He'd probably been offered a lot of money, or threatened, or both. I went to the madam's establishment, tried to arrange a meeting with her. A languid girl with her mouth full of chewing gum told me that the madam was busy. She'd contact me when she had the time. I scribbled a message, even though I was convinced that the girl would bin it as soon as I turned my back.

To say that I was depressed when I got back to my apartment a little before one would have been an understatement. I was almost – but not quite – longing for the depressing tranquillity of the Ivalo police station, with its charts, quarterly reports and impeccable filing system. At least back then I'd had a job, and a landlady who liked to cook. Ever since coming to Helsinki, I had been trying to reproduce some of her recipes, but the results always fell short. And now I didn't even have any money or coupons to buy food. A thorough search of the cupboard produced a packet of crackers and two raw onions. Better than nothing, I supposed.

At 1 p.m. sharp I was downstairs, the bag of crackers in my hand, waiting for a phone call I had arranged that morning. It came right on time.

I didn't know where Anita was calling from, but she was panting.

"There's a file," she said gleefully, "on Mustonen's desk, marked NELLIE RITVANEN. I caught a glimpse of it when I was talking to him this morning, but he locks his office door every time he goes out, so I couldn't see what was inside."

"Don't be too obvious about it," I said. "You'll get into trouble."

Anita's voice was muffled. "I won't."

"And it's all right if you don't get to see what's in the file. I suppose the important thing is that he's still working on it."

I could almost hear the triumphant smile in her voice. She didn't want to believe that her new boss was a bastard who would threaten a poor girl and chase her out of the city, or worse. But I wasn't so sure. In the past, Mustonen had been a good cop, diligent and smart, but even then his primary preoccupation had been his career. So no matter what I had just told Anita, the fact that he had a file on his desk didn't mean a thing.

"Anything else?" Anita asked.

"Yes. Do you think we can ask Ranta to look up if there have been similar cases in other parts of the country? One of the people I talked to this morning told me Ahti's family has a log cabin in Tuusula."

"Really?" Anita said. "Ranta has a cabin near Tuusula too. But I don't know. I was rather hoping not to talk to him unless it was absolutely necessary."

"It's necessary. Just ask him to look into it, all right?"

Anita sighed. "All right."

Come to think of it, her relationship with Ranta was weird. The man behaved like she belonged to him. I tried to imagine them together – Snow White and her favourite dwarf, Esmeralda and Quasimodo – but the image wouldn't stick. Maybe he was in love with her. That, certainly, was possible.

I fished in the bag for the last of the crackers. It was a little damp, so I held it up to the light, checking for mould.

"Hella?" Anita's voice quivered a little.

"Huh?"

"I was wondering if I could help you in a different way. Maybe I could pretend to be one of Klara Nylund's girls. You know, catch the guy red-handed."

I almost dropped the cracker. "What?"

"Well, I'm not proposing to actually, um, service the clients," Anita said lamely. "I could just —"

"Forget it."

"But Hella —"

"I said forget it. That's the stupidest idea I've ever heard."

My voice was unnecessarily harsh, but I was scared. I'd seen the photos of the dead girl – and Anita looked the type. I didn't want her death on my conscience.

"All right," she mumbled miserably. I could almost hear her wince.

"I'll see you tonight," I said, and put the receiver down.

When I came out of the booth, the caretaker's son was standing by the front door. Next to him was an officer from the court.

"Miss Mauzer?"

"Yes?"

"I have a summons for you. Please sign here."

The man held out a large white envelope.

I hesitated, my right hand crumbling the mouldy cracker, the left grabbing the door frame.

"Come on, Miss Mauzer, don't make me wait."

I signed, of course. What other option did I have? I even managed to exit the building with my head held high.

Another envelope was waiting for me at the office, stuck under the door that led to the reception area. Cream vellum, now smeared with dust. Still out of breath after climbing up the three flights of stairs, I stared at it for a long moment, wondering if more bad news was coming my way.

I was still reeling from receiving the letter. The court had notified me that they had made a mistake earlier and that the damages I had to pay to Kukoyakka were due in five days. Even if I sold all my possessions, there was no way I could meet that deadline. I didn't need any more hassle, and that new letter promised plenty. In the end, I flipped it with the tip of my shoe. It was from the madam, as I had expected.

The letter, when I extracted it from the envelope, started innocently enough:

Dear Miss Mauzer,

First of all, let me thank you for your generous offer. I am certain Maria will be delighted to spend some time with your friends in Lapland. The poor child is so worried, she needs rest.

I needed to write to Irja, warn her that Maria was coming. I tried to imagine Maria in Käärmelä: the high heels sliding cautiously on the ice, the hot coral lipstick drawing everyone's attention at Sunday Mass. Irja and Timo would give her my room, I thought. The one with a scattering of violets on the curtains, and a too-big wardrobe.

Anyway, this was good. It meant Maria could be tucked away safely, and it meant the madam wasn't mad at me for failing her so miserably. I read on.

The second objective of this letter is to beg your pardon for last night. I was taken aback by the revelation that the name of the attacker appeared to be common knowledge. That made me doubt your capabilities. I was expecting that, with your expertise and enthusiasm, you would be on top of the job. Maybe you had other priorities. Nevertheless, now that the girls' attacker has been identified, I must ask you to please hurry. You certainly understand that my business is suffering and that I am losing money. I would therefore appreciate knowing that the attacker has been apprehended (or otherwise stopped) before Monday.

Before Monday. Just two days left, meaning I was not going to make it. In which case, the madam would refuse to pay. The message was clear.

Yours truly,
Klara Nylund

And I'd been hoping I'd get some cash soon to pay the damages. Damn!

20

Hella

I spent the rest of the afternoon trying to think up creative ways to prove that Ahti Virtanen had been involved in the murders and the assault.

Questioning his domestic helpers would be no good – and likely to get me into trouble. His university friends? I had no idea who they were.

I did come up with the boy's photograph, which I tore out of a glossy magazine I found at the city library. One thing was clear: Ahti wanted to be a rebel, because there he was, clad in black leather, posing on a Harley. Unfortunately for the boy, his looks worked against him. The curly blonde hair, the round red cheeks, the bright blue eyes – he had the type of cupidesque face no one could take seriously. Would he go as far as killing someone to be in the spotlight? And there was one more thing: in Finnish mythology, Ahti is a god of water. Could there be symbolism in that? Was the boy trying to act out his name when he drowned these women, as if it were some perverse prophecy? I slid the page under my coat. It was 4 p.m. already, and I couldn't stay still. PIs are like wolves. If they don't move, they die of starvation.

"No," said Maria's neighbour when I showed her the photograph. "Never seen him." The woman was wearing the same dress as the day before, but now her hair was done up and her lips were painted a girlish pink. "But I didn't see Maria's attacker, I already told you that. Now, if you'll excuse me —" She slammed the door in my face.

Maria was gone already, on her way to Käärmelä. I tried the store on the corner and the fish dealer and a seamstress who had a small store on Maria's street. No luck.

The sun was already low in the sky, and the streets were filling up with people: men returning home from work, children playing in the snow, dragging their backpacks behind them. Not many women: they were inside already, cooking. You could smell it in the streets: roast mutton, pierogies, *kalakukko* fish bread.

I could try to pretend I didn't even know how I found myself on Steve's doorstep, but that wouldn't be true. Steve wasn't home, he was at work. As I stood under the street light, heavy snow landing on my lashes and melting on contact with my cheeks, his sexy voice was on Yle Radio, commenting on the latest American music hits. It was not him I had come to see. It was Elsbeth, his wife.

The front windows were dark. I thought that Elsbeth and Eva would be in the kitchen, towards the back of the house, having dinner. I wondered if my stomach would growl when I confronted them.

I stamped compacted snow off my boots and scraped the soles clean before climbing the steps to the front door and lifting my hand towards the bell. I pressed it hard, then waited with my ear to the door. It could be that Elsbeth had seen it was me and decided not to open it; or perhaps no one was home. I could hear no movement inside, no music and no voices.

I glanced at my watch. Half past six. Elsbeth could have gone to visit her parents, or a friend.

Before I could change my mind, I crossed the street, stopping in front of a cute little house, recently painted, its windows gleaming. Its door swung open as I was lifting my hand to knock. The young woman standing on the doorstep had a striped apron tied around her slender waist and two toddlers pulling at her skirt. Her face seemed to be caught between curiosity and righteous outrage. The outrage won.

"Are you looking for Mr Collins?"

"No. I'm looking for his wife."

The woman raised an eyebrow. For a moment, we just stood there, staring at each other. The inside of the house smelled of roast pork and burnt sugar.

"She's gone," the woman said at last, her eyes never leaving mine. "Took her daughter and left. All her things, too."

"When?"

"Mummy," one of the toddlers started whining. "I'm cold." Immediately, his brother joined the chorus, his mouth open, his whole body heaving.

"*Stop it!*" the woman muttered. And to me: "Look what you've done." She started to close the door and I had to put my hand on the door frame, because I was damned if I was going to leave before finding out more. "When? When did Mrs Collins go away?"

The edge of the door pressed against my hand. "I know who you are," the woman said. "She told me all about you." Both toddlers were hysterical now, and I could hear a man's voice calling "What's happening there?" from somewhere deep in the house.

The woman kept pulling at the door, but she was hesitant to crush my fingers. "Elsbeth moved out ten days ago," she snarled at last. "Now leave!"

I pulled my hand away, and immediately the door clicked shut. I stood at the edge of the street, massaging my bruised knuckles and thinking of all the lies Steve had told me, while damp snowflakes clung to my hair and lashes and blurred my vision.

21

Chief Inspector Mustonen

"Honey?" Sofia's voice was breathless with excitement.

"Hold on." I kicked the door shut. The office was almost empty at that hour, but I couldn't risk anyone eavesdropping on my conversations. "What is it, darling?" I pressed the telephone against my ear. It was not often that Sofia called me at the office. Something must have happened.

"I just learned that the house next door to my father's is for sale." My wife giggled. "Isn't that marvellous? Honey?"

"Of course," I said. "It is. Marvellous. But Sofia, don't you think that we maybe have enough on our plate at the moment? With the baby coming and all that?"

"Oh," Sofia whispered. "I thought you'd jump at the idea."

I ran my hand through my hair, sitting down heavily. I didn't need the added complication, not now, but I couldn't tell Sofia that. Ever since we had bought our little house by the sea, my wife had been dreaming of moving away. Our home was not grand enough, not chic enough. It had been deemed unworthy of an up-and-coming inspector and his socialite wife. She couldn't invite her friends over; she was afraid that if she invited them, they wouldn't come.

And then there was her family. As a wedding gift from her grandmother, Sofia had received a subscription to *Harper's Bazaar*. It was the only way, the old lady said, that Sofia could now keep up to date on the lives of her more fortunate friends, the ones who had made better unions. So the possibility of getting that house: yes, it mattered. It mattered a lot.

"I'll think about it, all right," I told my wife. "It might be a bit too expensive for us now, but maybe next year —"

"Aren't you going to" – Sofia hesitated – "Aren't you going to get that pay rise you were promised?"

"Only if I'm promoted to Jokela's position. It's not confirmed yet."

But my wife was refusing to give up. "Can it be soon?"

"I'll talk to Jokela," I said. "I promise you I will. I'm meeting him for a drink, but there's something I need to do before that, so…"

Sofia took the hint. "Of course," she murmured. "We'll talk about it tomorrow. I'll probably arrange to view the house, just in case. To make sure we really like it, you know? No point buying something we don't like."

"Good point," I said, even though I knew that to be the husband Sofia deserved, I *had* to like the house. I had to want it as much as my wife did. The gold brooch I'd been thinking of getting Sofia, as a gift for the baby's birth, wouldn't cut it. She wanted more. Much more. And I was not sure I'd be able to deliver.

"Love you, darling," I said, hanging up. Then I grabbed my coat and my gun, locked the door to my office, and made my way downstairs.

*

Jokela was thoroughly drunk when I finally arrived at the American-style bar that had lately become my boss's after-hours watering hole. He waved at me from a corner table.

"Over here, ma-ma…"

My boy, I silently mouthed. It really was time Jokela got rid of that stupid habit. Time, also, for my boss to stop patting me on the shoulder as if I was a prize horse.

I spread my lips into a smile and made my way over to the dimly lit corner. There were crisps scattered on the floor, sodden from the melted snow brought in on the patrons' shoes.

"Here," Jokela breathed, pushing a pint of flat beer towards me. And, suddenly annoyed: "You're late."

"Sorry."

"I mean, what took you so long? It takes what, from Headquarters to here, all of fifteen minutes? You took two hours."

"Sorry," I said again.

"You're hiding something," he slurred. "You look dishevelled. What have you been up to?"

For such a big, impressive-looking man, with his military bearing and shrewd, piercing eyes, Jokela was a cheap drunk. He invariably fell apart after his second glass of anything. Maybe that was the reason he demanded that we drink together every night, whether in his office or here, in the bar: he needed practice. And someone to cover up for his inadequacies and see him safely home.

A pretty red-haired waitress materialized by our table, a menu in hand. "Would you like to eat something, sir?"

"Better not," I said, smiling up at her. "My wife cooks dinner for me every night; she wouldn't appreciate me eating here." I pushed the beer aside. "May I have a brandy? What would you like, Jon?"

"Make it two," Jokela said. And, after the girl was gone: "You really aren't very bright, my boy."

"Why's that?" I asked, though I already knew. I also supposed that my boss didn't really mean to offend me: he was just speaking his dirty, one-track mind.

"That girl" – Jokela pointed at the waitress's receding back – "Want to bet that she's more fun than that boring, pure-bred wife of yours?"

"I love my wife," I said patiently. "I'm not tempted."

"Even when you can't fuck because the lady of the manor is pregnant?" Jokela snorted. "She did it to you the first time around as well, didn't she? If you keep going like this, from now until retirement, you'll only fuck once every two to three years, and only to procreate. I hope she has other virtues."

"She does have other virtues," I said. "She's supportive, and kind, and —"

Jokela smirked. "You're talking about your mother, right?"

I closed my eyes briefly. This conversation was my own fault. Three years ago, I had got a hard-on while looking at one of our female trainees. Jokela had noticed, and I had blurted out that my wife was exhausted by her pregnancy. Ever since, the topic would creep up every time a pretty girl crossed my path.

"Sofia is my wife and I love her," I said again, to drive the point home. "It may surprise you, and I have no doubt she's not your type of girl, but you should still be respectful of her. Now, could we maybe talk about something else?"

Jokela pursed his lips and stared into his glass. I knew he'd make me pay for my outburst, but I didn't care. The waitress glided up to our table with our order. I thanked her without looking up.

"Right," Jokela said at last. "What about Mauzer?"

"I followed your instructions, and she received the new payment date this afternoon. You know her better than I do. Will it deter her?"

My boss thought about that.

"Not sure," he said at last. "She's stubborn, like her father was. Jesus, the whole family was like that, uncompromising. Like they were a different species or something. I didn't know him that well, of course, but that's what people said. Even his enemies said that." Jokela shrugged. "Not a sign of superior intelligence, if you want my opinion."

"He was a spy, wasn't he?"

But Jokela was not finished with his monologue yet. "It's not that I don't have principles," he said sententiously. "It's just that, in order to succeed, one needs to be *practical*. I mean, it's obvious."

"So I suppose Mauzer's father didn't succeed?"

"Him?" A dismissive wave of the hand. "He did worse. Got himself killed. Family, too. Mauzer was the only one lucky enough to escape."

"I thought what happened to her family was a tragic accident? I heard something about a truck that got out of control on an icy road."

"Is that what Mauzer told you?"

I nodded.

"Then she'd better keep believing it. Safer that way. Not that she's the kind of girl to play it safe." Jokela stretched and yawned. "As I said, she's a different species. It must be in her – what do they call them? – genes."

I pretended to yawn too. "It's getting late, Jon," I said. I almost added *Sofia will be worried*, but thought better of it. "Shall we get going?"

Before Jokela could object, I helped him to his feet, pointing him in the general direction of the door. It *was* late. The bar was almost deserted: just the pretty waitress, looking bored out of her wits, and a couple of men in the opposite corner. One of them looked like Mauzer's boyfriend, only older. "Mauzer should be careful," I said. "She doesn't know everything, doesn't realize her Steve is a nasty piece of work."

"Ouch! Hold the door, my boy!" Jokela bumped into the door frame, angry with me because I should have watched him better. We stumbled outside. The street lamps' dismal light was struggling to pierce through the snow suspended in mid-air. The weather seemed to be getting colder, or maybe it was the contrast with the warm interior of the bar. I pulled Jokela's fur cap out of his coat pocket, put it on his bald scalp. I aimed him in the direction of the car that was waiting further along the street – he was clutching my arm, his fetid breath in my face – and was taking a step forward when it happened.

The woman slammed into us, sent us skidding on the ice. She must have been running. I noticed her gaping mouth and her terrified eyes even before I heard her scream.

I let go of Jokela's arm – my boss fell into the snow like a dummy – and grabbed hold of the girl. "Hey," I said. "What are *you* doing here?"

22

Hella

Anita was trying hard not to cry. She wanted to, of course, but she was also mindful of the fact that if she started, her eyes would be all puffy the following morning, and that was out of the question. "He looked like a vagabond," she said. "He smelled like one, in any case. Urine, rotten teeth and old sweat." She shivered theatrically. "And it was dark, and when he edged towards me in the shadows, I just —"

"But did you see him?" I asked. "Can you describe him?"

"No," she said, pursing her lips. "I ran. And, trust me, it wasn't easy to run in that dress. And in those shoes. I kept slipping. Don't laugh, Mauzer! I was doing it for you!"

"I know, I know. It's just that … it was a really stupid idea. Putting on an evening dress to wander the streets near Klara Nylund's establishment in the hope of catching the prostitutes' murderer… You were lucky you ran into Mustonen."

Anita looked down at her hands. An hour earlier, she had been brought over to my place by my impeccably polite former colleague.

"She's all yours," Mustonen said, with barely a look at my shabby living room. "We didn't manage to catch her attacker, though. I'll ask someone to look into it tomorrow." He paused, maybe realizing for the first time how small my apartment was. "Are you both living here with your boyfriend?"

There was no point in hiding it. If Mustonen wanted to, he could find out the truth in no time. "He doesn't live here any more," I said.

"Oh." Mustonen's voice was carefully neutral. "Well, I don't really think you ladies need police protection, but if someone scares you tonight, don't hesitate to call."

"Right," I said. "Thank you."

The moment he left, Anita slumped on the sofa, the picture of a damsel in distress, her eyes huge and liquid, her baby-blonde hair dampened to wheat. An hour later, she was still sitting there, shivering.

I handed her a dressing gown. "At least take your dress off. You're soaked."

"All right." But she still wouldn't move. She had that shifty look about her that made me wonder if she was hiding something.

"What is it? Do you have any idea who the person who attacked you might be?"

"No," Anita said, too quickly. She shook her head for more emphasis, but she wouldn't look me in the eye. "No idea at all."

I made her a cup of tea sweetened with honey and put her to bed; held her hand until she fell asleep. As for me, I doubted I would find sleep so easily. Plenty of things to worry about: the slow progress of the investigation, the damages I had to pay, the lack of money. Anita, too – I felt responsible for her. And, at the top of my personal worry list, Steve. Because now I knew that, contrary to what he had told me, he had only moved in with me after his wife had left him. Which meant he had deliberately lied to my face. Maybe, I wondered, maybe there had been no school play either. Maybe that, too, had been a lie.

The question was: why?

23

Hella

The obvious answer was that Steve wanted me to believe
he was the one leaving his wife. And then, after a week,
he had decided he wanted to break up with me but didn't
have the courage. So he had provoked a scene and made
me the guilty party.

Maybe he met someone else, a nasty little voice whispered
into my ear. *That was the reason Elsbeth left. It wasn't you –
she had known for ages that you existed. No, it was some
younger, prettier girl, just like the one delicately snoring on
your bed.*

But then why had he called me yesterday?

The usual reasons, the nasty little voice offered. I felt it
physically, a thing gnawing at my skull, gorging itself on
my misery. *Maybe the girl was unavailable. Maybe he was bored.
Maybe he'd had a bad day at work and wanted to hear the despera-
tion in your voice to reassure himself that he still mattered.* Plenty
of reasons.

Steve isn't like that, I thought, but I was just fooling
myself. Of course he was. All men were, provided we gave
them the liberty to mistreat us.

I wrapped myself tighter in my blanket, drew the curtains and lay down on the sofa. I didn't expect to be able to sleep, what with the cold and the hunger and the nasty voice that kept murmuring obscenities in my ear. But I was wrong about that too. I fell asleep as soon as my head touched the pillow.

When I woke up nine hours later, a lame Helsinki sun was creeping in through the gap in the curtains and I had a pounding headache. Anita was standing in the kitchen with her mouth half-open, clutching the belt of her dressing gown. At first I thought she was looking at me, then I realized her gaze was on the door behind me.

It was not a pounding headache. It was someone hammering on the front door, screaming bloody murder.

I scrambled to my feet, rushed to open it.

As soon as I let her in, the woman who had been banging on the door erupted into a torrent of screams and incoherent moaning. From what I could gather, there had been another attack, and police had been called to the scene.

My heart sank. Klara Nylund was right, I was not up to this. The police would be a safer bet. Surely Mustonen couldn't keep covering for Ahti Virtanen?

Our visitor was now slumped in the chair, sobbing uncontrollably. Anita stared at me, a glass of water in her hand, a puzzled frown on her pretty face. "Did you understand who the victim was?" she mouthed silently.

I shook my head no.

"Or how it happened?"

I kneeled next to the woman.

"The girl who died … did she drown as well?"

The *no* came between two hiccups.

I thought about what had happened to Anita the previous evening. "Was she attacked on the street?"

"No." My visitor grabbed the water from Anita and drank it in one gulp. It was only then that I recognized the gum-smacking girl from the day before last. She was struggling to get her words out. "Her head was bashed in," the girl managed at last.

I bit my lip. So it was different. And then another thought, a shameful one: it sounded like an unpremeditated murder. Still awful for the victim and her loved ones, of course, but just possibly I stood a better chance of uncovering evidence.

"Who was it?" I asked. "The dead girl? What was her name?"

My visitor stared at me like I was mad. "It wasn't a girl. It was Klara."

24

Chief Inspector Mustonen

"All right," Jokela said, his bloodshot eyes trained on me, "stop pacing my office and tell me what we've got on Klara Nylund."

"Female in an evening dress, late forties, head injuries, found in the brothel's back yard at five in the morning by a girl who had gone out in search of wood logs for the stove..." I glanced up from my notepad. "The pathologist wouldn't say anything – apart from the fact that the victim was dead and frozen solid. Given that she's got no face to speak of and no grey matter left either, if he dared to say he had doubts about that, I'd have bashed *his* head in."

"So no estimate of the time of death?" Jokela was frowning and I thought I knew why. If we didn't know what time the madam had died, we wouldn't be able to verify Ahti's alibi. Or arrange for it to be confirmed, depending on how desperate Jokela was.

"Not yet," I said. "The pathologist is Tom Räikkönen, by the way."

"I hate that guy." Jokela stretched his limbs, took a sip of his coffee.

And Räikkönen is Mauzer's friend, I thought but didn't say. One of the few she's got left.

"Any clues?" Jokela again. He sounded pretty much in control for a man who had thrown up like an open hydrant as soon as he had got into his car the previous night.

"Not yet."

"See that there are none." Jokela tilted his head to one side, his beefy fingers rubbing a spot on his neck. "You know. Limit the damage."

"This is a murder, Jon. I'm not messing around with this."

There was silence while Jokela tried to decide what to do about me. In the end, he laughed. He knew he had me by the balls, that I was in too deep already. He probably thought I was only protesting to save face, and in a sense he was right.

"OK," Jokela said. "Call it what you want. The important thing is that you know the stakes." He waved a hand at me. I was dismissed.

Over in the squad room, Anita was leaning on the secretary's desk, whispering something, her tight little derriere like an invitation. She must have heard Jokela's door close because she looked over her shoulder, catching my eye and blushing. She straightened herself up and hurried towards me. "Chief Inspector, I've been told that —"

I raised my hand. In my office, the phone was ringing. "Later, Anita."

I shut the door, picked up the phone.

"Has Sofia told you about the house?" No *hello*, no *how are you*, nothing. My father-in-law only believed in showing courtesy towards the rich and famous, and I was neither. I struggled to swallow the insult that was always on the tip of my tongue when I heard the familiar voice.

"Yes," I said. "She told me yesterday. We're thinking about it. Whether we'd be able to afford it. Look, I'm sorry, but I'm in the middle of something here. Can we discuss it tonight?"

"I'm busy tonight," Sofia's father said. "In any case, there's nothing to discuss. An opportunity like that only comes once in a lifetime. No one sells on our street unless they absolutely have to."

"We'll see —" I started, but my father-in-law cut me off.

"Be a man, for once, will you? My daughter and my grandchildren deserve to live in a nice place." The old man snorted. "I knew she made a mistake when she married you. She probably realizes it herself."

I stared out of the window at the pale Finnish sun, at the plumes of chimney smoke drawing arabesques in the air.

"That's not true," I said. "Sofia loves me, just as I love her."

"Then buy that goddamned house," my father-in-law roared. Then he hung up.

25

Hella

Klara Nylund's body had already been carried away from the crime scene – a narrow back yard behind the brothel with a solitary birch tree standing, crooked and skeletal, against the wall. Tom had come and gone, too. There was just one uniformed cop at the door; he looked about fifteen. I wondered if he'd even be able to gain access to this place as a client.

I explained who I was, told him I needed to talk to the girls and go through Klara Nylund's papers. Standing next to me, the gum-smacking girl sniffed and nodded.

"I don't know, ma'am," the young cop said. He was clearly searching his memory for a textbook entry on PIs and how to deal with them. "Wait until Chief Inspector Mustonen gets here. He'll tell you if that's possible."

"Can *I* come in?" my companion asked. "I live here." In her panic, she had run out of the house in just a flimsy dress. Now she was shivering.

The cop blinked twice. "I don't know, ma'am. Wait until Chief Inspector Mustonen —"

He didn't finish his sentence. The girl doubled over, heaving. I barely had time to catch her heavy blonde braid before she threw up. "Ma'am," the baby cop called out. "Ma'am! Move away, please. You're destroying evidence."

She gave him the finger.

When her heaving subsided, we climbed the steps to the porch. I broke off long icicles hanging from the roof; the girl crunched the ice with her teeth, her eyes closed. I was about to suggest we go back to my place when she grabbed my arm. "I have something for you."

Several steps away, the young cop was studying his wristwatch, his blonde eyebrows furrowed.

"What is it?"

"Klara's little black book."

"What?"

The girl drew a deep breath. "In my bag. It was in the garden, not far from her body. I took it. You can have it."

I was already thinking about the fingerprints. "Did you touch it?"

"No, I used my shawl to pick it up." She thrust the book towards me as if it was burning hot, and I slid it into my bag.

"Ma'am?" the baby cop called to me. "Chief Inspector Mustonen is here. You can ask your questions."

I turned.

Mustonen was several steps away, one hand on the railings, the other clutching his murder bag. The brim of his felt hat was hiding the upper half of his face; all I could see was a thin smile.

"Miss Mauzer. I suppose it is too much to ask what *you* are doing here?"

"I'm here to talk to the girls," I said. "But I suppose I'll have to come back later. Everyone must understandably be shaken."

"Actually," Mustonen smiled, "I'm not sure that will be necessary." He went up another step. "This is a police investigation now. No place in it for a PI. But I'll see to it that you get paid for your services. Please prepare an invoice."

"Not possible," I said.

Mustonen didn't stop climbing, didn't even look at me as he asked, "And why is that?"

"I haven't finished my work yet. I'm just getting started."

My assertion was pure impulse, an attempt to keep the upper hand in a game that I knew I'd already lost, an attempt to imprint a frown on that smooth benevolent face. I had no authority here, no resources; my client was dead. But the moment the words left my mouth I knew with absolute certainty that I was not giving up on this. Not until I was sure justice was done.

Mustonen finally turned to look at me, a concerned expression on his lean, handsome face. "Trust me," he said. "You don't want to do that. You really don't."

When I got to the morgue, the body was thawing in a saline bath. A rotary saw gleamed on the table, but Tom was nowhere in sight. I knew I wouldn't be welcome during the autopsy – Mustonen was due to arrive at any moment, and even an independent mind like Tom had a basic sense of self-preservation. So instead I went into the cafe on the other side of the road and used Anita's money to buy myself a big cup of hot chocolate sprinkled with cardamom. I sat there thinking about my limited options: my hands were tied, the police held all the cards. And now I had doubts that what Egg had said was true, that young Ahti was at the heart of this. He certainly didn't fit the description of Anita's attacker. How likely was it that not one but *two* homicidal maniacs, both obsessed with prostitutes, were roaming the streets of Helsinki?

Most of all, though, I was afraid of doing even more damage. The thought that Klara Nylund might still be alive if she'd only contacted some other investigator hung over me like a thundercloud.

I leaned forward, my hands wrapped around the cup. Klara Nylund's little black book was now in my pocket, wrapped in a handkerchief. The police technicians could certainly get fingerprints if someone other than the madam had touched it. The only thing *I* could do was read it.

I *was* going to read it.

Then I'd be able to make up my mind.

As with other really dangerous things – poisoned letters, trucks, teenage girls playing Shakespeare – the black book, when I pulled it out of my pocket and carefully unwrapped the handkerchief, looked harmless at first glance. Holding my breath, I picked up a clean spoon from the next table, wiped it with a napkin, then used it to turn the pages. Every page was identical: names on the left, numbers on the right. The names were nicknames: there were *fat o. b.* (old bastard? Someone's initials?) and *engineer sol.* (solitary?). The numbers were presumably dates of passage and prices of sexual acts. Klara Nylund's bookkeeping system was simple; it was also remarkably efficient. No one but her probably knew who these men were.

There were no other notes. No names underlined in red ink, no exclamation points.

I scoured the pages for descriptions that might fit Ahti: *y* (oung) *m* (oney)? Or Anita's unknown assailant: *vag* (rant)? The closest I got was *ten. pl* (tennis player?), who seemed to be a regular, and *filth*. This latter came up regularly, before apparently stopping the previous December. Could he be the one? But *filth* didn't seem an appropriate description for a man a beautiful young girl would hope to spend the rest of her life with. Unless of course he was also filthy rich.

My notebook was out and I started copying all the names and numbers into it. My intention was to drop it off for Mustonen after I saw Tom. I could always say Klara Nylund had given the book to me the previous day. Even if Mustonen didn't believe me, I doubted he would give me too much trouble.

It was lunchtime by then and the cafe was filling with people. The waitress kept shooting me worried glances – I was occupying one of the tables and not eating. As the doors opened again to let in a carefully dressed middle-aged couple, I picked up my bag and started for the door, the little black book open on the page that I had started copying. I didn't see the waiter carrying a tray piled high with cocktail glasses until I collided with him. For an instant, it seemed that the whole stack of plates and glasses would come crashing down, but he managed to recover his balance. "I'm sorry," I murmured. Some of the liquid had spilled from the tray, staining the book.

"No problem," the waiter smiled. "Here, let me help." He pulled a napkin out of his apron pocket and applied it to the stain. And there it was, in blotchy ink, as if the waiter had conjured it: *US DJ.*

"Are you all right?" the waiter said. "You look … a little pale."

"What? No, I'm fine. I'm fine." The world around me seemed to disappear, as if the spilled water had somehow penetrated my brain, deactivating all connections but one. I locked my eyes on the door, forced myself to move forward. Next thing I knew, I was out on the street, drenched in cold sweat, my head spinning.

US DJ, my brain kept screaming. Steve.

26

Hella

I needed to see Steve. I needed to know if he had been a client of Klara Nylund's the entire time he'd been seeing me. His name was one of the entries with the most numbers next to it. The last one was the night of the school play. I wondered if Elsbeth had found out about this. If that was the reason she had left.

Tom was just coming out of the hospital, winding a long striped scarf around his neck, when I stormed past.

"Fire in the cafe?" he called out.

Not stopping for an answer, I brushed past him and almost bumped into an old woman in a tattered fur coat who was standing idly by the hospital's entrance. The wind in my face filled my eyes with tears; I blinked them away. The last thing I wanted was for Steve to think I had been crying because of him.

The streets were packed with people. Maybe it was the sun, spreading like a yolk under a fluffy blanket of clouds. For the first time in a month, it wasn't snowing. And yet I couldn't see the city properly. When I looked at the tall austere buildings, it was not the peeling paint that I noticed but my past: a cafe where Steve and I had first held hands, a toy store where I'd bought a yellow bus for my nephew, Matti. My past had shaped this city more than the architects and the builders had. Beyond its walls of brick and mortar, I saw people who no longer lived and dreams that had dissolved into thin air. And my heart ached.

I was on the corner of Steve's street when a woman called out to me.

"Miss Mauzer? Yoo-hoo! Over here!"

I didn't recognize her at first. A short, stocky housewife, pudgy features, ferociously sprayed hairdo that would probably stay upright even if someone took out all the pins. Then I realized: she was one of my former clients. Her husband, a plumber, had started coming home late, smiling and freshly scrubbed, and the wife had got worried. She was right, too: the husband had been having an affair, with her own sister. Together, we had put a stop to it.

"How are you, Mrs...?" I said. The name wouldn't come. I had it on the tip of my tongue, but trying to remember only made it worse. "Glad to see you," I muttered.

She glanced at me nervously. "Miss Mauzer, you were very nice to me, so I'll just say this quickly and then we can pretend nothing happened."

I didn't have the patience for this, but she was blocking the way. "What is it? What have I done?"

"I don't blame you, actually," the woman said. "My husband told me I should never mention your name in good company, but I feel like —"

"Hold on. I don't understand. What happened?"

The woman looked away. "Well, he overheard it in one of the houses he was working in, just yesterday. That you decided that you'd make more money that way. And I know

I didn't pay you well – I couldn't spare more – but I never thought you'd be reduced to that."

I could barely stop myself from grabbing her by the collar and shaking the words out. "Reduced to what?"

"Prostituting yourself." It came out in a rush of breath. *Prostitute.* She glanced nervously over her shoulder.

I smiled. "That's nonsense. I am – was – employed by a madam, but as a PI, not as one of her girls."

Maybe what I was imagining was a reference to Steve was nonsense too. Look how easy it was to misunderstand. We'd laugh about it together once he had reassured me that he'd never set foot in Klara Nylund's establishment. Well, maybe not *laugh,* given that we'd broken it off, but at least chuckle wryly. And maybe it would be the perfect opportunity to discuss our feelings.

In front of me, the woman was smiling as well, but her face retained that nervous, strained expression. "That's what I told my husband too, that you weren't the sort, that there must be some reasonable explanation. But you know how it is. People talk." She swallowed, dancing from foot to foot. "Well, I'm glad we sorted that out, Miss Mauzer. I have to go now."

She scuttled off before I had the chance to say another word. I wondered if she believed my explanation; she didn't seem totally convinced. Maybe she liked her own theory better: a poor PI, struggling to make ends meet, throws herself into a career of prostitution. It could almost be funny if it wasn't my life.

I walked over the short stretch of road separating me from Steve's house and pressed the doorbell. By that point, the house had an abandoned look about it, milk bottles lining the front porch, the curtains tightly drawn. What I wanted was a matter-of-fact conversation. We were both adults. I just needed to know.

There was a shuffle of steps, and then the door was unlocked with a click.

"You're here," Steve said, blinking at me. He was barefoot, in jeans and a crumpled white shirt, pillow creases running along his left check.

"Sorry I woke you. There's something I need to discuss with you. Can I come in?"

Steve hesitated, his eyes on the little house across the street. I wondered if the young woman I had talked to the day before was watching. "Better not," he said. "Can we go to a cafe or something?"

"No, it's OK. There's not much to say anyway."

I'd decided to stick to the facts – no emotions, two adults talking – but it was hard. "I learned that Elsbeth left over a week ago. Before the school play." I swallowed back the *you should have told me*, but it must have shown on my face, because Steve shifted uncomfortably.

"She just went to spend some time with her parents. She was feeling unwell." He attempted a smile. "You know how it is."

Did I ever. Our relationship, which went back years, had been punctuated by Elsbeth's sick spells. Never anything specific – a headache, a nosebleed, feeling out of whack – but each time it sent Steve scurrying home to her. And when it was not Elsbeth, it was his daughter.

I pulled Klara Nylund's notebook out of my pocket, holding it with my handkerchief. "I found this. Do you know what it is?"

Steve looked genuinely puzzled. "No."

"It's a madam's list of clients, all referred to not by name but by some other characteristic. One of them is *US DJ*." My voice quivered, the confident elation that I had felt minutes earlier having abandoned me. "I was wondering if it could be you."

"A DJ?" Steve's eyes found the floor. "I'm not a DJ any more. I'm a music show host."

"You're the only American in this city who runs a radio show devoted to American rock 'n' roll music. And you used to be a DJ. The description matches."

Steve shot me a quick glance, probably wondering what else I knew. He wasn't denying it, why wasn't he denying it, how could a thing like that be possible? It felt like a bucket of icy water thrown in my face, it felt like one of those dreams where the earth suddenly disappears under my feet and I plummet into an abyss.

"And you believe that?" he said. "Is that what you think of me? You see a mention that could refer to a dozen other men around here, and you think it just *has* to be me?"

"If it's not you, why aren't you denying it?"

Steve gave an angry little laugh. "Because you'd believe me if I did? I'll save my breath. Goodbye, Hella."

He closed the door.

27

Chief Inspector Mustonen

The autopsy was well under way when I arrived at the morgue, a bunch of chattering trainees on my heel. Another one of Jokela's stupid ideas: he wanted to make sure the police academy students could see the pathologist at work, and the madam was the first indisputable murder victim we'd had in weeks. The trainees, three guys and Anita, had been talking non-stop since I picked them up at Headquarters, but as the heavy doors leading to the morgue swung open, they all fell silent. I hoped to God they'd stay that way.

Tom Räikkönen greeted us with a steely smile.

"Hands behind your back," he commanded the newcomers in his bellowing voice. "Now stand with your backs to the wall."

No one moved. I wasn't even sure they had heard him. The trainees' eyes were on the corpse. Naked, the ribcage sawn open, the head tilted to one side. From where I was standing, you could almost imagine the woman didn't have a face any more. Just some greyish-red pulp, like something out of the grinder Sofia used to make meatballs.

Räikkönen put down the white enamel jug he was holding. His eyes narrowed. "Listen up," he said, in a low voice that was somehow more effective than his previous roar, "one of you moves, you all leave. One of you talks, you all leave. One of you faints" – Räikkönen's gloved hand suddenly stabbed the air, pointing at a tall gawkish recruit whose name I could never remember – "You, answer!"

The boy's Adam's apple shot up. "We all leave," he said in a hoarse whisper.

"*Ex*actly!" Räikkönen smiled, turning his attention back to the corpse. He didn't look at me when he asked:

"Any idea who did this, Chief Inspector?"

"Not yet."

For a while, Räikkönen worked in silence. I knew better than to interrupt him. Tom Räikkönen was the best of our pathologists by far. He was also a first-class bastard. I knew that if I complained about the man's attitude, Jokela would give Räikkönen hell. But the pathologist's power to be a nuisance could not be underestimated, and it's not in my nature to get on the wrong side of anyone unless I absolutely have to. Especially not when there's so much at stake. Just the process of going through the motions made me dizzy and elated all at once.

At last, Räikkönen slid the last of the dead woman's organs back into place and peeled off his bloody gloves. Unlike the other pathologists, he always worked alone. Rumour had it that no one had managed to get on his good side yet. No one except Mauzer, that is. I knew I needed to watch my step.

"Well," Räikkönen said, "much as I dislike working on bodies that have not been thawed properly" – he nodded towards the blood-stained blade of the rotary saw – "I understand that time is of the essence, and I'm not going to make you wait for a formal report. Therefore I can confirm now that the lady died neither of curare poisoning nor of a broken heart." One of the trainees giggled, probably Anita. Räikkönen glared at her until she turned crimson.

"OK." I was used to Räikkönen's humour by now. "Go on."

"Multiple blows to the face with a blunt cylindrical weapon, by a right-handed person facing the victim."

"Like a poker?" I asked. I tried to imagine a man wielding a poker in the brothel's snow-covered back yard. The image wouldn't stick.

"No," Räikkönen said. "A bit larger than that. Like a metal tube or a rolling pin, though that would probably be too large. Or even the barrel of a gun."

I reached into my holster, pulled out the standard-issue Browning. "Do you want to see if that fits?"

Räikkönen weighed up the gun in his hand. "Could be something like that, yes, though why anyone would hit her with a gun instead of just firing it is not a question I can answer." He handed the Browning back to me. "Anyway. Once you find the murder weapon, bring it here and I'll see if it matches."

"What about the time of death?"

"Early evening. Around seven. Good for you, I suppose – lots of people on the street at that time, bars and restaurants still open. Someone might have seen something."

"Did she die instantly?" I asked. The trainees were still staring at the corpse with undisguised fascination.

"If your question is about whether she could have murmured her assassin's name into someone's interested ear, I think it's unlikely. She didn't die instantly, but she would have been unconscious in a matter of seconds." Räikkönen started wrapping Klara Nylund's remains in a white plastic sheet. For him, the conversation was over.

"Wait," I said. "Two more questions. Do you have any idea how tall her assailant was?"

Räikkönen glanced at me. "Probably about your height. Give or take. Meaning that close to fifty per cent of Finnish males would fit the description."

"Right. Could it have been a woman?"

"Are you asking because I mentioned a rolling pin?" Räikkönen pushed the trolley charged with the body against the wall. "I suppose, yes, it could be possible. Though of course it's not common to see a woman in a fit of murderous rage. Your typical woman would probably choose a different weapon. Poison, maybe. Or pushing the victim down the stairs. Something nice and clean." He started to unbutton his green surgical gown, which now looked like a butcher's apron. "Of course, it would help if you had managed to get footprints."

Somehow he was making it sound like it was my fault. There had been no footprints in the yard: the madam's attacker had smoothed the snow with a branch he had broken from the birch tree. The police had found the branch at the end of the alleyway that ran alongside the property.

The trainees stirred, but I wasn't done yet. "What about the victim's general health?"

"You said *two* questions, Chief Inspector," Räikkönen said quietly. "I answered two questions. You'll have all the details in my report tomorrow."

"I need to know now."

"All right," Räikkönen sighed. "Anything specific?"

"I was wondering," I said slowly, "if the victim was pregnant. She doesn't look very young, but I suppose it was still possible?"

There was silence. Räikkönen collected the instruments he had used for the autopsy and dunked them in a metal bucket filled with water. Then he strolled over to a filing cabinet that stood in the corner of the room and pulled a thin manila envelope from it. "You're an intelligent man, Chief Inspector Mustonen. Not that I ever doubted that. No, the latest victim was not pregnant. But" – the pathologist turned and his bright blue eyes locked on me – "the single blow received by the drowned prostitute Nellie Ritvanen could have been made with the same weapon. The autopsy file is here if you want it."

28

Hella

I couldn't bear to go home. Too many memories... The walls that Steve and I had both repainted in sunny yellow, a framed photograph of the Eiffel Tower – he had promised we'd go together one day – the knitted scarf that used to be his but that I had begun to regard as mine. The office was safer. Cold, lonely. No shared memories there, and no Anita to ask me about my day. The only thing waiting for me was the snow globe, which I shoved promptly in the drawer; I thought I had better try to forget it even existed.

I sat behind my desk, looked at my empty daily planner, then started to cry. As I sobbed, I realized that, up until the moment I had seen Steve's name mentioned in the little black book, I had still been hoping we would somehow get back together. It hadn't been the first time we'd argued. We had even been separated for three long years while I had worked for the Ivalo police department. But until now, the situation had been simple: Steve's wife had been there first, she'd had precedence, and I had been the outsider. I'd been *the other woman*. I hadn't been proud of that, of course I hadn't, but I had still felt justified because Steve had told me he was happier with me, that it was only in my arms he felt alive. That he and Elsbeth didn't love each other any more, that she was only still with him because she was incapable of managing on her own. So, stupid me, I'd thought Steve and I were soulmates. That we were meant to be. That Elsbeth had been a terrible mistake. Turned out the terrible mistake was *me*.

I realized with a sinking feeling that this was exactly how Elsbeth must have felt when she'd first discovered my existence. The shame washed over me like a wave. Maybe she had never been the stupid housewife that Steve had made her out to be. She had been a teacher once. She had given up work when their daughter was born.

And suddenly, I knew what I had to do. I'd write to Elsbeth. I'd tell her that I was sorry. The nasty little voice inside my head whispered: *About time. And it's not like you're risking anything. Steve and you are* over.

There was no food in my office and nothing to drink, but I could always rely on the abundance of ink and writing paper. I started writing without giving myself time to change my mind.

Before long, I had poured everything out.

The time when I had spied on Elsbeth having lunch with a handsome young man, hoping madly that she was having an affair with him and that I could report her to Steve. Did I really need to add that the man turned out to be her brother?

The time I was so insane with the pain of not being an official part of Steve's life, I had gone to the hairdresser and dyed my hair blonde, just like hers. Then, ashamed of myself, I had rushed back and asked the bemused hair stylist to reproduce my natural mousy brown. He had done his best, although it never even came close to my original colour. No reaction from Steve. He hadn't even noticed.

The time I made a decision that cost me my career, and Steve told me that my posting to the outer confines of the country could be a good thing – all that clean fresh air.

That wasn't even the worst of it.

The worst was those innumerable times Steve had told me I was a tough girl, not at all like his wife, and that I could live with the uncertainty. He told me he was proud of me because I never begged for him to commit – and so I didn't.

What an idiot I'd been.

When the letter was finished, I put it into an envelope and sealed it. The address did not present the slightest difficulty. If Elsbeth was indeed staying with her parents, I had their address jotted down in the most comprehensive file in my office: the Elsbeth file.

Then, I locked my office, ran down the stairs, and dropped the letter in the mailbox on the other side of the street. I felt curiously light, empty even. Ready for the first evening of the rest of my life.

Of course, as I was walking down the crowded streets, I didn't know that before long my old life would come crashing back.

Anita, perhaps sensing the state I was in, didn't ask any questions. She pointed to the table, where a bowl of chicken soup was already waiting for me, then busied herself in the kitchen while I ate. The soup was surprisingly good. I wondered what I would have been doing if Anita hadn't been home. I probably would have drunk myself to sleep. Some days, I really wondered if I was turning into an alcoholic.

I finished eating and carried the soup bowl into the kitchen, where the window was open wide to get rid of the musty smell. When I returned to the living room, Anita was waiting for me with her notepad open.

"So," she said crisply. "Let's get started."

I leaned my face on my hands. The food was working its way into my system and I felt exhausted, numb and almost happy, like someone who had found peace after making a decision that was long overdue.

"Do we really need to discuss the case now? I don't even know that Mustonen won't get a court injunction against me or something, for mucking up the investigation." I had of course forgotten to drop off the madam's little black book at his office.

"No he won't," chirped Anita. "He's a good investigator; he wants this solved. He'll appreciate your help." She looked like an eager puppy, staring at me with those bright blue eyes, holding her breath.

"Maybe," I sighed. "But Elena is still missing. What if he —"

Anita's eyes widened. "Did her in? Do you really think he could, that he could—? Why would he do that?"

"Sounds unlikely, I know. But I'd only be certain once I found out what happened to her. Why don't you tell me what you've uncovered so far?"

"First, there have been no similar cases in other parts of the country, according to Ranta. I mean, people drown, of course, but no cases where the victim was a young prostitute who announced she was going solo. Or at least, not recently. There was a string of unsolved young women's murders in southern Finland in the 1930s, but anyway, that's too far back in time, isn't it? I mean, it's not like we're looking for someone who's been inactive all this time."

I toyed with the idea, but it sounded unlikely. If the murderer from the 1930s had never been apprehended, he'd have no reason I could think of to lie low. And that man would now be at least fifty, probably too old to hop onto rooftops. "Uh-huh. What else?"

"Second, the pathologist seems to think that it was the same weapon for Nellie Ritvanen. So it *must* be the same murderer. We're looking for a multiple killer." For some reason, the idea seemed to fill Anita with boundless joy.

"Just someone covering his tracks," I said dully. "Klara Nylund must have known something after all. What did Mustonen say about this?"

"He said he's reopening the investigation into Nellie's death. That he's now convinced it was murder. What did *you* find out?" Anita waited, her eyes bright and hopeful.

I told her about the contents of the black book and showed her the names I had copied down in my notepad. That left Anita silent for a moment. I sat there wondering if she'd spill to Mustonen as soon as she got to the office the following morning, but part of me didn't care. All I wanted was to have the perpetrator arrested and charged; if Mustonen really was working on it and got there first, that was fine by me.

Finally, Anita raised her eyes. "There's something else, right? Something you're not telling me." Her hand hovered above the list of names and their matching numbers.

"No," I said quickly. "Just a bad day. I'm tired, and worried about the money. You see, I inherited my parents' house, but I can't live there, and I can't sell it either. Anyway, it's just a small —"

"Wait." Anita's index finger stopped on a line in the middle; her eyes widened. "The US DJ? Could it be...? Is that why you...? Oh God!"

I snatched the notepad from her, started to leaf through the pages. My hands were trembling.

"Hella?" Anita whispered in an awestruck voice. "Do you think it could be Steve?" I heard her swallow. "Do you think Steve could be involved?"

29

Hella

I had never thought Steve could actually be a suspect. I hadn't thought of anything beyond the hurt I felt. It was a shock to realize Anita could be right, that Steve's betrayal was not the worst thing. The worst thing was this: the only man I had ever loved, the man I had hoped to marry one day, looked like a serious contender for Helsinki's first-ever multiple killer. But I'd be damned if I was going to admit it.

"*Oh God.*" I echoed Anita's dramatic whisper. "Of course not! How could you even imagine a thing like that?"

Anita looked at her hands. "He's on the list."

"Yes, but hundreds of people are. OK, dozens."

"I don't know," Anita said slowly. "I mean, obviously we've got other, much more serious suspects and all, but ... don't you want to be certain?"

She was right, I would have loved to be certain. "I don't really see how."

"Well," Anita frowned. "I don't know." She lit a cigarette, twisted her mouth to blow a line of smoke towards the window. Then her eyes brightened. "Maybe I can pretend to —"

"No." I slammed both my hands down on the table, palms flat. "You're not going to be pretending to be anyone other than yourself. You tried that once already, remember?"

Anita swallowed, put out her cigarette. I was conscious of the note of hysteria in my voice; I didn't care. "Listen carefully, Anita. You're still very young. You're in training. You're not going to make any disastrous moves that could" – I stopped, unable to find the right words – "that could lead to disaster. This is not —"

"All right!" Anita screamed. The feet of her chair scraped on the wooden floor as she jumped to her feet. "Save your breath. I'm not doing anything. I'm going to bed."

She stormed off, slammed the bedroom door shut. I thought it was over, but just a moment later the door was thrust open again. Anita's face was blotchy with fury, but her voice had regained its composure. "Just out of curiosity," she said, "are you afraid of what I might uncover?"

Then the door slammed shut again.

30

Hella

The next morning, I woke up to a feeling of acute self-loathing which I immediately countered with a resolute *I don't give a damn*. I left the apartment before Anita was up. A heavy snowfall had blanketed the city during the night, and I had to lean on the front door to push it open. The newspaper boy, passing by, aimed a snowball at the street light; he was carrying a fresh edition of *Helsingin Sanomat*, with Stalin's pockmarked face occupying the centre of the page. I caught the words "conspiracy" and "doctors' plot" before the boy ran away. My plan was to catch up with Tom – I knew that he always started early – then go and see if there was any news of Elena. But as I trudged through the wet snow, I realized I needed to stop by my office first to pick up my bag, which I had left on the desk the previous evening.

The staircase was dark, and I could hear a shattered light bulb turn to dust under my heel. There was a heavy, expensive cologne scent floating in the air. I froze. Who could that be? Should I be afraid? But the scent was not that of a thug, and I had never believed in running away. I climbed the stairs slowly, on the lookout for potential danger. The smell got stronger as I reached the fifth-floor landing.

"Good morning," I said to the shadow leaning on the wall. My heart was beating too fast, but I was trying my best to keep my voice pleasant and businesslike. "Are you waiting for me?"

The man laughed. "I guess I am. The light seems to be out. Would you happen to have a paraffin lamp in your office?" His voice seemed polite, even friendly. A new client? This early?

I fumbled for the lock, trying to avoid turning my back on the man. As if realizing I was scared, he lit a match to help me. In the trembling light, I saw dark hair falling across his eyes and a chiselled chin. He was wearing a suit and tie, and a dazzling white shirt. The door swung open at last, but the man waited outside while I found the light.

The paraffin lamp sat on top of the filing cabinet; a moment later, its warm glow filled the room and I could see my visitor better. He was older than I had first thought. Expensive, well-cut suit, a diamond pin in his tie, manicured nails. Not exactly the sort of client I was used to.

"How can I help you, Mr…"

"Gustafsson." He smiled. "I own a small factory that produces spare parts for engines. Recently, my chief accountant brought to my attention that we've been receiving a higher than usual number of complaints about the quality of our products. Given our business, it's obviously a huge problem." He smiled again, thinking perhaps that the information he had provided was sufficient.

"I'm sorry, I don't understand. How could a quality problem be —"

"I suspect sabotage, only I have no idea who the guilty party is. This is why I need your help."

"I see." The explanation was plausible, but I still didn't believe it somehow. "Why not hire a man to help you? He'd surely be more credible."

"No," my visitor said. "That was my idea at first, obviously, but then I realized everyone would be wary of a new recruit the boss brought in. Now, if it was a woman... You surely have a minimum of secretarial skills." He winked at me. "A woman wouldn't rouse suspicion; she'd be much more efficient. And of course I'd pay you as if you were a man. I'm even ready to give you an advance." He pulled a leather-bound chequebook out of his briefcase.

"Oh," I said. "Well, thank you for coming to see me. Can I think about it for a couple of days? I'm actually working on a different matter, but that now seems to be coming to a close."

My visitor froze, the chequebook in his hand, looking slightly taken aback. He had probably been expecting me to jump for joy and rush over to his factory, forgetting the whole ghastly murder business. I wondered who had sent him. Mustonen? Would he stoop so low as to involve other people in his shenanigans? Should I consider this as proof of Ahti Virtanen's involvement? I didn't want to admit it, but the idea of a conspiracy was starting to feel appealing, like a minor itch taking attention away from the dull pain I'd been suffering from for days.

I rose to my feet, and the man did so too. "Out of curiosity," I said, "who recommended me to you?"

"Chief Inspector Mustonen," the man answered promptly. He knew I would ask the question. "Ten years ago, we were comrades in arms. After the war finished, we kept in touch." The man smiled, pulling a card out of his coat pocket. "My address and telephone number. Please try to make yourself available quickly. I would hate to lose orders if the problem persists."

"Of course," I said, even managing to muster a smile. "Just one murderer to catch, and then I'll be as free as a bird."

31

Hella

By the time my visitor left, it was too late to go and see Tom. He'd be busy working, and I didn't want to interrupt him. Instead, I decided to go and see if I could find out more about Elena. It was more of a formality really – I was pretty sure the girl was gone forever. It might not even have been directly related to Mustonen's visit. Ever since the war, Helsinki had become a magnet for refugees of all kinds: the reds, reluctant to go back to their country where Comrade Stalin's rehabilitation camps were waiting for them; the wayward Nazis, in search of a new beginning; the displaced peasants from Lapland. Outcasts of all sorts. Scores of them had arrived in the city, a hundred thousand, someone had told me once, and the worn-out, drawn faces of these men and women had become a familiar part of the landscape. For all her beauty, Elena was one of them. She was here by an accident of sorts, one that had made her native country impossible to live in. She was not moored, the people she met here were not her people, she could be here today and gone tomorrow. She could take off at the slightest danger.

I thought about my other options as I made my way towards the address Egg had given me. Should I try to find other witnesses to the accident? Could Elena's friends help? But when I knocked on the door of the ground-floor apartment and explained to an overweight man suffering from a very bad case of halitosis why I was there, he jerked his thumb upwards. "Why don't you ask her yourself?" he said, and I held my breath. "Where she's been. Only thing I can say, she's back now, and back to normal. Partied all last night."

"Are you certain it's her? Not some other girl?"

"I know Elena, OK? It's her. Go and see for yourself."

At last he closed the door and I could breathe again. So Elena was back. I wondered what I could say to make her understand that I didn't present a danger to her.

Elena's door opened on a chain. At first I thought that I must have got the wrong apartment. But then the man moved a little to the side and I glimpsed a beautiful dark-haired girl standing next to him.

The two spoke at the same time.

"What do you want?" asked the girl.

"Go away!" growled the man.

"I want to talk about Ahti Virtanen," I said, my eyes on Elena. "I'm a private investigator. My name's Mauzer."

The man shook his head and started closing the door. "We have nothing to say to you."

"I know what he did. I can help you."

The door clicked shut in my face.

"Not all the police officers in this country are like Inspector Mustonen," I cried. "I can take you to people who'll listen to you, take your statement. People who will be ready to help you."

There was no answer.

"Did he threaten you? Are you afraid of Mustonen?"

No one answered but I could swear they were waiting behind the door, listening to every word.

"All right," I said. "I'm leaving. But if I were you, I would press charges. People like Mustonen need to be stopped."

I had started walking down the stairs when the door behind me opened with a bang. "It's you who needs to be stopped," the girl cried out. "How dare you go about saying horrible things about him!"

"Shh," the man said. "Elena, get back inside. No one needs to know." But there was no stopping the girl any more.

"Inspector Mustonen sent us to someone who helped us get the papers," she said. "We're Finnish citizens now, Vlad and I. He's the best thing that ever happened to us."

PART II

PART II

Fighting Monsters

32

Chief Inspector Mustonen

That morning, Sofia woke up angry. I was in the kitchen, frying eggs for breakfast. Arne was sitting on the counter next to me, his short legs dangling over the edge. We both looked up when Sofia stumbled into the kitchen.

"Mummy!" Arne trilled, smiling from ear to ear. I set him on the floor and the boy ran to his mother, bumping into her legs. "Mummy!"

Sofia stared at him as if she wasn't quite sure he was hers. "Would you just take him, Erik? I'm feeling unwell."

"Sure," I said, and scooped Arne up one-handed. "What you need is a good breakfast, honey. It's just a bout of morning sickness. You'll be fine after you eat."

"I'll be fine once we move into the new house," Sofia snapped. The eggs were sizzling in the pan. I set Arne in his high chair, slid the eggs onto three plates, and carried them to the table. The coffee pot and the cups were there already.

"So that's what this is about?" The previous night, I had called Sofia's father to tell him that we weren't buying the house. We couldn't afford it, and besides, even if we could, it wasn't the right time. My father-in-law had snorted and hung up on me. Sofia had been standing next to me during the telephone conversation. When her father put the receiver down, she had turned and gone into her bedroom. She had refused to talk, blaming a headache.

"Sofia," I said. "I know you want that house. But it's come at a bad time. Maybe next year…"

She stabbed the yolk on her plate, not looking at me, the corners of her mouth twitching. She was as angry as I'd ever seen her. "There will be no next time. How often do we have to say it? This sort of house —" She threw her fork down, hid her face in her hands. On the other side of the table, Arne was staring at us, his eyes round. The kitchen clock chimed seven.

Sofia muttered something through her fingers. I leaned closer. "What is it, honey? I can't hear you."

"I said…" She was sobbing now, shoulders heaving, hot tears streaming down her cheeks.

I kept my hand on her shoulder, squeezing it gently. "Mummy is tired," I said to Arne. "The little baby is kicking her tummy."

Sofia took a big, shuddery breath. "My father says you don't really care about me. About us."

Arne looked at us gravely. "I hate little babies," he said.

"How stupid —" Sofia started. She pushed her chair back, hoisted herself up, both hands gripping the table. Her bloated face was a mask of fury. "I'm going back to bed. *You* take care of him! If you can't get us a decent place to live, you can at least take care of your child!" She stormed off.

"Pff," Arne said. "Mummies." He shrugged, trying to look grown-up and unconcerned, but his lower lip was trembling and his eyes were liquid with tears.

I drew a deep breath. I loved my wife. I really did. And I was not blameless; why would I deserve a perfect wife?

Besides, Sofia *was* perfect… Usually. Just not now. I looked at my son. "Want to go to my office, buddy? You can help me work. And when we come back home tonight, Mummy will be fine, I promise."

Arne nodded, hopeful now.

"Good. In that case, finish up your breakfast."

I pulled Sofia's plate towards me. The fried egg was torn into pieces, leaking yolk. I gathered it on a fork, stuffed it into my mouth. It was the first time Sofia and I had had an argument like that. Ironic, really, that it had to be about a stupid house.

When I finished eating, I sent Arne to get his jacket and hat, and then marched towards the bedroom door. It was locked; I could hear Sofia sobbing inside.

I rapped on the door.

"What?"

"I'll see what I can do," I said. "About the house. But I can't promise you anything, OK?"

"OK," Sofia said. Then she resumed her sobbing.

Arne loved coming to my office. It didn't happen often – there are better surroundings for a three-year-old boy than an overheated homicide squad room with its gruesome exhibits and portraits of criminals on the walls. But when he did come, he enjoyed the gentle cosseting of the squad secretary, Tarja, and the camaraderie he felt with the officers. He had already told me that when he grew up he wanted to become a detective too. Good thing his grandfather hadn't heard that; the old snob would have had a heart attack.

Arne's arrival that day provoked the usual whoops of delight. He sat on Anita's knee, smiling dreamily while she murmured something into his ear. All around them, the detectives were rushing about, the majority of them part of the team investigating Klara Nylund's murder. Neighbours, girls and those clients the police had managed to identify had been questioned, but none had provided any valuable information. The search of the back yard, the lane leading to it, and the interior of the house had been completed, to no avail. All the police knew was that someone, most likely a man, had met with the madam between 7 and 9 p.m. and bludgeoned her to death with an unknown weapon.

After discussing the case during our morning briefing – Arne spent that time helping Tarja water the plants – Inspector Pinchus summed up the situation: "Either it's random, or it's not. In either case, God help us."

"There's also Anita's attacker," I said. "The brothel is only a stone's throw away from where she ran into me. Inspector Pinchus, would you look into that?"

Pinchus rolled his eyes. "Just a coincidence. Some drunk. We'll never find him."

"I strongly suggest you try," I said through clenched teeth. Some days, I felt like nothing ever got done unless I insisted. And even then, it was not done properly.

"All right," Pinchus glared.

Jokela glanced at his watch, started drumming his fingers on the table. He had a lunch appointment with Dr Palmu, and he was afraid he'd be late. Pinchus got the hint and started to get up, but just then I surprised them by saying that it would be a good idea to involve Interpol.

"They've been asking for a sample file from us," I said. "This could be it. We'll provide them with what we have on Nellie and now Klara Nylund. Maybe they'll be able to come up with something useful."

Jokela drew on his cigarette; his nostrils flared. "Are you sure," he said, looking at me, "that this is a good idea?

What if the case is never solved? What would they think of us?"

I had hesitated for a long time before making the suggestion; I was not going to back off now. "I hope the case will be solved," I said. "To everyone's satisfaction. And anyway, this is not about our egos. In a situation like this, where we may be dealing with a mass murderer, we need all the help we can get."

Jokela glared at Pinchus, who had been following this conversation with an amused expression on his long, emaciated face. If Pinchus hadn't been there to witness the exchange, Jokela would have vetoed the suggestion, but now he couldn't do so without raising suspicion. In the end, Jokela gave a reluctant nod. "If you must," he said. "But bear in mind your priorities."

"The priority," I told Pinchus as we left Jokela's office, "is to locate the madam's little black book. All the girls know of its existence; none have been able to say where it is now." As for me, I had a pretty good idea of its current location – Mauzer must have got hold of it somehow – but no idea how to retrieve it.

"What if it was just a random attack?" Pinchus said, hunching forward like a heron. "We'd never get to the bottom of it. Unless, of course, we got lucky."

Thinking of luck, and by extension lucky escapes, made me realize that I still hadn't spoken to Anita about what had happened two days before. It was my responsibility as Jokela's deputy to make sure my officers were safe.

"Anita!" I called out. "Could you please come over?"

She stood up, smoothing her skirt. That girl looked like a ripe piece of fruit, a peach or an apricot; she made you think of summertime, of fancy cocktails and flimsy silk dresses.

I closed the door of my office behind her, offered her a cigarette.

"Thank you." She took one and smiled at me. "Arne is a lovely little boy."

"My wife and I hope our second child will be just like him," I said in a carefully controlled voice. I sat down behind my desk and faced her. "Anita, I need to talk to you about the other night. When you bumped into Jon and me in front of the bar."

"Yes?"

"Did Miss Mauzer ask you to help out with her investigation?"

"No," Anita said, startled. "No, she didn't. It was my idea. I didn't realize it could be so dangerous, I really thought that —"

I leaned forward. "Anita, are you telling me the truth?" The girl nodded energetically, the cigarette swaying between her long fingers; I held up my hand to stop her. "You must realize that Miss Mauzer is not like us. She is … impulsive. She doesn't follow basic safety procedures. I don't know whether she told you, but that was the reason she got expelled from the Helsinki homicide squad in the first place. Because she created a dangerous situation and one of the persons involved lost his life."

I let that sink in. "Now, Anita, you certainly understand that we don't want to lose you. So be friends with Miss Mauzer all you like but please, *please* be careful. Don't put yourself in danger. It's not worth it."

"Of course," Anita murmured, stubbing out her cigarette. She was blushing. "Of course. It was stupid of me to do what I did. I'll be careful from now on."

There was a knock on my door and Tarja stuck her head inside. "Are you busy, Chief Inspector? I have a person here from the Port Authority who says you called for him, and another visitor" – Tarja paused, dropping her voice to a whisper – "Miss Hella Mauzer."

"Speak of the Devil," I smiled. "But can you please ask Miss Mauzer to wait? I need to see the representative of the Port Authority first."

33

Hella

Tarja had colourless hair plaited in a ring loaf and dreamy wet eyes that looked with doting approval on everything and everyone except me.

"Are you enjoying yourself, Miss Mauzer?" she asked as we stood together in the reception area waiting for Mustonen. "Doing a man's work, being on your own?"

"Thank you, Tarja. Never been better. I know you lamented my departure."

The secretary pursed her lips and I pointed at Anita, waltzing out of Mustonen's office down the corridor. "Aren't you happy seeing another bright young woman joining the squad?"

"She's not the same," Tarja said, her pale eyebrows knitted in annoyance. "Anita knows her place, knows she can never replace a man. You are the only one who seems to think you're worth as much as any male officer."

Or maybe Anita's just better at fooling you, I thought. Because she knows the sort of person you are. Of all the woman-haters on the squad, Tarja, the only woman besides me, was also the most dangerous. As she turned and left without so much as a backward glance, I waved for Anita to join me.

My roommate looked different here: pulled together, sharp. In a moving picture, cast in the role of a promising young officer, a sole woman among weathered detectives, she would have been convincing. "What are you doing here?" she whispered.

I showed her the little parcel I was carrying. "First of all, I wanted to say sorry for yelling at you yesterday. And also, I brought the madam's little black book."

"You changed your mind?"

"Elena is alive and kicking. Apart from a highly suspicious potential client who showed up this morning promising heaps of gold, I have no reason to believe Mustonen is tampering with the investigation. So here I am. Being a good citizen."

Anita brought her platinum ponytail forward and started twisting it around her index finger. "I think you were wrong to suspect Mustonen. You know who the man in his office is?"

"No."

"Someone from the Port Authority. Mustonen is requesting their assistance to trawl the seabed. He's hoping to find evidence." Anita looked away, frowning. "Or maybe other drowned girls."

"Did he look into Ahti's alibi?"

"I suppose so," Anita said scathingly. "Just out of curiosity, is there some personal reason why you resent Mustonen as much as you do? Are you jealous of what he's become?"

"No!" I said, but the tips of my ears started to burn with shame when I realized that was what everybody would think. "I just want to be sure he's doing all that is necessary."

"OK," Anita sighed. "You still don't trust him, do you? I'll try to find out about Virtanen's alibi."

The words rushed out before I had time to check myself. "No! You should be careful."

"Be careful? That's funny," Anita said, though she didn't smile. "He said the same thing about *you*."

Ten minutes later, the Port Authority representative left and Tarja came to fetch me from the waiting area. A little blonde boy was clinging to her skirt.

"That's the chief inspector's eldest," she said by way of an explanation. They both watched me as I made my way towards Mustonen's office.

The air in the room was grey with smoke. In a heartbeat, I was thrown back in time. Nothing had changed; I could close my eyes and still know that the umbrella stand leaned to one side, that the desk lamp's green shade was chipped, that the wall to the left of me displayed two pictures painted by Mustonen: a snowy landscape featuring an ice-frosted lake, and a horse drawing a sleigh piled high with wood. But I knew it was just an illusion. Here, too, time had not stood still.

"I didn't know you had a child," I said. "Congratulations."

Mustonen was standing in front of the open window. He turned to face me as I came in. "Thank you. The second one is due soon." He nodded towards the little parcel I was holding. "Is that what I think it is?"

I started to unwrap it. "Klara Nylund's little black book. All yours now."

He didn't look at it. He looked at me instead, his expression benign and inscrutable. "Anything interesting in it?"

"I wouldn't know."

"Stop it, Mauzer!" Suddenly, Mustonen was leaning on his

desk, his face mere inches from mine. He looked paler than before, dark shadows under his eyes, his hairline receding ever so slightly, but otherwise it was the same man: handsome and fit and ruthless. "Don't you play games with me! This thing is evidence you stole from a crime scene. You could go to jail for that."

"Then prove it! She gave it to me herself. And there's one more thing." I took a breath, willing myself to remain steady, to keep staring into those cold blue eyes. "The so-called client you sent me this morning. Do you think I'm stupid?"

Mustonen was the first to back off. I could practically see the tension seeping from his shoulders. "What client?" he said.

"As if you don't know."

He sat down, rubbing his face with both hands. "Trust me, Hella, I don't. On the life of my son, I didn't send you anyone. Who did the client say sent him? You must have asked."

"He said it was you."

"Then," said Mustonen, and there was a dark look on his face, "he lied. I'll ask around, try to find out who that might be." He picked up the madam's book, slid it into an envelope. "You have to believe me, Hella, I'm just trying to do my job. And it's not always easy."

"What about the Port Authority?" I asked. "Are they helping you?"

He looked me in the eye. "The weather is too turbulent, apparently. Storm alerts. But as soon as it's possible, yes, they'll start trawling."

"All right." I got to my feet. "Thank you for the information. If you need anything, you know where to find me."

"I do." Mustonen hesitated. "And … be careful, Hella, OK? The police are not ready to charge anyone – yet – but we're dealing with an extremely deranged person here. You watch your step."

34

Hella

The court's letter was on the windowsill, where I had put it the previous day. I had circled the deadline for payment in red ink: Thursday, 5 March. There was no mention of what would happen to me if I didn't pay on time. Maybe it won't be so terrible, I thought as I took down the letter and dropped it into the wastepaper basket. Maybe they'll forget about me for a while. Part of me, the part that specialized in wishful thinking and which had grown out of proportion following my affair with Steve, almost managed to make it sound plausible.

I pushed the thought away and tried to concentrate on the task at hand. My visit to Mustonen had left me plagued by shame. Before my conversation with Elena, I had seen him as the evil spirit at the heart of this mystery, as the opposite of what a police officer should be. Turned out I was wrong. The man I had accused of pulling strings was playing a dangerous game, but deep down he was still an efficient and diligent police officer and perhaps even a decent human being.

But then again, that shouldn't have come as a surprise, and this was what bothered me most.

It was hard to believe it now, but we had almost been friends once, when I was new on the homicide squad. At that time, Mustonen had been the only one who didn't ignore me, the only one to treat me as his equal. Then he got married and his priorities changed. He had a family to support, a father-in-law to impress. By conscious choice, he had settled for just one facial expression: that of benign but purposeful detachment. He was there to do his job, rid the Earth of scum and rise quickly through the ranks. The rest didn't matter.

"Follow his example," Jokela used to tell me. "You cannot be so involved, little Hella. Keep your distance. Do your job, do it well, then go home to your family." There, Jokela usually stopped, remembering too late that I no longer had any family to come home to. A young girl fresh out of training, I was nodding away, trying to convince myself that my boss was right. Then we'd get called out on a new case, and I would snap again. Until that fateful December afternoon when I had shot a murder suspect at close range. That day had marked the end of my career, and the first promotion for Mustonen. Since then I hadn't stopped plummeting, while he had climbed the ranks and collected awards with disconcerting ease. Seeing him today made me realize how far he had come over the last three years. The realization was anything but comfortable.

Maybe, I thought, I had accused him because I was jealous of his success. Apart from Egg's insinuation that he had done Elena in – which turned out to be spectacularly false – what proof did I have that Mustonen had been meddling with the investigation, covering for Ahti? It could have been Jokela all along. Or even someone else, such as Ahti's family. But if my motives, even unconsciously, had been that low, what did that say about me? Was I a bad person? The only thing that had kept me afloat over the last few days, as I struggled to cope with the rejection, the hopelessness and the lack of self-esteem, was this: I was one of the good guys. I was fighting evil. All it had taken was a few harsh words, screamed at me by a pretty dark-haired stranger, to shatter that image I had of myself. What was I but a hysterical, middle-aged, delusional spinster tilting at windmills while the real investigation continued elsewhere? While people I deemed unworthy did good in silent, unobtrusive ways?

I felt an overwhelming need to talk about this with someone who would understand. I needed Irja and Timo, their undivided attention, their impartiality, their kindness and trust in me. But Irja and Timo were too far away, in their secluded village in Lapland. They were busy, too, with the new baby and now with Maria, whom I'd sent to stay with them. But maybe I could still go, sometime during the spring. I was staring at the calendar, trying to make up my mind, when I heard a noise coming from the staircase. I turned to look: a thin white envelope had just been slipped under my door. My name was on it, nothing else.

I swung the door open and heard retreating footsteps. "Hey," I called out. "I'm here. Come and talk to me."

No answer. The footsteps gained speed. A moment later, I heard the heavy oak door leading to the street screech open then slam shut.

I slid a finger under the flap of the envelope, tore it open. The letter was just one page, covered in an angry scrawl:

Miss Mauzer, as Klara Nylund's successor, I wish to inform you that your assignment with us is terminated. Please avoid being seen in the vicinity of our establishment.

There was no signature.

I stared at the letter. So it *was* over. I had failed, it was as simple as that. There were things I hadn't done yet – like trying to find out who had really sent the latest prospective client to me – but I didn't feel it was worth it. I was out of the game, and I didn't even care. Suddenly, I knew what I had to do: go back home, put my things in order. Then, the following day or the day after, I would board a train to Ivalo.

35

Chief Inspector Mustonen

The man sitting across the desk from me, puffing on an expensive Cuban cigar, looked even smaller than I remembered.

"Is that your son over there in the squad room?" the diminutive man asked. "The cute little blonde boy?"

I was tempted to say no, but if Virtanen was asking the question, it meant he already knew the answer.

"Yes," I said. "Why don't we get down to business? How can I help you?"

The fact that Ahti's father had chosen to come and see me at the office meant our relationship had just reached a wholly different level. I was now required to publicly take sides, tacitly admit I was corrupt. I could feel cold sweat gathering between my shoulder blades, my heart rate picking up.

There was a silence during which Virtanen stretched, shook his cigar into the overflowing ashtray on my desk and flicked a tiny speck of dust from the sleeve of the camel-hair coat that he hadn't bothered to take off. I waited.

"I was assured by your boss that you were smarter than that," Virtanen said at last. "Apparently, he was wrong."

"I thought you were pretty smart too," I countered. "Looks like we were both mistaken."

Virtanen stared at me.

"The so-called new client visiting Miss Mauzer on my behalf," I said. "It was someone you sent, wasn't it? I've checked with Jokela and he's adamant he wasn't the one who set it up."

"And what if it *was* me? The factory exists; my friend is ready to give her that job and pay her well. What's the harm?"

"Mauzer doesn't operate like that," I said. "Trust me, I know. The moment she realized someone was trying to take her attention away from the madam's murder, her antennae went up." I tilted my chair back, adopting the nonchalant attitude of my visitor, showing him I was not afraid. "Mauzer's like a bulldog. Once she sinks her teeth into something, she doesn't give up. All you managed to achieve is getting her to distrust me."

Virtanen shrugged. "Didn't she already? Anyway. Maybe you're right, maybe it was a bit excessive. But I had to try. That woman really is a pain in the neck." He leaned forward suddenly, his tiny eyes gleaming. "And so are you! What the hell were you doing going around asking about my son's alibi for the night the madam was killed? I told you he was home with us. My wife can confirm."

"That's the usual procedure, I'm afraid," I said easily, hoping my visitor would believe me. "It's routine. Your son's name came up in connection with the investigation, and he was a client. We are looking into the background of everyone we can identify based on the information contained in the madam's notes."

"Well, I have made some inquiries of my own," Virtanen said through clenched teeth. "And I've got a couple of other suspects to offer you." He pulled a folded piece of paper out of his pocket. "Here. Just in case you haven't been able to identify them on your own." He held out the paper for me to take.

I shook my head, folded my arms across my chest. "I do not want to hear your arguments. This investigation needs to remain impartial, if it has any chance at all of succeeding."

Virtanen thought about this, then slid the paper back into his pocket. "So you have a suspect?"

I nodded.

"I want to hear you say it!"

There was no way around it. My son was in the next room, and Virtanen was furious with me already.

"Yes," I said. "This is off the record, but yes. We have a suspect, an American DJ, the only one in Helsinki. His name is Steve Collins."

36

Hella

Anita came home just as I was finishing packing. She seemed in a good mood, and started to tell me about her day, but then she noticed the suitcase and her voice died down.

"Where are you going?"

"Lapland."

"Why?"

"I need a change of air. Besides, I'm off the case. Do you think this sweater still looks OK?"

I pulled a burgundy wool sweater out of the wardrobe and held it against my chest. Anita looked at it critically. "No. Too old. And is that a hole near the hem? But the colour suits you well, you should wear burgundy more, it sets off your pale skin. And you know what?" Anita stepped back with her head tilted to one side, appraising. "I've never noticed it until now, but you're actually quite good-looking. You've got nice high cheekbones, huge eyes and lovely legs. It's just that you're too tall and skinny. You're what, five foot seven?"

I nodded, eyeing myself self-consciously in the full-length mirror fixed to one side of the wardrobe.

"And your hair's dark," she added. "You need to make it sparkle. Maybe we should get you some nice earrings. I saw a pair at the jewellers on my way home, like a long chain with a ruby pendant. The store assistant said they weren't for sale, they were there to be mended, but maybe if you insist —"

"Anita," I said. "Thank you. But I don't have any money for earrings. Is that where you've been, at the jewellers? Is that why you're home so late?"

"I had things to do. What do *you* care anyway?"

"For one, I promised Ranta I'd keep an eye on you. And two, given your romantic notions of what a criminal investigation involves —"

But Anita wasn't listening. "You know what?" she said brightly. "Maybe fashion will change one day. Maybe this time next year, gap-toothed women with hollow cheeks will be all the rage."

"It doesn't matter," I said. "Really. Can we just stop this now? I'm trying to finish packing, not get into fashion modelling."

"Well, aren't we two spoonfuls of grumpy in a bowl full of bitchy this evening? Of course it matters! Life is different when you're beautiful! People go out of their way to help you, and everyone is just *sooo* nice. You'll see for yourself when I'm done with you." Anita fumbled in her purse, pulled out a pair of tweezers. "We'll start by giving a nice pointed arch to your eyebrows, and then —"

"No. I'll leave my eyebrows as they are: straight. The Marilyn Monroe look wouldn't go well with my face." I stepped back. "You know, I'm not really comfortable doing this. It makes me feel like I'm some sort of mass-produced garment, with eyebrows like this and a waist like that." Anita looked hurt, so I hurried to add: "In any case, I'll never be a natural beauty like you. So it's not even worth trying. I have my work, that's what matters."

Anita smiled, placated. How she admired herself. There was something lovely, childish and unselfconscious in liking oneself so much. She turned towards the mirror, striking a pose, and I thought she was going to leave it at that, but I was wrong. "I don't understand," Anita said, her jet-black eyebrows prettily furrowed. "Are you trying to be like a man?"

"No." This conversation was getting us nowhere. "I'm trying to be real."

"Do you mean I'm not real?" Anita had just said when there was a sharp knock on the door. I glanced at the clock: 7 p.m. I wasn't expecting anyone. Could it be Ranta again, coming over to check up on his cousin?

"Aren't you going to get the door?" Anita said. "What if it's Steve?"

"It's not. And I'm not in the mood for social calls. Would you please —"

Anita was opening the door already. The woman standing on my doorstep could have been her older sister: a mass of shiny blonde hair, porcelain skin and big blue eyes that now looked tired. My gaze slid down over the generous breasts and the narrow waist, noticing the shapely legs in nylon tights and elegant black leather pumps.

For the last five years, my attitude towards this woman had been oscillating between hatred and guilt.

"Hello, Elsbeth," I said.

37

Hella

"Can we talk?" Elsbeth glanced from me to Anita.

"Of course."

I ushered her into the living room, my heart flailing. There were heaps of clothes on the two chairs and the sofa. I carried them into the bedroom, dumped them on the bed. By the time I got back to the living room, Anita had already put her shoes on. "I'm going for a walk," she said. "Maybe get some milk or something."

"Thank you. This is … thank you." At this hour, the stores were already closed; Anita would have to sit on the stairs and wait. Still, I couldn't bear to talk to Elsbeth in her presence.

After she was gone, Steve's wife and I remained silent for several minutes. I didn't know what I wanted to say any more. Everything had been in that letter I'd sent her. There was nothing else to add.

"I didn't know you lived with a friend," Elsbeth said at last.

"I don't. Not really. Anita is staying while she's looking for her own apartment." With a little shock, I realized that wasn't true, that Anita wasn't even looking. Over the past few days, we had fallen into a curious routine, like an old married couple who spend their time arguing but can't imagine getting a divorce.

Elsbeth looked around. "Is this where my husband used to spend his evenings? You even started living here together, didn't you?"

"It's over now," I said, for what it was worth. "Steve and I are over."

"I don't want him either," Elsbeth stated bluntly, sitting down. "I've had enough." She held my gaze. Up close, she didn't look like the fragile little thing I had imagined. She looked steely. Tough. There was a question I needed to ask her, but I was so afraid of the answer, I probably wouldn't dare.

"How's your health?" I asked instead.

Elsbeth grinned. "Never better. Are you asking because Steve told you I was on the verge of succumbing to some mysterious illness? That I was incapable of surviving on my own?"

I felt a hot flush washing over my face. "Don't bother answering," Elsbeth said. "Steve actually told me the same thing about you. That he needed to support you, otherwise you'd just crumble and die. I suppose you're also well?"

I nodded, incapable of coherent speech. The idea I'd had of my relationship with Steve was unravelling with breathtaking speed. "I'm happy to hear that," Elsbeth said. "Because I didn't come here to complain."

"Why, then?"

"I found a job. At a high school, teaching biology. I'm due to start next Monday."

"And?"

"So this morning, I went back home to collect my clothes and other personal stuff. I've rented a nice apartment not far from here, and" – Elsbeth paused to rummage in her handbag – "don't ask me how, but I found this." She pulled an envelope out of her bag, holding it by one corner. "Please read it."

There was a typewritten letter inside the envelope. I shook it out on the table. No date on the letter and no signature; there was just one phrase, its meaning terrifyingly clear:

I KNOW WHAT YOU DID TO THOSE POOR DROWNED GIRLS. GET READY TO PAY FOR YOUR SINS.

38

Hella

The room started spinning around me, its edges blurred and darkening. Elsbeth must have realized I was about to faint, because next thing I knew, she was pushing my knees up and putting my head between my legs. "Deep breaths," she instructed me. "In through the nose, out through the mouth. It will pass." After a moment, when she saw the colour flowing back into my cheeks, she got up and left the room. Soon, I could hear the whistling of the kettle and the clanking of china in the kitchen.

"Are you trying to slim down?" Elsbeth asked when she came back into the living room. "Or is money tight?" She set down the tray holding two ill-assorted cups and a chipped teapot. "I didn't find any sugar."

"I'm trying to slim down." The tea was scalding hot but I sipped it anyway, hoping Elsbeth would attribute my burning cheeks to the drink.

"I can help you out," she said as if she hadn't heard. "Or give you an advance, if you accept the assignment."

"What are you talking about?"

"This." She pointed at the letter. "Find out who sent it.

Make them stop." I opened my mouth to object, but she laid a hand on my sleeve. "No matter what Steve did to me, he doesn't deserve this. And our daughter doesn't either. It's because of Eva that I'm here. I need to protect her interests." Elsbeth looked away. "I thought of going to the police first, and then I had a better idea. You. You can figure it out."

"Nice try," I said, when at last she stopped talking. "But even if I was ready to accept this assignment, which I'm not, what makes you think I'll keep quiet about Steve's eventual involvement? This" – I pointed to the letter – "is blackmail. But that doesn't mean it's necessarily…" I swallowed. "That it's necessarily misinformed."

Elsbeth sprung to her feet. "How can you imagine that there is a word of truth in that, in that —"

"I've seen the dead woman's notebook. You haven't. Now sit down and let's talk."

Elsbeth hadn't stayed together with Steve because she was frail and needed looking after, I knew that already. More worrying was the realization that she had stayed in her marriage because she loved him, and because she knew *he* wouldn't survive on his own.

"He's the one who needs looking after," she said to me, unshaken in her belief in Steve's innocence even after seeing the handwritten copy I had made of the madam's black book. "But then, he's a man, so I guess it's not really surprising."

I was dumbstruck by her reaction. I'd said what I had to provoke her, because I wanted to see how far she would go to defend the man who had cheated on her for ten years. She didn't hesitate for one second. Did that make her a saint, or a fool? I couldn't tell.

"Let's get down to basics," Elsbeth said. "Is there a set fee for your services or do you charge by the hour?"

"I will not take any money from you. And, just so we're clear, I haven't agreed to take the case." I collected the tray and carried it over to the kitchen. I waited until I was safely hidden by the door before I dared to ask the question.

"Was your daughter in a school play a few days ago?"

I held my breath.

"She was due to play Ophelia. *God hath given you one face, and you make yourself another.*" Elsbeth laughed. "That applies to all women, doesn't it? Always feeling like we have to pretend to be something different than what we really are. Men too, probably, though I wouldn't know. Anyway. The play was cancelled a couple of hours before the performance. Hamlet slipped on ice and broke his leg."

I reflected on this. So Steve hadn't argued with me that evening just because he wanted to spend his time with a prostitute. He really had been intending to go and see that play. "All right," I said. "I'm not accepting yet, but I promise I'll think about it."

"You know what?" Elsbeth stood up as I made my way back into the living room. "I hated you too, because I knew about you almost from the start. And I knew he was serious about you."

"He was *not.*" I bit the inside of my cheek until I could taste blood.

Elsbeth smiled sadly. "Believe me, he was. And because of that, I hated you. But now I'm mad with Steve, because I feel that, had we met under different circumstances, you and I might have become friends. We're not that different."

39

Chief Inspector Mustonen

Bonaparte once said: never interrupt your enemy while they're making a mistake. As I sat well hidden in a booth in the far corner of Kappeli, I wondered if that applied to colleagues as well.

The restaurant was known for its stuffy waiters, its old-world cuisine and its steep prices. It was also conveniently located just around the corner from Headquarters, and the current police chief, Dr Palmu, was a regular. He was now sitting alone in his usual spot by the window, waiting for his order of blinis with sour cream and caviar.

I took a sip of my mineral water. Several tables away from Dr Palmu, out of earshot but in plain sight, sat Virtanen and Jokela, their heads bent close together in animated conversation. I wondered what those two were talking about. Me? No, they were smiling too much. More likely than not, they were discussing the guest list for the reception Jokela was planning to organize once his nomination to the position currently occupied by Dr Palmu was made official. According to the grapevine, it was a matter of days now. I'd had to learn that from Tarja, not from Jokela himself. Jokela wasn't talking to me; not since he had discovered that Ahti Virtanen was officially still a suspect and that I had gone to formally interview him with Anita in tow.

"Why don't you focus on that DJ?" Jokela asked, his tiny eyes trailing me as I paced his office. "Or, I don't know, other clients?"

"The other clients all have alibis," I countered.

"Well, so does Ahti."

"Provided by his parents."

"What's wrong with the parents?" Jokela roared. "You're a parent too. You know your child. If Virtanen says he didn't do it, then he didn't do it. Does the DJ have an alibi as well?"

"No. The night Klara Nylund was murdered, the programme schedule at Yle Radio had been altered to allow for extended coverage of the upcoming parliamentary elections. Which means Mr Collins was free to roam the streets alone at the time the murder was committed."

"You see?" Jokela said. "Did you bring him in for questioning?"

"Tomorrow."

"A confession would be best." Jokela's eyes narrowed. "You can interview him in a cell, use a sock stuffed with snow like they do in the Soviet Union. No traces, all nice and clean. People speak, believe me."

"Beat up the suspect with a stuffed sock? I wouldn't dream of doing that."

"Do whatever it takes. I just hope you are not hesitant to go after the man because he's Mauzer's boyfriend?"

"He's not her boyfriend any more. And it's not that. I want to be sure we explore all the options before focusing on just one suspect."

"Ahti is not an option," Jokela said.

"Even if he's guilty?"

The whisky glass flew past inches from my head, shattering against the wall behind me. When Jokela spoke, his voice was seething with rage. "The boy's *not* guilty. The fact that he was fooling around in the port doesn't mean a thing. Coincidences happen, we all know that." Jokela pulled a handkerchief out of his jacket pocket, wiped his hand. "I want you to focus on the radio guy. Make an arrest and make it quick."

He hadn't talked to me since. He had even pretended not to notice me when, ten minutes earlier, I had followed a waiter to my table. The only one to acknowledge my presence was Dr Palmu, who smiled and shook my hand.

"Are you also having lunch with business associates, Chief Inspector?"

"No, sir," I said, smiling back. "I'm having lunch with my wife."

And now Sofia was being ushered in by a waiter. She looked stunningly elegant, the angles of her long body softened by her pregnancy, her head carried high. Contrary to me, Sofia was at home in this sort of place. She knew how to speak to the waiters, she was dressed just so, she made all the other women, even the beautiful ones, look tacky.

"Hello, darling." I kissed her on the cheek.

The waiter pulled out the chair and my wife sat down. "I'll have mineral water too," she said.

"No." I took my wife's hand. "We'll drink champagne. Darling, I have good news for you. I made an offer on the house and it's been accepted."

I was back in the office two hours later. Jokela's door was closed, and judging by the low rhythmic snoring coming from that direction, my boss was inside. It was a wonder he had even managed to find his way back, given the quantity of alcohol he had polished off; I had been watching him out of the corner of my eye while Sofia talked with breathless excitement about the new life that awaited us.

I felt dizzy myself, but it wasn't because of the champagne. The enormity of what I had committed myself to had started to sink in, and my brain was a jumble of numbers. What if I had misjudged the situation? Would I even be able to pay? I had asked Sofia to keep it a secret, to tell no one about our plans, but I knew she wouldn't be able to resist sharing the news with her father, cousins and closest friends. In a matter of hours, all of Helsinki would know.

"Chief Inspector?" Little Anita was standing in the doorway, clutching a paper file. "I've collected the information you requested this morning."

I threw my jacket over the back of my chair, beckoned for her to sit down. "What have we got on him?"

"Mr Steve Collins," Anita said, and her voice wobbled, "was born on 11 August 1918 in Helsinki."

"Hey," I said gently. "Anita. You're not betraying your friend. You're just compiling background information on a suspect. Have you ever met him?"

She nodded, her eyes bright. "Once, briefly. He came over to Hella's place to fetch something."

"And what did you think of him?"

A helpless shrug.

"Anita," I said, "we need to find out all we can about Mr Steve Collins. If he's not the one who is killing those innocent young women, the earlier we cross his name off the suspect list, the better. And if he turns out to be the killer, our job is to stop him. Put him behind bars. I'm sure even Miss Mauzer would agree with that. Wouldn't she?"

Anita mumbled something I couldn't hear. She was still clutching the paper file.

"Say that again?"

"Hella says she doesn't believe he – Steve – could be involved. She … she was furious when I suggested it."

"No kidding? And you're still living with her? Shouldn't you start looking for a different place?"

Anita nodded and let go of the file.

I was careful not to seize on it too quickly. "Did you find anything?" I asked, as I leafed through the pages. "Something that could make us think he's our guy? Something that… Oh, I see." So she had found it. I'd been right about the girl: she had beauty *and* brains. A good addition to any team. Maybe too good. My men were already having trouble concentrating on their work as it was. "Well, thank you, Anita. Good job. How did you find out?"

"I talked to his colleagues at the radio station. The receptionist told me about a woman Mr Collins knew some years back. She drowned."

"Right. This changes everything, doesn't it? What was the woman's name?"

"Matilda Reims."

"Reims, you said?" I stood up quickly. "Go to the archives, see if —"

"I already did." Anita smiled nervously. "I called Ranta. He's coming up with the file. Does the fact that…" She hesitated. "Is it really significant? I mean, from what Ranta told me over the phone, another man was the prime suspect."

"I don't know. I didn't investigate that case. I only heard about it in passing. But the fact that Mr Steve Collins was involved with another mysteriously drowned woman… It's too much of a coincidence to be ignored."

"We need to question him," Anita said, reluctantly, perhaps feeling that that was what I expected to hear. She kept glancing at the Nellie Ritvanen file that was sitting on my desk; she wanted to consult it, had asked for it twice already, but each time I had denied her access.

"Exactly," I said. "Good thinking." I smiled at Anita, but she was biting her lower lip and didn't smile back.

40

Chief Inspector Mustonen

When I got home that evening, after a short stop at the jewellers to discuss the design of the brooch I had ordered for Sofia, my wife and child were both screaming. At first I thought Arne had fallen and hurt himself, so I rushed towards my son and grabbed him, checking his body for injuries. Immediately, he stopped sobbing and stared at me.

"What are you doing?" Sofia asked in an icy voice. She, too, had stopped screaming; she was standing in the middle of the living room, arms folded across her chest, eyes narrowed.

I set Arne on the floor. "What? What happened?"

Sofia unfolded her arms and stabbed at the air. "This happened!" There was a tremor in her voice now. I looked in the direction she was pointing. *This* turned out to be the hideous art nouveau floor lamp, Sofia's family heirloom, the glass globe that crowned it neatly broken down the middle.

"Arne..." I kneeled next to my son. "Did you do this?" He screwed his eyes shut, shook his head no. "Who was it, then? Was it Sara?"

Sofia snorted. "Right, blame the cleaner now!"

"Arne?" I prodded gently. Two big tears rolled from under my son's closed lids. I pulled a handkerchief out of my pocket. "Arne, a good man can sometimes do wrong, but he always admits to his mistakes and asks for forgiveness. Tell me who did this, and I promise I won't punish you."

"*I* will punish him," Sofia said. "Your dear son was playing with a ball. I've *warned* him."

"I'll buy you another lamp, Sofia," I sighed. "I'll try to find one just like it. It's important that Arne learns to tell the truth. When a child is penalized for his honesty, he begins to lie."

"Out of curiosity," Sofia scowled, "is that how you were brought up? No punishment, whatever you did?"

"No," I said. "But that's the whole point. My father was straight out of the Old Testament: lots of rules and no mercy. I don't want to turn into him."

"Still," Sofia said in a clipped voice. "Your father brought you up to be a good man. A good man who's too soft on his precious son, and who'll turn him into a misfit. And that lamp was *one of a kind.*" She turned on her heel and left the room, slamming the door shut behind her.

Arne stifled a sob. He was trying to say something, but I couldn't understand him.

"What is it, buddy?"

Arne threw his hands around my neck and buried his snotty face in my shirt.

"Are you asking me if I always told the truth when I was a little boy?"

Arne nodded.

"I always tried." Now that Sofia was gone, Arne's sobs were quieting down. "Now you tell me."

"It was me," Arne said and sniffed. "I didn't mean to."

"I know you didn't." I picked him up and carried him over to the bathroom. "I'll wash your face and then we'll go and see Mummy, and you'll tell her you're sorry."

41

Chief Inspector Mustonen

On my way to the office the following morning, I stopped by the antique store on Aleksanterinkatu. There were no lamps on display that looked similar, or even vaguely art nouveau, so I pulled the broken piece of glass out of my pocket and showed it to the owner. "Could you find me something like this? My wife loved that lamp."

The antique dealer peered at me from above his glasses. "Not sure I can promise you anything. And if I do find something, it won't come cheap." He cradled the shattered remains of the globe in his palm.

I nodded, resolutely pushing away the unwelcome thought of another fancy object that Sofia wanted and I couldn't afford. "Of course. Please get in touch with me." I left my card with the dealer then hurried to the office, squinting in the bright sunshine that was suddenly flooding the city.

The pile of documents on my desk had grown by an inch or so in my absence. The Matilda Reims murder file was on top. I started working through it, on the lookout as much for the hard facts as for the things that hadn't found their way into the paperwork but kept simmering under the surface: the inconsistencies between witness statements, the hidden motives. It was a pity I couldn't talk to the investigating officer any more: Inspector Krigsholm had died of cancer in 1946, in the months following the investigation's closure. All I had to go on were Krigsholm's notes, and these were few and taken in a shorthand that at times I had trouble deciphering.

The case seemed straightforward enough. A young, pretty banker's wife, a string of lovers. Steve Collins had been one of them. There were just two mentions of him in the file: the first one to say that he was in Helsinki at the time of the drowning, the second to mention that he didn't have a motive. It didn't mean anything either way. Where was the motive in the prostitute's murder? I supposed any half-decent detective would think first and foremost of her pregnancy, but wouldn't a married woman be able to pretend she was carrying her husband's child? I leaned back, making my chair squeak. Could Steve Collins really qualify as a suspect? Could a jury find him guilty? I didn't really know the man, not personally in any case, but from what I'd heard, Collins lacked the drive, intensity and passion to make a successful murderer. I could quite well imagine the DJ killing someone in self-defence; a premeditated, cold-blooded murder, let alone several, was a different matter.

In the end, the consensus of those working on the case was that the husband had done it. Mr Reims was questioned, repeatedly, but he never cracked under pressure, never confessed to anything. It was thus no surprise that the prosecutor refused to press charges. The handwritten note, scribbled across the case file, was clear enough: *more evidence needed.* There must not have been any, because after a couple of months the case had been archived and forgotten. I wondered what would happen if the police reopened it. Would any new witnesses come forward, perhaps someone who had been suffering from a guilty conscience all these years? On balance, I thought that unlikely. The police would be stuck where they had left off, chasing after shadows, never able to prove anything, even less able to prosecute. Unless they attacked it from a different angle. Questioned the husband again, found out what he had to say about Mr Collins' involvement in his wife's death. Would he become more cooperative now that he was not at the centre of the investigation?

There was a knock on my door and Tarja's anxious face peered at me. "Mr Steve Collins is here to see you, Chief Inspector. Shall I bring him in?"

The man that Tarja had ushered into my office was handsome in a loose-limbed, feline kind of way. Nothing American about him except maybe his accent, which had a mid-Atlantic twang to it; I wondered how much of it was fake. After all, as Anita had discovered, the guy had been born in Helsinki.

"Why don't you take a seat, Mr Collins."

The man sat down casually, his eyes scanning the room. He refused my offer of coffee. "Don't the police always come in pairs?" he asked.

I smiled back at him. "Frequently we do. If it makes you more comfortable, I'll ask one of our trainee officers to join us." I picked up my phone, called Anita and waited. I watched the suspect closely as Anita came in and there was no mistaking the look on the man's face: she was his type of woman. She was also the polar opposite of Mauzer, so I wondered how Mr Steve Collins had managed to stick with my former colleague for so long. Might he have been interested in the sort of immunity a relationship with a police officer could provide? Was this something that could be exploited?

"Thank you for coming to see us at such short notice," I said as Anita sat down.

"My pleasure." Steve Collins looked relaxed, but I knew he couldn't possibly be. "Would you mind telling me the reason for this sudden interest?"

"This." I pointed to the madam's little black book. "It mentions you as one of the clients. We're investigating the alibis of everyone involved."

Collins extended a hand towards it. "Can I take a look? I have a hard time believing my name could be mentioned in here."

"No, you can't. Why don't you answer one simple question, Mr Collins. Were you a client?"

"I wasn't. But even if I had been, it wouldn't make me a murderer."

Next to me, Anita was scribbling away on a legal pad, the tip of her pink tongue protruding slightly out of her mouth.

I tried another angle. "Your house is up for sale, Mr Collins. Are you thinking of running away?"

The man laughed, but I thought I spotted a shadow crossing his face. "My wife left me. I don't need a big place like that any more."

"Did she leave you before or after Nellie Ritvanen was murdered? Because the police received an anonymous letter urging us to take a close look at your whereabouts on the night of the murder."

Steve Collins looked aghast, and for a moment I thought I'd scored a point. But then Collins shrugged. "I'll only be able to answer that question if you tell me when exactly the poor girl was murdered."

"February the seventeenth. We looked at the programme schedule, and you weren't on the radio that night. Were you with your wife?"

"I doubt it. The seventeenth is Hella Mauzer's birthday. I was with her." Collins rose from his seat, smiling slightly. "Why don't you ask her for confirmation?"

"So tell me, Anita, is Mr Collins a liar? I've heard women have the intuition for such things. Or is he too handsome to kill anyone, except by breaking their heart?"

"I don't know," Anita mumbled.

"I think you do – you're only afraid to speak your mind. So let's do it another way. Did Hella Mauzer think he could be a murderer? She saw that little black book. She must have spotted the reference to him."

"She did. But as the man who attacked me outside the brothel couldn't possibly be Steve Collins, she thinks he was just a client, that's all."

"Well," I said. "Maybe the man who attacked you will prove to be irrelevant to our investigation. Probably some drunk who spotted a pretty girl and thought he'd give it a try. If he was a mass murderer, you wouldn't have got away so easily."

"Maybe." Anita was looking at the drawing on my desk to avoid making eye contact with me.

"Not maybe," I countered. "Certainly. And your friend Hella Mauzer knows it very well. Do you realize that she's possibly shielding a murderer? Just because he was her special friend?" I leaned forward. "I really appreciate Hella, you know. She's brave and opinionated, and even though she sometimes acts in a reckless manner, she always means well. But this time she's gone too far, don't you think?"

Anita nodded, looking miserable. I thought I had her on board when she asked, "Did we receive an anonymous tip about Mr Collins?"

"No. That was my invention. Any other questions?" I could see that Anita was burning to ask me something.

"You didn't question Mr Collins about the Matilda Reims murder. Why?"

I drummed on the table with my fingers. "Because I wasn't ready yet, and I want to be a hundred per cent certain of my information before I move in to interview a potential murderer. So far, I've only read the case file. I haven't even talked to the victim's husband."

Anita wriggled on her chair. "But didn't you…" she started in a small voice, then looked away.

"Go on."

"No," she said quickly. Too quickly. "It's OK. It was just a stupid comment."

"There are no stupid comments in a murder investigation. Every little idea, every little uncertainty matters. If we are to work as a team on this one, I don't want us to have secrets from one another. Tell me what's bothering you."

Two bright spots were now blooming on Anita's cheeks. "Inspector Krigsholm," she said. "The one who investigated Mrs Reims' murder. He was your partner. In 1945 and 1946, you worked all your cases with him. So how could you not know about the Matilda Reims case?" She bit her lip. Probably expecting a nasty comment from me, or a dismissal, or both.

I smiled instead. "Glad you asked. This is something I believe we should address during the next morning briefing, so there are no questions about my motives." I picked up my phone. "Tarja, could you please come over here?"

We waited in uncomfortable silence. Anita was wringing her hands, not daring to look at me, looking anyway.

"Tarja," I said when the door opened at last. "Would you care to tell Anita where I spent the summer of 1946?"

42

Hella

St John's Church in Ullanlinna is a fine example of Gothic Revival. It stands on a hill that for many centuries was a place for Midsummer bonfires, and this is where its name, that of the feast day, comes from. I took a seat on one of the benches at the back, my eyes on the girls huddled together in front of the altarpiece that showed Saul's conversion. The girls were wearing lace and mink, their faces heavily made up. I wondered which one was the new madam.

I didn't try to talk to the girls – the wary glances they shot me were enough to convey their state of mind. Instead, I concentrated on the pastor's words. In a tuneless voice, he spoke of redemption and forgiveness, of life choices and the mistakes we all made. I wondered if he'd known the victim, or if there was a set speech for those who, like Klara Nylund, had chosen a different path.

There was no body – it was still in Tom's morgue. So once the final prayers were over and the girls had left, their arms locked together, I stood outside, trying to convince myself that I'd made the right choice. That morning, I had written two letters and received another, from Irja, informing me that Maria had arrived in Käärmelä and that she was settling in well. I had written back to her, saying that I was coming. Somehow it had felt necessary, even if in all likelihood I'd arrive before my letter did. The other letter had been for Elsbeth. I had informed her that after having thought it over, I had decided to decline her offer. Steve was a big boy, I had written, he could take care of himself. I had posted the letters, then, on my way to the church, I had stopped at a children's goods store and exchanged my last coffee coupon for a knitted bunny for baby Margarita. Its long ears were now sticking out of my bag.

The train for Ivalo was leaving in less than an hour from Central Station. I picked up my cardboard suitcase and started to cross the street.

"Hey, pariah? You want a hand?"

I almost dropped the suitcase. Ranta? "What are you doing here? Don't tell me you were at the vigil?"

"Didn't you see me?"

"No."

Ranta seemed satisfied. "That's because I took care not to be noticed. Apparently I was scaring the girls, so I'm not welcome any more."

"You were a client too?"

"Every other man in Helsinki was," he grinned. "Thought I'd go and pay my respects."

"That's very noble of you."

"Another reason was that I thought I'd find you here," he continued, unperturbed. "Anita told me this morning that you were going back to Lapland. Are you visiting that happy-clappy Christian friend of yours?"

"Her name is Irja. And actually, I'd better hurry if I don't want to miss my train."

But Ranta was still blocking my way. "Your Steve is a suspect now. Mustonen is interviewing him as we speak. Don't you want to do something about it?"

"No. He's not my problem any more."

"They've dug up an old case. Matilda Reims. Ever heard that name?"

"No," I managed to say. "Look, I really need to be going." I turned away and almost broke into a run.

He shouted after me – "Just think about it, pariah!" – but I didn't look back. It was only after I'd run through Central Station's doors that I realized I hadn't asked him why he was so interested in Steve's well-being.

Steve and I had met through music. People nodded when I said that – they imagined a concert, or a chorus, or even piano lessons, but it hadn't been anything like that. I had been making a fool of myself on the radio and Steve was called to the rescue, cutting me off mid-sentence, replacing my voice with Johnny Mercer's "Zip-A-Dee-Doo-Dah".

In the silence that fell on the studio after the microphones were cut off, my boss ran a trembling hand across his sweaty brow, throwing an apologetic glance at the radio host who had been interviewing me. "Are you out of your mind, Miss Mauzer?" he asked. "You were here to discuss the work we do to help homeless children. Do you really think anyone could be interested in knowing what a *polissyster* like you thinks about criminal investigations? The public will think we are a bunch of … amateurs!"

"Sorry, sir," I replied, keeping my voice level. "I assumed I was here to talk about my work."

My boss dabbed his forehead with a handkerchief. "You are impossible, Miss Mauzer! Your work consists of dealings with juvenile delinquents and female criminals when male officers cannot intervene for reasons of decency. Whoever put it into your head that women were equal to *men*?" He glanced at the radio host for support. "Was this programme about equality?"

"Not that I know of," the man said, an eye on his watch. "Pity it had to end like this." He hurried out of the studio, and my boss and I followed suit.

We were coming down the stairs when I heard my name. I looked up. A tall blonde man, his wavy hair cut short, was smiling at me. "Thumbs up, Miss Mauzer," he said and winked at me. "You made my day!" He ran down the steps and held out a hand. "I'm Steve Collins. They only let me do rock 'n' roll here, but I hope that one day I'll be big enough to interview someone like you." His hand was warm and soft to the touch, and he held mine a second too long. I felt myself blush, painfully conscious of my ill-fitting uniform and my nails bitten to the quick.

"It would be a pleasure, Mr Collins," I said.

He laughed as if I'd said something funny and hurried up the stairs again. Thirty seconds later, I heard his voice coming out of the speakers fitted on the ground floor. I scurried after my boss, trying to convince myself that the way I looked didn't matter because I would never see the blonde man again. Only I did. I ran into him at the corner store exactly seventeen days later, dropped the cabbage I was buying, and blushed even worse than the first time. My heart was lost, and I didn't even have the time to run a background check on him. And now I was paying the price.

I did ask Steve about the other women in his life, of course I did. Not immediately, because in those early days of our relationship, I chose to believe that his marriage had been a terrible mistake, and that he had spent his entire life waiting for me. That he would divorce, and we would get married and live happily ever after. That's how conceited I was. In my defence, he was the first man I had loved and who, I believed, loved me back. I couldn't bear to think I was just one of many, even as rumours of all the girls Steve had dated before started to creep up on me. When I finally asked him, summoning up all my courage, he snorted: "That was in the past." I must have gone white, because he added hastily: "It meant nothing."

Too late. I didn't believe him. The soul-destroying thought that I, perhaps, meant nothing too, would not subside. I started questioning Steve's every word, spending sleepless nights picking apart our conversations, even the most casual ones, searching for secret meanings. The spontaneity seeped out of our relationship, gradually at first, and then all of a sudden, like water draining. My departure for Lapland had been a deliverance for him, I knew. Ever since we'd got back together, I'd been walking a tightrope of trust and self-esteem, careful not to look either way, to focus only on the next step, on the now. Until that rope had been snatched from under my feet, leaving me in free fall. Matilda Reims. A name I had heard before but had done my best to forget.

The train pulled into the station. I was one of the first to climb in. As I crossed the departure hall, I made a point of not looking at the newsboys, for fear of seeing Steve's photograph on the front page. And now I was too far away to decipher the blurry headlines.

The old lady settling into my compartment smiled kindly at me, pointing at the bunny ears sticking out of my purse. "Is that for your baby?"

"For my god-daughter," I explained. "No children of my own."

The old lady nodded sympathetically. "It takes a while to find the right man. But it will come, my dear, don't you worry about that."

"I don't think it's going to happen. Not any more."

"And so you're leaving?" The woman tut-tutted. "Running away?"

I wondered if she had guessed right. Was I running away? Did I really believe Steve could be guilty of murder?

The answer to this was no. I felt it in my bones, in the darkest recesses of my brain. Steve was guilty of a lot of things, but not that. But if I believed in his innocence, how come I was turning my back when he needed me the most, while the wife he had cheated on during their entire married life was standing by him? Because I couldn't stand the sordid, the shameful, because I thought that would *teach* him?

The train whistle cut through the noise, freezing people in mid-motion. "Why don't you sit down?" my travel companion said. She was already pulling out her knitting needles and a ball of light-blue wool. "Would you like me to show you how to knit? You can make a friend for your little bunny."

I didn't answer. The sound of the needles gently clicking away brought it all back. The tiny room I had occupied during my police training, crammed with my parents' belongings. The sweater I had knitted and offered to myself at Christmas, tearing through the gift wrap as if I didn't know what was inside. The loneliness, the mourning, the questions. And then: Steve. I had been a fighter then. I hadn't given up. Had the three years I spent in Ivalo really changed me that much?

I thought of the snow globe I had left in the office, of the wire-thin translucent girl inside it, standing knee-deep in the synthetic snow. I thought about Eva. If the worst came to the worst, not only would she grow up without a father, she'd be tainted by shame. I thought about my own father, and what he had meant to me. I didn't owe anything to Steve, or to Elsbeth, but maybe I owed something to Eva.

The train shook itself into motion. I had only a second left to make a decision.

Click-click-click, went the knitting needles.

"Oh dear," sighed the old lady. "It's so hard to do the right thing."

43

Inspector Mustonen

July 1946

It was Tarja who brought me the letter.

"I opened it by accident," she said, and blushed. "I'm so very sorry."

"It's all right." I was alone in the squad room; I liked to be the first to come in, the last to leave. I glanced at the letter: the handwriting on the envelope was unfamiliar, the envelope itself looked cheap. I dropped it into the incoming mail tray, turned to Tarja. "Did Inspector Krigsholm say what time he'd be coming in?"

Tarja started fussing with her shawl. "Maybe you'd better read that letter now, Inspector. I didn't read it myself, of course, but I couldn't help seeing the first sentence, and —"

I picked up the envelope, pulled out the letter. One page, poorly formed characters leaning to the left, an ink stain in the corner. "Oh, I see."

The letter was about my father. The person writing to me, a certain Mrs Saari, hadn't made any attempt to soften the blow. *Your father has had a stroke*, the letter said. *He is conscious but he can't move, and he can't speak. You need to come at once.*

"Looks like you'll have to do without me," I said.

The secretary started crying, as if on cue. "Oh, Inspector, this is so awful. Of course you need to go and stay with your poor father." She must have realized, from the fact that the letter had been written by a stranger, that my mother was already gone, so she asked about brothers and sisters.

"Five sisters," I said, already thinking of the time it would take me to pack my things and get to Central Station. "I'm the youngest."

"The apple of your father's eye," Tarja sobbed. She was prone to hackneyed imagery.

When I finally managed to get hold of Jokela between two meetings, he was harder to convince, but even he gave in eventually. That evening, I boarded a night train for Tampere.

44

Hella

The sun-melted snow was dripping from the rooftops when I got back to my place. When the water froze again the following night, the Surgical Hospital would have a field day with all the broken limbs. I made a mental note to tread carefully, both literally and metaphorically. A sensible, grown-up resolution that lasted as long as it took me to climb the four flights to my apartment. Then my heart gave a loud bang against my ribcage, and the suitcase tumbled down the staircase.

"Steve," I said, when my voice was back under control. "You're here?"

He ran down the steps to grab my case. "I didn't know you'd been out of the city."

"I haven't. I was planning to go away, but then I changed my mind. Anyway, it's a long story. Boring, too. How did it go with Mustonen?"

"I'm innocent," Steve said in a mumble, taking my hand but then letting it go immediately. "Jesus, the way you look at me..."

"Any proof? Of you being innocent?"

We entered the apartment, Steve still staring at my suitcase, me trying to push the bunny's knitted ears deeper into my bag. The apartment smelled like Anita now, almond oil, powder and honey. Her clothes brush lay forgotten on a sideboard.

"Is she still living here?" Steve asked, looking around. "Your friend, Anita. She was there during the interview this morning."

"You didn't answer my question." I wondered if I should offer him coffee but decided against it. I was back to help him, but that didn't come with an obligation to be nice.

"No proof," Steve said, taking a deep breath. "Hella. We've known each other for how long?"

The answer – 1,844 days – was always at the back of my mind, like a thread enmeshed in everything I did, but I was damned if I was going to admit it. The new post-break-up me was cool, cynical and independent. Much like the pre-break-up me used to act, only this time it was for real.

"I don't know," I said. "Four years? Five?"

"Five years. Probably a bit longer now, even." Steve fumbled in his pocket for his cigarette case and lighter. "Remember how we —"

"Steve. Enough already. State your case or bugger off."

He smiled weakly. "That's the spirit. It must be what I'm lacking to break through. Do you know that the Soviets reported this morning that Stalin had a stroke? But I'm not covering that, oh no, I'm not good enough." He drew on his cigarette. "Maybe if I could get straight to the point, like you do, they'd let me do serious stuff and I wouldn't need to bury my head under some girl's skirt to forget about my inadequacies. No. Sorry. OK, then," he added when I didn't answer. "I need your help. I'm the damsel in distress that courageous Hella Mauzer in her shiny armour must save before the dragon eats her."

"Mustonen doesn't look like a dragon to me. More like some mythological snake, a youthful Jörmundganr, maybe. And, just out of curiosity, how exactly am I supposed to save you?"

"You're the only one who can confirm my story. I told Mustonen I was with you on 17 February. And I know, I know" – Steve's voice took on an unpleasant pleading tone – "that given the circumstances, helping me out is the last thing you want, but here we are."

"The day Nellie Ritvanen went missing. Did you tell Mustonen the reason I would remember 17 February?"

"Because it's your birthday," Steve said. "We spent it together, remember? Dinner at that little French restaurant on Albertinkatu, and I offered you a book. *Introduction to Criminalistics*, by Charles O'Hara and … and James Osterburg." He glanced around the room. "You still have it, don't you?"

"On my bedside table. I imagine Anita reads it every night."

"You see?" Steve forced a smile. "Can you tell that to Mustonen?"

"What else? While you're at it."

Steve flinched as if I'd hit him. "Nothing. I know you don't believe me, and God knows you have your reasons for that, but I've never set foot in that brothel."

"But?"

"But the police say they've got an anonymous tip telling them to investigate my whereabouts. And I suppose it's only a matter of time before they dig out the Matilda Reims case."

"Oh yes," I said. "There was her, too."

Steve started rubbing his face with both hands. "Yes. And before you say it, I know how it looks."

I asked the police receptionist to call Mustonen, tell him I had come to give my witness statement. They ushered me in immediately: the Harbour Murders, as the tabloids were calling them, were gaining traction. Tarja pursed her lips as I crossed the squad room in the direction of Mustonen's office; Anita didn't look up from her reading.

"Hella," Mustonen said, enveloping my hand in both of his. "Glad you came. Care for some coffee?"

"Yes please." There was a drawing on Mustonen's desk, propped against the photograph of his wife and son. Something complicated, a jumble of tiny hearts, with a ruby dot in the centre like a drop of blood. Mustonen noticed me looking. "It's the design of a brooch I ordered for my wife, as a gift."

"Beautiful." I accepted the coffee cup from Tarja. "I won't take up too much of your time. As Steve Collins already told you, we celebrated my birthday together. I came to give you the details."

"Really?" Mustonen asked, arching an eyebrow.

I looked him in the eye, careful not to blink. "Yes."

He folded his arms across his chest. "Tell me about your evening." A nod to Tarja. "Start writing."

I told Mustonen everything I could remember. The maître d' and his measured smile. What we had eaten – duck à l'orange and chocolate fondue – and what we had drunk – the Martinis, and too many of them. The clumsily wrapped package that Steve had placed in my lap. The expression on the faces of the nice middle-aged couple at the neighbouring table when they had seen what the book was about. And – the hardest part – how we had come home, drunk and happy, and made love.

As I talked, Mustonen kept checking against his notes. "You know that Mr Steve Collins was a regular client of Klara Nylund's?"

"That's what I heard, yes."

"All right," Mustonen said at last. "Could you please wait in the reception area while Tarja types your witness statement? Then you can sign it and go home."

I did as I was told. Half an hour later – even though it felt much longer than that – I was out on the street again, my heart jammed in my throat. There was no going back now. I had made a decision that could possibly cost me my career and land me in jail. Worse than that: this witness statement turned my entire world upside down. It redefined me. I was no longer an uncompromising investigator, but a woman led by emotion.

Hella Mauzer, born 16 February 1924. A liar by omission. A perjurer. All for the sake of one resentful teenage girl. The old me would certainly have refused to shake the new me's hand.

45

Chief Inspector Mustonen

"How did it go?"

Jokela was looming in the doorway, his moustache spiked and twitching. He had obviously been waiting for Mauzer to leave so he could pounce.

"Collins has an alibi," I said. "Maybe we can break it; I'll have a look into it. Also, he's probably too tall."

"Too tall for what?"

"According to Räikkönen, our guy is a bit shorter than Collins."

"Don't see how he can tell," Jokela said. "That's pure guesswork, if you want my opinion."

I didn't, but now was not a good time to say that. Instead, I said: "The news is going around that Dr Palmu will be retiring at the end of the month, and that your appointment to his position is on the Justice Minister's desk. How come I had to hear about it from Tarja?"

Jokela pushed into my office, closed the door behind him. He looked younger, happier than I had ever seen him. Once promoted, he would hold on to his job forever. Forget early retirement: he'd be around for almost as long as I would, blocking the way.

"Well," Jokela said, "you've only got yourself to blame, haven't you? I warned you." A shrug. "Maybe you *are* too young. Or maybe you're not made for the pressures of this job. You should think about joining the traffic police – you've got good enough ideas for that."

"So you won't be recommending me for your current position?" That much was obvious, of course, but I still wanted to hear him say it.

"No, I won't."

No more *my boy* here. No more drinking sessions either. I'd finally got what I had wished for, but it tasted bitter.

The day was only half-gone, but I couldn't stay in the office after that. I needed air, and space. So I stuffed the drawing of the brooch into my jacket pocket and made my way downstairs. I was passing through the revolving doors when a man called out to me.

"Inspector?"

"Yes?" I couldn't place him, maybe because my mind was on other things. Medium height, big inexpressive eyes, lank blonde hair clinging to a large knobby forehead.

"Ljungkvist," the man said, extending a hand for me to shake. "Port Authority. I was coming to see you."

I steered him outside, offered him a cigarette. "Why? Has something come up?"

"No," Ljungkvist answered, squinting in the sun. "But the weather is better now. We can trawl the harbour."

"Today?"

The man glanced at his watch. "We can start today, yes, if the police divers are ready. But tomorrow should be good too, according to the weather people on the radio."

"Then let's make it tomorrow. I'd like to be there, and I have things to do right now."

Ljungkvist smiled. "Sure. With sun like this, everyone should enjoy a bit of the outdoors. Make it ten?"

"I'll be there."

The sun was sliding below the line of the horizon when I returned to Headquarters. I didn't know how long the girl had been sitting there, waiting for me. Certainly long enough to make her stoop a bit, wipe away the sparkle in her eyes.

"Anita. What's happened?"

Anita exhaled, straightened herself. Put a smile on, sucked her belly in. A little-girl voice: "I wanted to apologize. For asking that question about the Reims case and Inspector Krigsholm."

The squad room was empty, dark. Even Jokela was gone; to celebrate or to lick boots, I didn't know and didn't care. I unlocked the door of my office, switched on the lamp, then ushered Anita in, leaving the door open.

"I'm not angry."

"Then you're a saint. I shouldn't have doubted you. It's just when I saw that Krigsholm had been your partner, I couldn't help wondering if you'd known about the Reims case even before I brought it up."

"You asked a perfectly reasonable question. I would have done the same."

"Really?"

"Yes. Really." I waited a beat, enjoying the smile that lit up her face. When I knew she was able to focus again, I added: "Actually, I'm glad you came. It could have waited until tomorrow, but now that you're here…" I fumbled in my desk drawer without taking my eyes off Anita. "Here it is." Expensive, creamy paper, an envelope with many stamps. "As you know, I'm in charge of our cooperation with Interpol.

They're setting up an exchange programme for sharing work methods, implementing common standards. We need to give them the name of our candidate." I smiled, pushing the envelope towards Anita. "I thought it could be you."

A sharp intake of air, a manicured hand flying to her mouth. "Me?"

"It involves a training period in Paris, starting next week," I said, the unspoken words – the Eiffel Tower, Louvre, Montmartre – charging the air around us with electricity. "What do you think?"

46

Hella

"I refused."

I glanced up at Anita; it was not a joke. There she was, standing in the middle of my living room, back straight, eyes blazing. She had come in as I was unpacking my cardboard suitcase and started telling me her story as soon as she crossed the doorstep. But seriously? Paris, the capital of fashion, the most romantic city on Earth, the place that everyone – *everyone* – longed to see at least once in their lives. A girl would be stupid to decline an offer to live there, even for a short while. And Anita was anything but stupid.

"Why?"

"I haven't finished my investigation. I told that to Mustonen too. That I wasn't planning to go away until I uncovered the truth, and too bad for him if he tried to stop me."

"What did he say?"

"He was floored. I also told him I knew that he was hiding things from me." Anita pointed an accusatory finger at me. "Just like you do. You all think I'm just a dumb blonde. But I'll show you what I'm capable of."

"Anita," I sighed. "This is not some pulp fiction plot, where the blonde heroine is always rescued at the last moment by a handsome stranger. This is real. This is dangerous."

"I went to see Ahti Virtanen yesterday, did you know that? With Mustonen. We went to his house, which is huge, and I dropped my glove behind an armchair, and then, that very same evening, I came back for it and talked to him. If there's one thing I'm good at, it's establishing contact."

I closed my eyes. The girl worried me. She imagined herself single-handedly restoring order while looking stunningly gorgeous. She pictured a spark of admiration in Mustonen's eyes, grudging approval from Jokela, Dr Palmu shaking her hand ceremoniously. She saw herself giving interviews to national dailies and being acclaimed by Steve on the radio. I was sure she had already chosen the new dress she would buy to wear to a small but prestigious reception given in her honour by the city's mayor – champagne and petits fours, and all those adoring glances.

"This is dangerous," I said again. "I don't want you to end up another bloated corpse, floating face down in the harbour."

"I won't. I'm smarter than that. And anyway" – Anita snorted her disdain – "a liar like you doesn't have a say in the matter, not any more." She pulled her suitcase from under the wardrobe and started throwing her clothes into it.

"What are you doing?"

"Leaving." Anita picked up the crimson suede pumps from the back of the wardrobe, wrapped them in tissue and placed them on top of the suitcase.

"Why?"

"Going back to Ranta's."

She stormed off to the bathroom. I followed her, saw

her collect the little vials of cream and perfume scattered around the sink. The hairbrush. The curling iron.

"Why?"

Angry breathing, no answer.

"Is this because I provided Steve with an alibi?"

"No," Anita said, clicking the suitcase shut. "It's because you lied."

"Steve is innocent," I said. "I know it. He's being set up."

"Is that what you really believe, or what you *want* to believe? You've been accusing Mustonen of partiality, but are you any better?"

Never before had I seen Anita so furious. "Go on, tell me you're better than him," she needled. "Tell me your lies are justified because you can't possibly be wrong. Because you're so good, so pure and true, you get to define what the truth *is*? Go on!"

I shook my head. "I'm sorry."

"Sorry's not good enough." Anita kicked the suitcase onto the landing. "I don't know who I hate more, you for being a liar, or myself for being gullible enough to believe you were anything different."

47

Inspector Mustonen

July 1946

Mrs Saari, who turned out to be the baker's wife and my father's next-door neighbour, ran out of her house as soon as she saw me push open the gate.

"How good of you to come, Mr Mustonen! Would you like some coffee? Or tea? Or *anything*?"

"Maybe later, Mrs Saari. I would just like to see my father right now."

I thought she would stay at the door, but the woman followed me inside the house. I didn't know what to expect. In my mind's eye, my father was as formidable as ever, and when I breathed in the familiar scent of home – wood polish and mothballs – I almost turned back. Only the thought of Mrs Saari hovering behind me in the narrow corridor forced me to climb the creaky stairs and open the door to the bedroom.

"Hello, Father," I said from the doorway.

There was no reaction, so maybe Mrs Saari had not been exaggerating after all. I came closer. My father's strong regular features had melted away, leaving behind a lined, beaky mask, immobile except for the watery blue eyes that blinked as I approached.

"It's Erik." I leaned over to kiss my father's damp fore-head. "I came to keep you company."

"Isn't it great, Mr Mustonen?" the woman chipped in. "Your son's here. No doubt, your daughters will be arriving soon."

"I don't think they will, actually," I said, taking the woman by the elbow and steering her towards the door. "But I'll be staying a while. As long as my father needs me."

Once Mrs Saari was gone, I made coffee in the downstairs kitchen and carried it to my father's room. "Why don't I tell you about my life?" I said. "After all, it's thanks to you that I've become the man I am."

48

Chief Inspector Mustonen

I blinked and my father's photograph came sharply back into focus. I glanced at my watch; it was only eight in the morning, though it felt like hours since I had tiptoed across the empty squad room and sneaked like a thief into my own office. Now the first morning light was sweeping brush-strokes of yellow over the rooftops, and all around me the familiar furniture, clean, uncluttered, impersonal, seemed to acquire a life of its own. It stared at me accusingly. It oozed with disapproval.

The furniture was telling me it was time I made a decision. Not only because of what my father's life, and death, had taught me. Because of Anita, too. When the previous night she had said thanks but no thanks to Paris, the high blush on her cheeks had told me everything I needed to know. The reason she had declined. What she thought of me. I had to reverse the flow, and fast. Make the right choice. Act like a better man.

I picked up the receiver but dropped it back on its base immediately. Checked the door first. Made sure it was closed. Locked it, for more security, so no early bird could overhear my conversation. Waited for the furious thumping of my heart to subside. OK, here goes, I thought. I picked up the telephone again and waited for the secretary to answer.

"It's Mustonen," I said, my voice strangled but my mind clear. "From the homicide squad. I need to speak to Dr Palmu. Yes, I'm afraid it's urgent."

The hours that followed rushed past like an extract from a movie, a kaleidoscope of tight, action-packed scenes.

My second call was for the garage on Ratakatu. A girl answered, already bored. This time I gave my name and title. "Do you still have Virtanen's Chrysler?"

She didn't know.

"Could you find out, please?"

I held my breath as she wandered off. Doors slammed shut, someone yelled, and I'd started to think she'd forgotten all about me by the time she finally came back on the line.

"Inspector?" She was chewing gum now.

"Yes?"

"We have it."

I breathed out. "Good. I'm sending over an officer with a warrant. We'll be towing the car to Headquarters for inspection. No, don't say anything to Mr Virtanen. Not yet."

A glance at my watch: 9 a.m. The squad room was filling up with people; I could hear their yammering through the thin partition wall. Jokela was not in yet – I had been straining my ears for the unmistakable heavy step. Just as well. It was time to get going.

I lifted my coat from the hook, grabbed my bag, my hat. Down the stairs at a running pace, hoping not to bump into Jokela. I didn't take the car; I knew I'd be faster on foot, and there was an added benefit too. I could stop by Elena's place, warn her that she needed to testify against Ahti Virtanen. It was a good thing I had helped the girl; there was nothing Virtanen senior could do to her now that she was a Finnish citizen, and her testimony was going to be crucial. I reached her building in less than ten minutes. There was no going back now: the next twelve hours would either make or break me. No, I told myself as I climbed the stairs. Don't even think that; it will work. No reason it shouldn't, I was doing the right thing. A bit late, but still, I was doing it.

"What do you want?" Vlad droned, as if he had never seen me before. As if he didn't *owe* me.

I gave him a fuck-off look. "Where's Elena?"

"Busy," Vlad said. "In the bathroom."

"All right. Tell her not to leave the city. She'll have to testify."

Vlad grumbled something which I decided was a yes. Down the stairs again, taking them two at a time. Cold morning air in my face, snow pricking my skin like needles. Thinking along the way, hands in my pockets because I had forgotten my gloves, heart racing. The familiar landscape – cranes, boats, docks – flew unseen past my eyes. I only became conscious of my surroundings when I arrived at my destination. The nondescript Mr Ljungkvist was standing guard above an open trunk full of debris: broken bottles, a doll's porcelain leg, a handbag's chain, other junk that was impossible to identify.

"I'm sorry," Ljungkvist said when he saw me. "I know I promised we'd wait for you, but my guys told me there's a storm alert for this afternoon, and they didn't want to be caught in it."

"Of course," I said. "Perfectly natural. Anything useful?"

"Don't think so." Ljungkvist stuck a cigarette in his mouth, cupped his hands around a match. "But I'm no expert. We're almost done, by the way. Just one last stretch to go and we'll be good. Then you can take our treasure chest" – a nod towards the gaping trunk – "to the police station and inspect it at your leisure. You never mentioned what exactly you were looking for, did you?"

"That's because I wanted your guys to keep an open mind. You never know what might come up."

"No weapon so far," Ljungkvist said. "No bodies either. A nice tie, if you're interested. Looks almost new."

"No thank you," I grinned. "My wife chooses my ties for me. Let's keep our fingers crossed for that gun."

Ljungkvist nodded again, didn't say anything.

In this part of the port, cordoned off by police, the silence was only disturbed by the humming of the air compressor. Two lines ran from it towards the water, disappearing into the murky depths. A man in a fisherman's cap and a fur coat was frowning, his gaze on the gauges at the front of the compressor; two others, in matching sweaters, were turning the wheel. Yet another man, in a diving suit but no helmet, leaned above the water, watching the bubbles. The whole operation felt impeccably rehearsed and synchronized, as I supposed it should be. I stuck my hands deeper into my pockets and tried to rein in my impatience.

Next to me, Ljungkvist was smoking, blowing perfect rings into the cold damp air. I hesitated to ask him for a cigarette – I had run out of smokes and was dying to have one – but decided against it. Finally, the cord running into the water tensed and the men perked up. I came closer.

The diver's huge round head was already above the water. "Anything?" Ljungkvist cried out.

No one answered. They waited another minute while the diver was pulled onto the embankment and his faceplate lifted.

"Anything?" Ljungkvist asked again. He seemed even more eager than I was.

The diver – pale and puffy-eyed after his time on the seabed – squinted at us. "Sorry, no."

Ljungkvist shot me a worried glance. "All for nothing, huh? A pity." He looked like he was ready to plant incriminating evidence himself, if only I cared to tell him what it should be.

I bit my lip, frowning. "Maybe not," I said at last. "Can I have a look at that tie you mentioned?"

49

Hella

I hadn't run after Anita. I'd wanted to – to make her stay, talk to her, explain the dark and tangled reasons making me believe in Steve's innocence – but I knew it wouldn't be any good. Furious as she'd been, she wasn't going to listen to me, and even I could recognize an argument that was going nowhere. Instead, I'd spent another bad night tossing and turning in the too-wide bed, the thump-thump-thumping of Anita's suitcase travelling down the stairs still loud in my ears. I woke up late; my hair was clinging to my damp cheeks, and my eyes were red and swollen.

Slumped in my bed with the covers pulled up to my chin, I thought about the events of the previous day. I had underestimated Anita. To me, she was just a pretty, foolish amateur detective. But I knew nothing about her other than what I had seen, and I had only seen – or had chosen to see – what she had let me.

Shivering, I made my way towards the kitchen. The plan was to throw cold water onto my face and then make a cup of tea. To try and do something useful. The sort of useful didn't really matter at this stage. So when I put the kettle on and noticed the slimy wall tiles, I decided that would do. *Spring cleaning! Come on, girls!* My mother's cheerful voice echoed in some distant chamber of my mind, and I nodded to myself gloomily. My apartment could do with some cleaning, whether spring or otherwise. Besides, the stench had got stronger in the last twenty-four hours. It was coming from the pipes and I couldn't help wondering if something had died in there. The image made me shiver. I put on an old shirt and got to work, like my mother would have done.

First, grate some soap above a basin, pour hot water over it. Then, grab a brush, plonk it into the soap solution and start scrubbing at the tiles. The situation called for a song. Some childhood tune, domestic, sweet and unthreatening – only I couldn't remember any. At some point after my parents' accident my musical memory must have wiped itself clean, because all I could come up with was "Eeny Meeny Miney Mo", and that didn't really lend itself to humming. In the end, I switched on the radio – classical music, not Steve's programme – and went back to my scrubbing. Two violin concertos later, my hands and calves and lower back were hurting like mad, and I'd only covered twenty square feet of tiles. Maybe this cleaning idea had been stupid to begin with. I had hoped it would give me a feeling of order, of being in control, but it hadn't. While I scrubbed, I couldn't stop thinking about Anita's last words. What if she was right and I was wrong? What if I was deluding myself? No amount of cleaning was going to take away the realization that I had lied to the police, that I had placed myself firmly on the other side of the divide, based on nothing more than a hard to define malaise and blind trust in my former lover's integrity.

I paused, wiping the sweat off my forehead with my sleeve. All that furious scrubbing had got me closer to the pipes, and the stench was becoming unbearable. What if there *was* something dead in there, like a rat? A stinking little corpse, leaking into the walls? Tom told me once that when you smelled something, it meant tiny particles of that thing were already in your nose. I gagged, pressed my sleeve to my face and ran out of the kitchen and down the stairs, not bothering to lock up behind me. I banged on my landlord's door for a few minutes until I realized that either no one was home, or no one was going to answer. I ran up the stairs again, breathing through my mouth. I would leave him a message. I fished a fountain pen out of my bag and started writing: *Dear Mr Norrlund, I am afraid there's a dead rat or mouse in my wall. It's filthy and it stinks. I need your help sorting this out. Can you please—* My hand froze in mid-air. I stared at the note. Then, holding my breath, I went into the kitchen and threw the window open.

What was that word in Klara Nylund's little black book? *Filth?*

The rat would have to wait. I could barely believe it, but it was possible that I'd just made a breakthrough.

The strings I had to pull cost me the last of my food coupons, but it was worth it. The dates matched. The description matched. Whether Anita would be ready to cooperate was another story, but I decided that I was not going to think about that yet.

I snapped the file shut, put on a coat and left the apartment. My plan was to discuss the case with Mustonen first, lay the facts before him and let him draw his own conclusions. But when I turned up at the police station, the receptionist informed me that he was not in the office yet. I scribbled a short note for him, left it with her. The hands of the clock behind the receptionist indicated that it was a quarter past three.

I decided to try my luck at the morgue, though I had no illusions: Tom was the early to bed, early to rise type. He was probably already on his way home, where his mother awaited him with pierogies and a pot of freshly brewed tea. I knew I wouldn't be welcome. Mrs Räikkönen, a slim, startlingly beautiful woman who looked nothing like her son, disliked me intensely.

"She thinks you're after my irresistible body," Tom told me once. "She also thinks you're unworthy of me. Much too bony. With one N."

"Just tell her friendship is the best I can offer."

"The F word is not part of her vocabulary, you should know that by now. And anyway, I prefer her trembling with fear at the idea that you'll get me one day. Her cooking benefits from it greatly."

The thought of Mrs Räikkönen's piercing blue eyes made me quicken my step. Some people were like that: never threatening, impeccably polite, they still managed to convey the impression that they could slip arsenic into your coffee at the first opportunity.

I was also wondering what Tom would make of my theory. At this point, he seemed to be the only person likely to listen to me, the only one, too, to tell me if I was being delusional. I realized of course that my findings were pure conjecture; I didn't have any evidence. *You have to be pretty desperate*, my inner voice whispered, *to accuse a man of assault without the slightest evidence.*

Especially if that man is a police officer.

The daylight was beginning to fade and a bitterly cold wind was blowing off the sea. I paused on the corner of Kasarmikatu, waiting for the lights to change. No one would believe me, I knew that. Even if I came up with the most irrefutable proof there was, people would still be wary. Unless you were a crackpot who was convinced that the world was run by giant grasshoppers, you wanted to believe the police were there to protect you. It was the basis of civilized society, the backbone of every democracy. You didn't expect a police officer to turn out to be a criminal. Because what is a police officer breaking the law? The end of a civilization.

I didn't realize I was out of breath until I pushed open the door leading to the morgue. "Dr Räikkönen?" I called out. I had no desire to stumble onto another unknown corpse being stitched up.

Immediately, a dishevelled head popped out of the autopsy room, grinning broadly at me. "Dr Räikkönen already left," the man told me. "He said he was feeling a bit under the weather, so he went home."

"Thank you," I sighed, wondering if I could still catch Tom. "How long ago did he leave?"

"At least an hour," the man said. "Sorry." He ducked out of view and almost immediately I heard a strange scrubbing sound that reminded me of my own cleaning efforts. I turned to leave.

Twenty minutes later, I was standing in front of another door, this one belonging to an elegant little mansion just off Ludviginkatu. The house, in grey Finnish granite, was the epitome of art nouveau, an urban fairy tale complete with gargoyles; Tom hated it with a passion.

I've always believed cities are like people, they have stories to tell. They entice you with a glint of a store window, a whiff of cardamom; they hide their scars under layers of paint. This part of Helsinki was a wealthy widow, her face transformed by powders and lotions, cornices and gleaming brass knockers. The widow kept to herself, most of the time, and bad-mouthed her neighbours. I was not at ease here.

I braced myself and knocked, putting on a smile that was as brilliant as it was fake. A short instant later, Mrs Räikkönen answered the door, her lips stretched in a smile that matched my own. "Miss Mauzer! What a pleasant surprise! My son is not in yet, but do come in. Would you care for some tea? Maybe with cinnamon buns?"

"Thank you." I followed Mrs Räikkönen inside, and immediately my feet sunk into a deep plush carpet. With its Aubusson tapestries, dark velvet curtains and luscious potted palms, the house around me felt like one of those flesh-eating plants one read about in science magazines: it was sticky; it swallowed me whole.

"My son," Mrs Räikkönen was saying, "has taken up drawing. Twice a week after work he goes to an art studio, where he learns how to draw." She shrugged. "I never look at his work, of course. From what I understand, they draw nude models." She pointed to a love seat upholstered in yellow silk. The furniture in the room was arranged in such a manner as to offer a view of Tom's butterfly collection that occupied the north-facing wall.

"Milk, sugar?" Tom's mother shoved a dainty teacup at me. "Truth be told, Miss Mauzer, I would have preferred if my son had carried on with the butterflies. Such an innocent hobby. I hope he doesn't expect me to hang his *draw*ings on the wall. And if only it was just that. He's decided to get himself a motorbike!" She smiled but her hands trembled. "It's been a while since I saw you last, Miss Mauzer. I even thought you and my son had had a lover's tiff. I'm very happy to see that you're back."

The doorbell rang before I could answer, and Mrs Räikkönen hurried away. I heard urgent whispering at the door, a nervous laugh, but Tom's appearance was an anti-climax: he looked his usual cheery self, rosy-cheeked and dapper. There was a manila folder under his arm.

"Hella!" He enveloped me in a bear hug. "I trust this is not a social call."

"And why wouldn't it be?" Mrs Räikkönen said in a clipped voice. "You have the right at your age to entertain young ladies."

This was when it finally clicked. For a detective, I'd been slow on the uptake. I almost laughed out loud.

"I'd love to see your drawings," I said to Tom.

Mrs Räikkönen went white around the mouth, started folding the edge of the tablecloth into neat little pleats. I almost felt sorry for her. The warm welcome she'd had for me, so much at odds with her previous icy politeness, could mean only one thing: she thought I was the lesser evil.

"Come to my office, then," Tom said, with a wary glance at his mother. "I'll show you."

The office, large but oppressive, was filled with more butterflies in mahogany cases. The pencil drawings were tacked to the wall in between, and they were exactly as I had imagined them – anatomically correct, with just a tiny hint of artistic feeling thrown in. All nude. All men.

"They're not mine, by the way," Tom said. "All these pictures were drawn by a guy I met at the studio. Touko Laaksonen, but he calls himself Tom, like me. Works in advertising. What do you think?" Tom turned to face me. A vein was pulsating in his right temple; he wanted to give the impression that he didn't care, but he did.

"So there's more to it than healthy living?" I said. "I should have guessed when I saw those beefcake magazines at the mortuary. Silly me."

"Not that silly," Tom grinned, relieved. "My mother didn't notice anything either – I only told her who I was a couple of days ago. This thing has been building inside me, so I thought I needed to tell someone, otherwise I'd go mad. But I still hope no one else connects the dots. Maybe Sweden's King Gustaf could have weathered this sort of publicity, but I certainly couldn't."

"No problem. If people start to talk and you need me to play the part of an amorous girlfriend, I'll be there for you. But I didn't come to talk about your sexual preferences. Hear me out on this."

Tom sat in silence as I showed him Klara Nylund's notes, the travel dates, my suspect's infatuation with Anita, everything. I mentioned his obsessive personality, the fact that he had become a *persona non grata* in the brothel. The question I needed to ask Tom was whether the physical characteristics of the killer matched.

"You've seen the man, right? Could he be the one?"

Tom took his time, chewing on the tip of a pencil. "Things aren't always what they seem, huh?" he said at last. "For everyone. But how would he lure them? He doesn't look like a possible romantic interest to me."

"Not to me, either. But maybe we got it wrong, maybe the romantic interest was someone else altogether and he attacked Nellie because he couldn't bear the thought that she was leaving. Or do you think I'm totally crazy?"

"Hmm," Tom said. "From what I've seen of the man, he's a bit on the small side – he's what, about the same height as you are? – but yes, I suppose it's possible." He put down the file and stretched. "Officer Ranta. Who would have thought?"

50

Hella

Outside, night had fallen. There was a bit of snow, tiny sting-
ing flakes that melted as soon as they touched the window.
The room was dark, except for a Tiffany lamp that threw
a circle of golden glow on the papers strewn on the desk,
leaving Tom's face in the shadows.

"It matches," I said at last. "The description – *filth* – the
dates when Ranta came over from Lapland, the fact he wasn't
welcome at Klara Nylund's any more, his unhealthy interest in his cousin's love life, the description of her attacker.
Even if Anita refuses to help, I can line up the madam's
girls, prove that Ranta was a client."

"It's a big thing," Tom said, not looking at me. "Accusing
a police officer. The police look after their own. Even if they
believed you, and that's a big *if*, they'd most likely never act
on it. Instead, they'd make your life hell. Make you pay for
the humiliation, for the threat to the powers that be. You've
already spent years paying for a crime you didn't commit –
with this, you'd likely become the most hated person in all
of Finland."

"Do you think I don't know that?" It came out sharper
than I intended; but then, I was scared.

Silence.

"Don't count on me to help you," Tom said at last, with a sheepish grin. "I love you – platonically – and all, but this thing could end my career."

I was tempted to point out that he didn't really need a career – not like I did, in any case – but I knew of course that wasn't true. Even if he had more money than he knew what to do with, Tom was still very much attached to the prestige of his job, and he loved nothing more than having a medical enigma to exercise his mind. So I said: "Of course. I don't intend to involve you. Our conversation is totally off the record."

Tom nodded, relieved. "So what are you going to do about this? Confront Ranta all on your own? Go and see Mustonen, try to convince him?"

"No," I said slowly. "The first thing to do would be to talk to Anita. When she told me about the attack, I couldn't shake the feeling that she knew who her attacker was. If I'm right, even if she chooses to deny that it was Ranta who scared her, I'd still see her reaction." I got up to leave. "The most dangerous lies are those we tell ourselves, aren't they?"

"I wouldn't know," Tom said. "I only tell lies to others. So kiss me goodbye, baby!"

"*Baby*?! Is this for your mother's benefit?" Tom's voice rose on this last word, and I was wondering if Mrs Räikkönen was hovering outside, trying to eavesdrop.

Tom winked. "Give me a hug, my sweet love." I did, giggling madly. The anxiety was gone, replaced by an elation that set my whole body on fire. The case was about to be solved; it might take a while to collect the evidence, if Anita refused to testify, but I was certain we'd get there in the end. And the best part: it wasn't Steve. I had known that, of course I had; I still felt better because I had a credible suspect now.

"I should hurry up," I said. "With a bit of luck, I'll catch Anita before she leaves the office."

"Be careful. I'd hate to have you on my autopsy table. Besides, my schedule is full for the next few days."

Anita was not at police headquarters – she'd left early, Tarja informed me gleefully, after receiving a sumptuous bouquet of pink roses at lunchtime. She was not at Ranta's either. There was no one at Ranta's. I knocked and I called, but the thin, wobbly door remained stubbornly closed. I peered into the keyhole: no key in the lock. Ranta's house was on the wrong side of town: overflowing garbage bins, peeling paint, not a tree in sight. There was an old woman in a tattered fur coat, sitting on a bench near the house with her eyes downcast. When I said hello to her, she turned away and started muttering under her breath. I crossed the street towards a tiny corner store, asked the owner if he'd seen Ranta or Anita recently. The man shook his head, probably wondering who I was. It's how it goes in that sort of place: people mind their own business. It's safer that way.

I stuck around for an hour, feeling increasingly jittery, like an overanxious mother waiting for her teenage daughter to come back from a date. It felt wrong, because I knew that Ranta, too, had left the office early. He had told his colleagues in Archives that he was going out of town, fishing. A passion of his, or so he claimed. I wondered about Anita. Could she be with him? Unlikely. And even if she was, it didn't necessarily mean she was in danger. Wasn't I the one who had told her she was as capable as any man? Anita was a police officer. She knew how to shoot, she knew how to fight. She was not stupid. I tried to imagine Mustonen in her place, going fishing with Ranta. Would I be afraid for him? The answer was most definitely no.

When the little hand on my watch reached seven, I decided I'd waited enough. It was time to go and see the only person who could help me now.

Time to see Mustonen.

51

Hella

"I read your note," Mustonen said, "but I refuse to believe it."

He ran a hand through his hair. His eyes were bloodshot, tired. "I haven't seen Anita this afternoon, it's been an awful day. I can't really go into details, but there could be changes here soon. Besides, we've made a breakthrough on the harbour drownings case. The evidence we have doesn't point to Ranta, it points to a man called Ahti Virtanen. His initials are embroidered on the tie that was used to attach a piece of metal scrap to Nellie's handbag. We are now performing an inspection of his car. So no, I can't really believe Anita would disappear like that. And that Officer Ranta could be involved."

"Maybe it's both," I said. "Maybe Virtanen is a mass murderer while Ranta is an occasional rapist. Look, maybe it's nothing, but I'm worried about Anita. I want to make sure nothing has happened to her."

Mustonen looked at his watch, frowning. "You know what? I was planning to go and interview Ahti Virtanen, because I happen to know that his parents are at their summer cabin, entertaining some important guests. He'll be alone. You stay in the background, don't say a word. You'll see for yourself. And if it has nothing to do with him, we'll try to track down Ranta." He pulled a shoulder holster from his desk drawer and put it on, grabbed his jacket from the back of his seat. "Team? Just like in the good old days?"

"Thank you." I wanted to tell Mustonen that I had been wrong about him, but it didn't seem like the right place, or the right time. So I nodded and followed him out of the office.

The traffic was heavy on Unioninkatu. In the three years I'd been away, Helsinki had filled up with cars, Opel Kapitän sedans and Tatras, gleaming Volvos for the affluent, Soviet-made GAZs for the penniless or the optimistic. All were honking, starting and stalling, and the air was thick with fumes. The city was badly in need of traffic police. But then it was also badly in need of new, affordable housing, and food, and order.

Almost without thinking, Mustonen and I settled back into the routine we knew by heart. Him at the wheel of the brand-new Studebaker he'd got from Headquarters, swerving expertly between cars, a smile on his face. Me with a city map on my lap, giving out directions. It felt like I had never left the squad. It felt like home.

"What kind of changes?" I asked.

"Huh?"

"You said there could be changes on the squad."

Mustonen gave a mirthless little laugh. "The squad has changed a lot since you left, Hella. It's grown corrupt. It has started to defeat its purpose. Or maybe" – he swerved the car into one of the narrow streets off Tehtaankatu – "it's always been that way but I was too naive to notice. I'm partly to blame too. I should have reacted earlier. Only I could never imagine we'd get to a point where political considerations would take precedence over a murder investigation. So I…" He bit his lip.

"What did you do, Erik?"

"I put a stop to it. I should have done so a long time ago, but I was afraid for my career. I guess you've got a lot more courage than me." He smiled ruefully. "This squad needs people like you, Hella. People who are uncompromising and bright."

I felt myself blushing. Was he offering me my old job back? What about Jokela? He surely wouldn't like that. I mumbled something that could mean yes, or no, or thank you, depending on what Mustonen chose to hear.

He smiled again, nodding to himself. Ten minutes later, we stopped before an imposing nineteenth-century mansion painted light blue. "Don't tell them who you are," Mustonen said as we stepped out of the car. "Just follow my lead, OK?"

A redhead with no neck but plenty of bosom answered the door. Her gaze travelled from me to Mustonen, then back to me again. Behind her, I could see a brightly lit foyer, marble floors and chandeliers and a stuffed polar bear standing guard in one corner.

Mustonen showed the woman his warrant card. "Is Mr Ahti Virtanen home?"

"He is," the woman said. "He just arrived. But you probably need to speak to his father. He'll be here soon."

"We don't need his father. It's him we've come to see, and he's of age. May we come in?"

Mustonen wasn't really expecting an answer. He had already pushed past the woman and was walking towards the large oak staircase. "Mr Virtanen?" he called out. "Ahti Virtanen?"

A muffled sound came from somewhere upstairs. "Police," Mustonen said. "We need to talk to you." And to me: "Wait here, Mauzer, would you?"

"All right." I turned towards the woman. "You said Mr Ahti Virtanen just got back? Do you know where he was?"

The woman shrugged, licking her lips. I could hear voices coming from upstairs, rising. "Maybe," the woman said, "maybe I should come up and see what's going —"

A gunshot ripped through the house.

Time froze in mid-breath, the gleaming foyer reverberating around me. The chandeliers, blazing with light, the bear's open jaws, its pointed teeth.

Two shots. Three.

The woman screamed, her hand pressed hard to her mouth, her eyes wild. I ran up the stairs. A long carpeted corridor, with doors opening on either side. "Erik!" I cried out. "Are you all right?"

The door farthest down the corridor flew open. Mustonen was standing in the doorway, heaving, clutching his gun. "Yeah," he said. "I think I am." He motioned towards the inside of the room. "That bastard tried to shoot me. I had to" – his voice caught – "you know."

"Let me in. Do you think he's dead?"

"I don't know. Be careful."

But the boy was dead all right. He was slumped against the wall, a gun in his hand. He had no face any more, just some bloody pulpous mess and, above it, blonde hair slicked back. "Jesus," I whispered. "What did you two talk about? Did you know he had a gun when you entered the room?"

"No. He had it behind his back, I guess. I asked him where he had been and he started shooting."

"Jesus," I said again. "I thought this sort of stuff never happened."

"Did you really?" Mustonen asked, drawing a ragged breath. "It happened to you. Go downstairs, call the other cops and your pal Räikkönen. Can you do that?"

Behind him, the maid paused in the doorway, gasped, then started screaming again.

52

Hella

I refused to stay inside. The air in the house was heavy, viscous like congealing blood. I made the phone call to Headquarters, then went outside and sat on the stone steps. After a while Mustonen came out too. He lowered himself onto the steps and offered me a cigarette. He lit another one for himself, cupping his hands round the lighter and its flame; he screwed his mouth to one side to blow the smoke away from me. "Sorry about that. I shouldn't have brought you here."

I didn't answer. I was thinking about that other case, when the roles had been reversed and Mustonen had found himself on the outside while I had shot a suspect who was threatening me. I thought about what he knew about that case, and what he might have guessed. I tried to imagine Jokela's reaction. Most of all, though, I thought about Anita.

"If it was Virtanen who took her," I said, "chances are we'll never find her now."

"Oh, we will." Mustonen dragged on his cigarette. "Believe me, we will. If she was even taken, which I don't believe."

It started snowing again, tiny brittle snowflakes. Somewhere in the distance I could hear the wailing of a police siren. I stood up too quickly for my head, then had to wait for the dark points floating before my eyes to dissipate. "I'd better be going. You don't need me right now. And if I have to testify about what happened, you know where to find me."

"I'd rather you stayed here." Mustonen turned his head to glance up at me. In the darkness, I couldn't see his eyes.

"I would love to catch up with the team," I said ceremoniously. "But I'd rather look for Anita. I have a bad feeling about her."

Mustonen flicked the stub of his cigarette into the snow-covered flowerbed. "Stubborn, aren't you, Mauzer? I'll keep you posted."

One thing my father had taught me was not to panic. Not to jump to conclusions, either. So Mustonen had fired at a suspect who was threatening him. Killed him. It happened. I was living proof of that.

I observed Mustonen carefully while he sat with me on the stone steps, smoking and waiting. He was shaken, but he wasn't worried. This meant he had all the evidence he needed. He could prove that Virtanen was indeed our guy. And why not? All the evidence pointed to him. Except for the evidence pointing to Ranta.

A police car whirred past me, its blue lights flashing. And then another. And another. I believed I saw Dr Palmu's pinched face in one of the cars, but I couldn't be sure, so I just kept walking. My priority was finding Anita. Then I'd have the time to think about everything carefully, come up with a decision.

It took me close to forty minutes to get to Ranta's place again. All the windows were dark. I paused on the doorstep, but only for a second. I needed to appear as inconspicuous as possible, as if I had every right to be there, to do what I was doing. I pulled a bunch of picklocks from my shoulder bag, shielding it with my body. If anyone was watching, they would see a woman fumbling for her keys. And I was right about the lock, too. Standard pre-war, opened with a hairpin. I let myself in, shut the door behind me.

The first thing I noticed was Anita's fake pearl necklace lying on a side table, amid a jumble of keys, fishing hooks and bolts. Maybe Ranta *had* gone fishing. Maybe it hadn't just been an excuse. Or maybe he was one of those accomplished criminals who knew that for a lie to be convincing, you needed to get all your props right. Inside, the house was unexpectedly big. A living room, a kitchen, two bedrooms, all a mess. Anita's clothes, dirty plates, papers. And photographs, but not everywhere, only in Ranta's bedroom. The photographs were of Anita. Some of the pictures dated back to her childhood. There she was in her first communion dress, a thin veil masking her features. As a toddler in pigtails. As an older child with a huge ribbon in her hair. As a young woman, dressed in a freshly pressed police uniform, smiling self-consciously.

In one of the photographs, a forty-something man, wiry and strong, was standing next to her, his hand on her shoulder.

"*Jesus,*" I said out loud.

Then I turned around and hurried towards the exit.

Another thing my father had taught me was to trust my instincts. I knew then, knew with absolute certainty, that I had been looking in the wrong place.

53

Chief Inspector Mustonen

It was a few minutes past 9 p.m. Dark shadows danced on the walls and I could hear the muted sound of car horns and sirens from downstairs. The squad room was buzzing with excitement. Even though it's the capital of Finland, Helsinki is still at its heart a sleepy provincial town. The last shoot-out involving a police officer had happened almost exactly four years ago. Hella Mauzer had been involved, and she had ended up being banished to Ivalo. Would the same thing happen to me?

I hadn't seen Jokela; I'd barely seen Dr Palmu. The police chief went up to the crime scene, took one hard look and left. He nodded at me as he passed but didn't meet my eye.

The pathologist came too, wrinkling his nose as if he'd smelled something rotten. "This unfortunate young man is very probably dead" – Räikkönen's sense of humour is inimitable – "but I will only have absolute certainty and the list of probable causes after an autopsy." I had to stay behind and wait until the mortuary team took the body away. Only then did I feel free to leave the house.

Going down the drive, my car crossed that of Virtanen senior and his wife, dressed to the nines – black tie and tiara – and staring open-mouthed at all the police cars blocking their driveway. I pressed my foot down on the accelerator; I had no desire at all to talk to them. Let Jokela sort this out. If he was still around, that is.

Tarja stayed late too. At 9.10, she knocked on the door of my office. "Inspector Pinchus would like you to join him in the interview room, sir. He thinks he may be on to something. A witness."

"Does he?" I toyed with the idea of saying no. I still had things to do, and no intention of being held up at the office. And it had been a long day. What I needed was a whisky and a cab home, but I knew that was not possible. Not yet. When I got back to the office, I called Sofia briefly, told her in a few words what had happened. She sounded annoyed. Could this interfere with my promotion, she wanted to know. "I don't think so," I said, speaking the truth. At that point I didn't care either, though I had enough sense not to say that.

"Shall I tell Inspector Pinchus you're coming, sir?" Tarja again, hovering in the doorway.

I stifled a sigh. "Yes. Tell him I'll be with him in a few minutes."

Pinchus was, in my view, the most annoying of the homicide squad detectives. One of those people who always hoped for the worst, only happy when their darkest predictions were realized. At the opening of every new case, he tut-tutted around the evidence gloomily, his whole body sagging with the weight of his dark unerring knowledge. And inevitably, when Pinchus was in charge, the worst did happen, though it was never his fault. He drew those cases to him by some mysterious alchemy. They lent credit to his incipient pessimism, made him come across as a prophet, not just an overanxious doomsayer. If it had been any other officer, I would have said no and gone away. But it was not any other officer, it was Pinchus. I was curious.

I leafed through the Nellie Ritvanen file, though there was really no need. I knew the file by heart now. My motto is *always ready*, and I was. Then I went over to the interview room. Pinchus was sitting hunched over a table, his bald head glowing under the artificial light. Across from him sat a small dark man, dressed in some sort of work outfit. His glasses were secured behind his head with a shoelace.

"Inspector," Pinchus said, waving a hand. "Take a seat." He never called me Chief Inspector, presumably because I was younger than him but higher in rank and he considered that unjust. I had never let it bother me until now. I slammed the file onto the desk and ignored Pinchus.

"My secretary tells me you have information for us," I said to the little man. "What is it?"

The man swallowed nervously and glanced across the table at Pinchus, who said in a gloomy voice, "Mr Nurmi thinks he was an eyewitness to a kidnapping. He came here all the way from Tuusula."

The little man started nodding away, his eyes never leaving Pinchus. "A young woman," he said. "Red dress, beige coat, hair just like so." He put up his hands and twisted his fingers into something complicated. "She said she was from the Helsinki police. And that she had laid a trap for a suspect."

"Did you see the kidnapper?" I asked. My heart was going fast.

"Not too well, sir." The man put his hands back on the table, like an obedient child. "I was too far away, on the opposite platform. And then a train passed." The witness sniffed. "I wouldn't be able to recognize him or anything. But he dropped something. The kidnapper, I mean."

Pinchus coughed. I hadn't noticed it until then, but my colleague had a brown paper envelope lying in front of him. He slid it towards me.

"It's a scarf, Inspector." He paused while I shook the scarf out of the envelope and bent low to inspect it. "The description of the victim matches Anita," Pinchus said, when I straightened myself up again.

"Yes," I said. "I know."

"The scarf has its owner's initials embroidered on it – do these people embroider every piece of clothing they own, even socks? And there are bloodstains, too."

"We can't be sure it's blood. Get it to the techs, ask them to analyse it as a priority."

Pinchus glanced at his watch. "The tech on duty is at the Virtanen incident. The other one has gone home."

I took a deep breath, let it out slowly. "Take it to Räikkönen, then. He's capable of doing this, and he's already at the morgue. Tell him it's urgent."

Pinchus shook his head. "He'll refuse. He'll say it's not his job."

"Flatter him. Tell him he's a great artist. Tell him I offered to put his works on display in the squad room."

Pinchus stared at me as if I was mad.

"Just do it, OK?"

54

Chief Inspector Mustonen

"She's dead, mark my words," Pinchus said gloomily, on his way out. "Anita left the office at 3 p.m. She was last seen alive on a train platform in Tuusula shortly before five." He sighed noisily. "That's four hours."

"How can you be certain about the time?" I asked the witness. "You don't have a wristwatch."

The man stared down at his wrist, as if unsure whether he had a watch or not. "I saw the 4.47 train go past just as that guy grabbed her from behind," he said at last. "I looked again after the train had passed, and she was gone."

"She couldn't have climbed aboard the train?"

"The 4.47 doesn't stop at that station." The witness fished in his pocket for a handkerchief, brought out something grey and stained. "It used to, but then they changed the schedule."

"All right, do you think anyone aboard that train could have seen the kidnapper?"

"Maybe," the man said, but I could see he thought it very unlikely. "I suppose you could always ask."

I pulled Ahti Virtanen's photograph out of the file, slid it towards the witness. "Could it have been this man? He's of medium height, about the same build as me." I stood up and walked towards the window so the man could observe me from some distance. A black Volvo stopped directly under the window, and I saw a uniformed chauffeur rush out and open the passenger door for Jokela.

"Could be," said the little man behind me. "I told you, I didn't see him well."

"Thank you," I said without looking at him. "You have been a very responsible citizen. Please write down your name and contact details. If we ever need you to testify, we want to be able to reach you easily."

"What about the compensation?" the man said.

I whipped round. "What are you talking about?"

"There's a reward," the man said stubbornly, his jaw jutting out. He didn't look like an obedient little citizen any longer. "For helping the police with inquiries. I know there's one – I wouldn't have come otherwise. How do I claim it?"

"What I don't understand," Pinchus said when he was back in the squad room, "is what Anita was doing on that railway platform in the first place."

I shrugged. "That's pretty obvious, isn't it? How did it go with Räikkönen?"

"How do you expect?" Pinchus countered. "He was already in a foul mood because of that dead boy you sent him. When I told him there was biological evidence to examine as well, I thought he was going to bite my head off."

"Well, he didn't. Consider yourself lucky. Did you mention his drawings?"

"Is that like some sort of secret password? I did. That got him angrier still. But in the end, he said he'd do it."

I arched an eyebrow. "Good. It wasn't such a big deal, was it? All Räikkönen has to do is dab on some oxidant, then swipe with luminol. I could practically do it myself. Do you have confirmation, yes or no?"

"No. We'll have to wait until Räikkönen is done with the autopsy." Pinchus looked around, squinting. "Where's everyone else?"

"Interviewing the train conductor," I said, ticking off on my fingers. "Trying to trace any passengers who could have seen what happened." I didn't mention Jokela. Jokela had been summoned for questioning by Dr Palmu; it was unlikely he'd come back any time soon, if at all.

"Bad idea, the interviews," Pinchus said. "It will never work."

I felt like slamming him into the wall, shaking him until his eyes glazed over and the synapses in his brain collapsed. But I couldn't lose my nerve now. I bit my tongue instead, until I could feel blood seeping into my mouth.

"So, what did you say Anita was doing on that train platform?" Pinchus asked conversationally. His one talent was ignoring the effect he had on others.

"I think she was trying to solve the case. Mauzer came to see me earlier this evening. She was afraid that Anita had been taken. I didn't want to believe her then, but maybe she was right." I shook my head. "I showed our witness a photograph of Virtanen, but he wasn't able to identify him."

"Well, it *was* Virtanen's scarf, wasn't it?" Pinchus said, matter of fact.

"Looks like it, yes. Once Räikkönen has finished with it, we can show it to the family."

"OK." Pinchus glanced at his watch. "But until then?"

"Two things," I said. "*You* will call Virtanen's family, try to find out if they have any idea where the boy spent the last few hours."

"What about you?" Pinchus asked. He was clearly not happy with the assignment.

"I'll go talk to Mauzer. I'm willing to bet serious money she was the one who got this stupid idea into Anita's pretty head. With any luck, she'll get Anita back to us."

55

Hella

I needed to see the one person who wouldn't think I was completely crazy. Someone who had no stakes in this game. Tom. As I walked down the dark empty streets, I went over the arguments in my mind. Means, opportunity: it was all there, and I thought I could glimpse a motive. And at least my new theory explained the reaction I'd got from Nellie's friend Maria. Given my past work as a police officer, she had every reason to be afraid of me.

On the corner of Eteläranta, I had to stop because I felt sick. My head was spinning, I was struggling with nausea, with a rush of blood in my ears. What if I *was* going mad? Should I have gone home instead and tried to sleep on it? Or consulted a doctor? I'd been wrong before. I'd been wrong that very afternoon. But Anita was out there, and she was in danger. Not because she was a pretty girl, but because she had uncovered something.

"Are you all right, dear?" A tiny old woman was looking up at me, her face creased in concern. She was wearing a big old fur coat, raccoon or wolfskin, with the seams coming apart at the sleeve. "You look unwell. And you're" – she held out a hand, touched it lightly on my forearm – "you're swaying."

"Thank you. I'm fine. I was going to the hospital. Is it this way?"

"I'll walk you there," the woman said. "It's not far. And it's dangerous for a young girl to be out on her own at night."

I tried to smile. It must have come out odd, because instead of smiling back, the old woman grabbed my elbow firmly and steered me down the street. "Boy trouble, is it, my dear?" I mumbled something vague, and she took it for an acquiescence. "Trust me," she whispered, leaning closer, "it's not worth it. And you're putting yourself in danger. You've heard of that maniac, the one who stays close to the port, just a stone's throw from here, and murders young girls? Drowns them?"

"Yes. I've heard."

The old woman had surprisingly strong hands. Her fingers were digging into the flesh of my forearm like claws. I had a feeling I'd seen her before, though I couldn't remember where. "They were asking for it, of course," the woman added, matter of fact. "Walking around the dark streets alone – don't tell me those girls weren't looking for trouble."

"They were not. No one deserves to be killed. Certainly not young women whose only crime was being out on their own at night."

The woman stopped abruptly. "You really think that, do you?" She was standing close, too close, staring at me with her mouth open, her teeth yellow and decayed. Her breath smelled like a corpse left to rot. "But what if it was our Lord's way of separating the wheat from the chaff?"

There was no light where we were standing, and no people. At some point, without me even noticing, we'd left the large avenue we'd been walking on and headed down tiny crooked streets I didn't recognize. In my panic-fuelled confusion, I couldn't remember how long I'd been walking like this, dragged along by this tiny steel-clawed crab. I tried to shake her hand off, but she only gripped me more strongly.

"I bet the girl who died had boy trouble." The woman chuckled. "Just like you."

A dog howled somewhere in the distance; the air smelled of sea salt and fear. I willed myself to remain calm. She was just a tiny old woman. Mad, no doubt about that. But dangerous? Could she have been the one who had drowned Nellie? Killed Klara Nylund? And then I remembered what Tom had said about the murderer's height. I burst out laughing. "You almost had me fooled," I said. "Are you going around town scaring young women? I don't have time for this. Which way to the hospital?"

She gave me a dirty look. "If that girl had met me, she would have been fine." She tugged on my arm, and a few moments later the street curved and there it was. The Surgical Hospital.

I detached myself from the woman's claws. "You shouldn't be doing this," I said. "But thank you."

"Hey," she cried out. "This isn't the hospital entrance. This is the morgue."

"The morgue is where I'm going. You and I are after the same person. It's only our methods that are different."

56

Hella

Tom was hunched over a microscope, peering at what looked like a piece of fabric.

"Looking for moths?"

The feet of his chair scraped against the floor. "Jesus, Hella, can you wear heels or something, so that I can hear you coming? What if I knock the evidence over?"

"This is evidence?" I leaned in for a closer look. "Of what?"

"Of dinosaurs, I would say. Seriously, your pal Mustonen probably thinks I'm a palaeontologist. This bloodstain is *weeks* old. The guy must have had a nosebleed or something."

"How do you know?"

"Dried and decomposed blood reacts to luminol in a different way," Tom muttered. "The reaction lasts longer than for fresh blood, and the stains glow brighter."

"Oh. And whose scarf is this? Virtanen's? Was he wearing it when he died?" I closed my eyes, trying to remember. I was almost certain there had been no scarf.

"Yes and no," Tom said. He was bent over the microscope again. "Judging by the embroidery, it's his scarf all right, but he wasn't wearing it at the time he was shot. This scarf was found on a train platform, left behind by a mysterious stranger who kidnapped a girl matching your friend Anita's description."

"Where? When?"

"Shh," Tom said, pushing the microscope away. "Don't get all excited. All the king's horses and all the king's men are already looking into it."

"That's what I was afraid of. Can I ask you something?"

"You keep asking me things," Tom sighed. "But OK, go ahead."

I pointed at the body lying on the autopsy table, covered by a sheet. "What happened to him exactly, do you know?"

"You want the official version or the off-the-record one?"

"Off the record."

"I don't know." Tom glanced up at me. "Absolute truth, Hella. I'll write in the official version that this boy has residue on his right hand, compatible with firing one shot, and that he was consequently killed by two direct shots, one to the head, another to the torso, but that would be it. I don't know what happened in there. And you know what's worse? I don't *want* to know."

"OK. Can you listen to what I have to say without interrupting?"

Tom cocked his head to one side – *Do I ever?* – but, to my surprise, he did as he was told.

"What if Anita's attack was a coincidence?" I said. "And it threw me off the scent, made me blind to what was staring me in the face. Someone in a position of power. Someone who is above suspicion. Who has a lot to lose if his relationship with Nellie Ritvanen comes out. This person isn't a mass murderer, there's no compulsion in what he does, just the desire to cover his tracks. Probably he enjoys the risk too, thinks he's invincible. And let's imagine Steve was telling the truth when he said he'd never set foot in that brothel."

When I finished talking, Tom stood still for a long moment, his face drained of colour, his lips pursed.

"What do you think?" I prompted him when I couldn't bear the silence any longer.

"You're not mad," Tom said at last, not looking at me. "You're worse."

"How so?"

"Your actions are perfectly logical, it's only your conclusions that are wrong." Tom licked his lips, a quick, reptilian movement of the tongue. He turned towards the filing cabinet in the corner. "I mean, OK, it's possible he could have done it, he's the right height, and the weapon matches, but why take such a risk? That's the real question, Hella. Why would a man who's got everything to lose do a thing like that when he could just buy her off? And don't start on that gibberish about homicidal compulsions or some such psychological reason. The man's not mental." Tom stopped rummaging in the filing cabinet and turned to face me. "Answer me, Hella. Why would he do it?"

I looked at Tom's white, swollen, suddenly *old* face.

"I've been asking myself the same question, and there's only one answer that I can come up with. Because he thinks he can get away with it."

I didn't remember the journey home. It must have been quick – my wristwatch indicated it was 10.15 when I paused on the corner of my street. The roof of my house was white with snow, but the windows were as black as tar. A police car was stationed outside, its driver slumped in the front seat. I stepped back into the shadows and thanked my lucky stars that I had decided to find Tom before going home. I thought about what that police presence implied for me.

One thing was obvious: my apartment was out of bounds. Chances were someone was watching my office too, so I knew I'd have to do without a weapon. It wouldn't be the first time. Better to get moving before anyone spotted me lurking there in the shadows.

Ranta had told his colleagues where he was going – to a lake near Tuusula – and I decided I needed to start there. I threw one last glance at my own dark windows, trying to conjure an image of all the good times I had spent there with Steve, and then turned resolutely away. No time for feelings of any kind. Even my own uncertain future didn't bother me at that point.

The only thing that mattered was finding Anita. I had failed her on every front, but maybe it wasn't too late to bring her back. Over the last few days, and even though we had spent half of our time fighting, she had become one of my closest friends. And now I ran the risk of losing her.

PART III

The Abyss

57

Inspector Mustonen

July 1946

After just a few days at my father's house, I had settled into a nice, predictable routine. In the morning, those glancing in through the brightly lit kitchen window would have seen me enjoying my breakfast with Mrs Saari. It was an arrangement that suited us both: she supplied me with freshly baked bread and village gossip, I provided a jar of good coffee. Company, too. Her husband, the baker, started work at 5 a.m. She was lonely. Not horny lonely, she just wanted to talk, which suited me just fine. We'd sit together in her kitchen, sip our coffee, and the picture of my father's life would come together, filling me in on the last ten years I'd missed.

"I didn't know him very well," Mrs Saari said. "He kept to himself most of the time, but I heard so much about him. Such a good, upstanding citizen. Always in church. And you turn out to be an *inspector*. He must be so proud."

I shook my head, smiling. "I doubt it. He wanted me to be a lawyer. It didn't work out that way."

"Why did you choose detective, then?" Mrs Saari laughed. "You could have studied law. It's the same."

"No," I said. "Totally the opposite. Lawyers play with the truth, alter it in order to suit their goals. Our job is different. We serve justice. Besides, I like the danger, the adrenaline."

"You're an idealist," Mrs Saari sighed. "Until I met you, I always thought that young men joined the police because they wanted to be above the law."

"Maybe some of them," I admitted. "But not the majority. Not me, in any case."

After breakfast, I would help her wash the dishes, then I'd wish her a good day, although I knew it wouldn't be the last time I'd see her. Mrs Saari had a habit of popping up unannounced at the old man's house, and I had to keep that in mind. As for me, my days really started when I climbed the stairs leading up to my father's bedroom. The old man needed washing too. He hated it when I touched him, glared at me from under drooping eyelids, but once that was over he was clean and smelled nice, and Mrs Saari could tell everyone who would listen what a good son I was.

The rest of the day was spent reading. My father's favourite book: *Counsel to Parents on the Moral Education of Their Children*. I couldn't be sure whether his mental facilities had remained intact, so I read the book slowly, the words falling like stones into the dark and filthy waters of the old man's mind. The beautiful thing was, my father listened exactly like I had when I'd been a child: petrified. Every once in a while, when I paused, the old man would move his lips.

"What is it, Father?"

There would be no answer.

"That's what I thought," I would usually say. "It's not a book to discuss, it's a book to listen to, just like everything else. Remember this? *A mighty power which fathers hold in trust for the future of their children is the character of the legislation which they establish or sanction.* Beautiful, huh?" I'd lean over to rearrange the blanket, breathing in my father's scent – pine resin, incense and moss – and my childhood would lunge at me. I'd hide behind the book: "*It is too frequently the case that the father, absorbed in outdoor pursuits, regards the indoor life as exclusively the business of his wife, and takes little or no part in the education of his children.* That wasn't you, no. When Mother ran away with that circus guy, you took care of our education. For as long as I can remember, you were there."

I stopped before we got to the chapter on purity. I lit a cigarette and tried to imagine what my five sisters had become. If I met one of them on the street, would I even recognize her? It had been too long, and we'd never been close. My last contact had been with Anna, who was a year older than me. She had got married the previous year, to a civil servant from Rovaniemi. I had sent her a gift: a porcelain teapot with a set of matching cups, and in return I had received a thank you note but no invitation to come and visit. It didn't matter; I hoped she was happy.

"Did you carry on swimming in ice water, Father?"

A moan.

"Did you? I'll ask Mrs Saari. If you were in better shape, we could have gone swimming together. Remember when you told me that one day I would enjoy it? That what doesn't kill us makes us stronger? You were right. I love it now, never miss a day. You'd be proud of me, living like one of the characters from this book. It was tough, but I learned how to do it. All thanks to you."

My father's eyes darted towards the book, panicky, pleading.

"I wonder if the girls still dream of their childhood at night," I said, "or whether they've managed to push it to the back of their minds? The rules, the fasting, the interdiction against looking in the mirror – *Vanity, saith the preacher* – the endless sermons. Was there some warped love in this, or just the desire for your daughters to grow up as different from their mother as possible? And are you satisfied with the result? Don't you want to dictate a letter to your daughters? I can write. No? Well, where were we? Oh yes. Purity."

I resumed my reading: "*The wilful ignoring of right and wrong in sex; the theory that it is a subject not to be considered; the custom of allowing riches, talents or agreeable manners to atone for any amount of moral corruption. The purest family contends with difficulty against this general corruption.*

"You know what?" I said suddenly. "I just thought of something. To make your life better." I ran down the stairs and out of the house, knocked on Mrs Saari's door. She was doing laundry. When she opened it, her shirtsleeves were rolled up to her elbows and bubbles of soap clung to her skin.

"Can I cut some flowers?" I asked her. "I think my father would enjoy looking at them."

"Of course!" Mrs Saari said. "What a wonderful idea! I should have thought of it myself."

She gave me a pair of very sharp scissors and pointed to a well-tended flower bed. "Help yourself. Do you know what sort of flowers he likes?"

"Daisies."

"Well, I've got plenty. You can take as many as you like!" She smiled again and disappeared back inside the house while I went to work, clipping the long stems at ground level in order to keep them suitable for my purpose.

When I'd had enough, I left the scissors on the porch and went back to my father's room. The old man started blinking, fast, when he saw me. "I thought at first I'd put these in a vase," I said, "but you don't have one. I'll make you a garland instead." My father's lips moved and I leaned closer. "I can't hear you." A single fat tear rolled down his cheek. I started work on the garland, humming to myself. It had been an eternity since I had made one, and it came out clumsy, flowers sticking out every which way.

"La!" the old man whispered, his eyes on the daisies.

"Lara! Are you trying to say *Lara?* So you remember her?" There was no answer, but then I hadn't expected one. Still humming, I tied the last knot, inspected the garland. Not perfect, but it would have to do. I placed it carefully on my father's head and smiled. "Do you know that I'll miss you? As long as you're alive, I know where the evil is. But shh…" I took the old man's parched hand in both of mine. "You don't have much time left, so let's both think about Lara, the village prostitute. How she thought it would be fun to initiate the fifteen-year-old me. How she needed to be puri-fied. Try also to remember how she begged you to spare her. Her exact words would be best."

My father died that very same day, while I was reading the book to him. One moment the old man was there, his breathing fast and shallow, a touch of foam at the corner of his mouth. When I looked again, he was gone.

58

Hella

The hole Ranta had drilled in the ice looked like a dark mirror. I leaned over, glanced at my reflection: a stranger was staring back at me, a wide-eyed girl with unruly hair, her mouth set in a grim line.

"Aren't you afraid I'll push you into the water?" Ranta said. His voice was tuneless, barely audible. As if he was speaking to himself. As if he had forgotten I was there.

The reflection in the dark water quivered, breaking the spell.

"I'm sorry," I said. "I already told you I was sorry. But I would never have suspected him if I hadn't suspected you first. Only then did I become open to the idea that anything was possible and that the clothes don't make the man. We can dwell on it all we like, or we can focus on what really matters."

"If she's already dead, nothing really matters any more." Ranta searched for bait in the tin open at his feet, picked up something red and sparkly, slid it just above the hook.

I stared at him. I'd been expecting a stronger reaction. I had thought he would scream, call me a liar, *do* something. Instead, he just sat there on his overturned bucket.

"What about justice?"

"That's just a pretty word. Besides, what kind of justice do you really expect? No one will ever believe you. Us." Ranta shrugged, stretched out a hand, and the fishing line went into the water. A tear slid down his cheek, the first sign of emotion.

"I saw the photographs in your room," I said. "That's how I knew. Even though I barely recognized you."

"Do you mean to say I was a handsome young man?"

"Yes." I didn't ask what had happened to him; it didn't matter. "Why did you lie? All those years, you pretended to – How could you live like that?"

"It was to protect Edith. Anita's mother. My dead uncle's wife. People … people were talking, but as Anita was born nine months exactly after Edith's husband died – he fell off a ledge – we thought it better if everyone assumed Anita was his child." Ranta drew on the line, swirling it through the dark oily water. The bait caught the moonlight, shining like a tiny flicker of fire. I wondered if the fish were stupid enough to think that sparkly thing was real.

"Anita knew, of course," Ranta said, still not looking at me. "We told her when she was old enough. It was only in the eyes of other people that we were cousins. It started out like that, but I don't remember why we kept it up after Edith was gone."

I think I knew why. When her mother had passed away, Anita was an adult already, and Ranta had grown old and unattractive. She didn't want to be associated with him more than necessary. She was probably thinking about her reputation. The lie was convenient, and there was only one person in the world who knew things for what they were – and he could be easily persuaded to keep his mouth shut.

"I would never have guessed," I said. "But the photographs didn't look like stalker material. More like a proud dad. Were you the one who scared her near the brothel?"

"She was the one who scared herself. I saw her standing there in that ridiculous dress and I made a move towards her, but it was dark and she panicked and ran before I could stop her. I wanted to go after her, but then I saw her talking with Jokela and Mustonen and I thought maybe it would do her good to be scared a bit. I never approved of her becoming an inspector, but you know how children are, they never listen. And I suppose at some point she understood it was me, but by then it was too late, and she was probably enjoying playing a damsel in distress and being saved by Inspector Mustonen."

"That's what I thought. You never touched her. And she did look shifty about it."

"Yeah," Ranta said. "Well." His voice quivered. "Are you certain of what you just told me?"

"I am."

"When you gaze long into the abyss, the abyss gazes also into you? Ever read Nietzsche?"

"Yes."

"Then you had better stay as far away from this as possible. Travel somewhere." He glanced up at me. "You can still visit those friends of yours, over in Lapland. They seem like nice enough people."

"What about you?" I said, and then it dawned on me. All this lack of reaction, this resignation: it was just a facade. It was exactly how Ranta always acted – in the shadows. Biding his time. And if Anita had been hurt, it was not justice he wanted, it was revenge.

"It would be easier for you if I was out of the way, right? If no accusations were made, if you could approach Anita's kidnapper unsuspected?"

Ranta's hand froze above the hole in the ice. His knuckles, clutching the fishing rod, were white.

"Because I can't let you do that. Call me an idealist, but I want the truth to be known. Besides, there's the small matter of Ahti Virtanen."

"Not my business —" Ranta began.

I cut him off. "I'm not going to Lapland." I got to my feet. Around me, the pristine surface of the frozen lake looked like it was covered in muslin. "I'm going to stay here and fight that bastard. Now, you can keep on fishing if you've got nothing better to do. Or you can come with me."

For a moment I thought I had lost him. Ranta kept staring into the dark hole, his face expressing nothing at all. Slowly, he pulled the line towards him. A little silver fish was twitching at its end. Ranta unhooked it gently and sent it back into the water. Then he got up and brushed the snow off his knees.

"Right. Then I'm with you. Where are we going?"

"Ahti Virtanen's summer cabin," I said. "Unless you've got a better idea."

59

Chief Inspector Mustonen

"I really don't understand," Pinchus drawled, "why you're not asking for a warrant to search Virtanen's summer cabin. It's only a mile from that train station." He locked his bony fingers under his chin, staring at me with sad, reproachful eyes.

"We have no evidence yet that Virtanen was involved in Anita's disappearance," I explained patiently. "Jokela is already breathing fire. So is Virtanen senior. You want to go and tell them we're accusing the boy of kidnapping a police officer? And that the only evidence we have is some old bird – who, by the way, didn't even recognize Virtanen in that photograph – and a scarf found lying on a train platform? *So what?* they would say." I mimicked Jokela's angry rant: "*Are we even sure it's his scarf?*"

Pinchus seemed unconvinced, but then I'd always suspected the man of being smarter than he looked. I added quickly: "Once we can prove that Anita is missing, and the stains on the scarf are blood, we'll definitely ask for a search warrant."

"I suppose." The inspector stretched and yawned, but his eyes remained alert, watchful. "Are you going home?"

"There's nothing else we can do here, is there? All the detectives have come back empty-handed. And God only knows when Räikkönen will get around to analysing the evidence."

I picked up my coat, held the door open for Pinchus.

"See you tomorrow morning?"

He nodded. I could almost see the little wheels turning inside his head. "You want to share a taxi?" he asked. Pinchus lived somewhere in the general direction of my house, but still, the request seemed strange. Or maybe I was getting paranoid.

"No thanks. I'll walk a little. Clear my thoughts."

Before he could add anything, I started down the deserted street. As I walked, I counted on my fingers what still needed to be done.

First, recover Anita's body.

Second, dump it in the lake next to Virtanen's summer cabin.

Third, hurry back home and slide into bed next to Sofia.

60

Hella

Walking on the frozen lake was hard, and I had to hold onto Ranta's arm to keep from slipping on the ice and falling.

"How did you figure it out?" he asked me.

"It's because he executed that boy, Ahti. When he brought me over to Virtanen's place and ten minutes later the boy was dead, it made me wonder. Mustonen is an experienced officer. And when I checked with Tom Räikkönen, I got the impression that maybe Mustonen had shot first then placed the gun in the boy's hand."

I glanced at Ranta, not certain if he had understood. "That's when I started thinking about the reasons Mustonen might have for doing away with the boy. Because he knew Ahti was a killer but he couldn't prove it? That didn't seem like Mustonen. To advance his career? Much too risky. And then I thought, what if the boy was a scapegoat too, just like Steve? And what if Anita had spotted something while she was on the squad, and that was the reason she had gone missing? And there was another thing: there's the word *filth* in Klara Nylund's notes. I thought it meant poor hygiene.

But it wasn't that, it meant a corrupt cop. I should have thought of that sooner."

"The dirty one," Ranta muttered, shaking his head. He didn't say anything more until we reached his car, a dark-green Volvo that had seen better days. Ranta got in first, then slid across to open the door for me. "What's the address?"

"Koskitie Road," I said, and then paused. "No, it doesn't add up. Mustonen told me that Ahti's parents were entertaining guests at their country place. He couldn't have taken Anita there."

Ranta drummed on the steering wheel with his gnarled fingers. "What if he lied?"

"Because you think he's that good? A double bluff?"

"Why not?"

"No. It must be a different place. He could have borrowed one of the squad cars. What if —"

"What if Anita's in the car?" Ranta said flatly. He hadn't started the engine yet. He was staring ahead at the snow-covered road and the narrow tree branches that were swaying in the breeze. "I don't think he would dare. He must have driven it back to Headquarters. Would he really be driving around with a … with Anita?" His voice caught.

"No. He wouldn't do that."

"And he couldn't have just dumped her into the lake in broad daylight. Then there must be a different place. Mustonen is the sort of guy to have a backup plan. Someone to take the blame if things don't work out as expected." Ranta swivelled on his seat towards me. "Did you tell him you suspected me?"

"What?"

"Did you?"

I nodded miserably. "I did tell him, yes."

"Then I know where she might be." Ranta released the handbrake and put the car into gear. "Just pray that this damned thing doesn't skid on the ice."

We didn't say a word to each other, Ranta and I, until we reached our destination. He kept leaning forward, his knuckles white on the steering wheel. I glanced at him once or twice, wondering what was on his mind, but his face gave nothing away and I knew better than to ask. So I stared ahead at the white ribbon of the road and the tree branches laden with snow. The right headlight of the car blinked on and off, and the images flashed before my eyes like something out of a kaleidoscope, stark black and white, here and then gone.

For the first time in my life, I realized that my parents had been the lucky ones. They had never known that they had lost their daughter and only grandson. They had never known they had lost each other. The truck careering out of control had swept them up all together, swallowed their lives whole. Maybe Father Timo was right and they were in heaven together. But – and I only thought of it then – even if Timo was wrong, if there was no heaven, no hell, no purgatory, it didn't matter all that much, because my family was still together: my parents, Christina, and Matti, who would be four years old forever. I was the one who had been left behind. Mourning, grieving, my life a despicable mess. Would I have felt better if the truck driver had been apprehended, brought to justice? I doubted it. No amount of punishment, no pleas for pardon could bring my family back. I could understand Ranta's train of thought – but only up to a point. Anita was only one of Mustonen's victims. In a little village close to the polar circle, a family was hoping for justice for their daughter. There was Nellie's son, Ahti's parents. They all deserved to know what had happened. Mustonen had to be brought to trial. Otherwise the victim's families could never be sure.

The car swerved right, bounced down an icy, overgrown track. Ranta pointed: broken branches, tyre marks in the snow. Another car had passed there recently. The falling snow had almost covered the tracks; almost, but not quite.

"Where are we?"

"My summer cabin. You've turned me into the perfect suspect, so Mustonen must have brought Anita here. If she's found before he has the time to tidy up after himself, everything will point to me. But even if she isn't, this is a good hiding place, not too far from the Virtanens' cabin."

I didn't believe him. I didn't *want* to believe him. I grabbed my flashlight and jumped out of the car, sinking ankle-deep in soft translucent snow, and ran towards the tiny cabin painted a fiery red. The tyre marks stopped maybe five yards from the porch. From there towards the door, the snow was trampled. Someone had dragged a heavy burden behind them. I flung open the unlocked door.

In the middle of the room there was a big canvas sack, the sort they use to store potatoes in. Something red peeked out of it: Anita's crimson suede pumps, one of the heels broken. I rushed towards the body in the bag, fumbled for a pulse. Dead. She was dead.

Behind me, Ranta let out a long shaky breath.

61

Chief Inspector Mustonen

Once, when I was eight or nine years old, my father took me to a small village outside Tampere. We went there to attend the funeral of a young girl, a distant relation of our family. As we climbed into the horse-drawn carriage, I finally summoned up the courage to ask my father what had happened to her.

"She was from your mother's side," came the laconic answer. I waited. Even at that young age, I knew that insisting on an answer, however politely, would accomplish nothing at best and probably get me punished. My father would tell me what had happened to the girl if he wanted to. Which he did, half an hour later, once we found ourselves in the middle of a snowy field, our carriage the only spot of colour in the sad, inexpressive universe. "She burned to death," my father said. "She was helping with dinner and her dress caught fire." He shrugged. "Some fancy dress. These people think very highly of themselves."

My father's eyebrows were spiked with snow crystals but his mouth quivered, red and moist as he spoke. "They bought her a wedding dress to wear in the coffin." He laughed harshly. "Can you imagine a burned girl, Erik, her skin charred like coal, wearing a white dress? I suppose they think it would make her a fiancée of Our Lord."

"Well, it would," I said, "if she died a virgin." Virginity was a frequent topic of conversation around the dinner table.

"No," my father said, in a slow, careful tone I knew only too well. "Think about it, Erik. Her skin burned away. Even between her legs." He bent closer to me, his breath smelling like vinegar. "Could she still be a virgin?"

I swallowed, hard. I didn't want to imagine what the girl looked like, but now that was all I could see: a charred stump of a body covered with lace. "Um, no?"

My father cracked the whip and the horse jerked forward, its hooves slipping on the snow. "No," he said quietly. "*No.* It's blasphemy, Erik. That's why only you and I are going to the funeral. I don't want your sisters exposed to this, because women are not capable of understanding. Now, if that poor child had drowned" – he paused, his voice dropping to a murmur – "it would have been much, much better. They could have dressed her in a wedding dress with a veil, she'd be a tiny fiancée of Our Lord, all would have been well." My father glanced sideways at me, to make sure I understood.

"Yes," I whispered, because that's what was expected of me. My father nodded with an encouraging smile, so I continued: "Yes, death by water would have been better for her."

"For everyone," my father said. "This is what Our Lord does when he wants to show mercy. It's like a second baptism." He turned away, satisfied with my obedience, and I could lift my eyes to the sky and let the snowflakes land on my lashes.

That word – *mercy* – kept resonating in my ears for years to come. I choked on it when Lara drowned. And it was there, on the tip of my tongue, when Nellie stopped thrashing in the water and looked at me one last time. I knew, of course, that mercy had nothing to do with it. I was not like my father; I didn't kill for purity, I didn't kill for pleasure. I only killed because I had to. It wasn't my fault that harlot threw herself at me, saw me as a means to change her life when all I wanted was a little distraction on the side. If Sofia hadn't been exhausted by her pregnancy, none of this would have happened. Just like nothing would have happened if I'd had enough money to pay her off, like I wanted to. But I couldn't change the past, and my family was more important than anything. I needed to hide my infidelity from Sofia – I could never risk her running out on me and Arne. The rest didn't matter; Nellie had been expendable. I had looked at Nellie, but all I could see was a lace wedding dress, and the charred remains within. That, and Lara's face under the ice, her blue eyes frozen solid.

I thought about this as I walked down the street, heavy wet snow clinging to the soles of my shoes. Was Pinchus watching me go? I didn't look back; instead, I turned left at the first intersection. Two minutes later, I was standing in front of the squad surveillance post, looking at all the parked cars around me.

62

Chief Inspector Mustonen

"Chief Inspector." The elderly guard stretched, his eyes flicking up at me from the dirty magazine he hadn't bothered to hide. "Working late?"

"Yes," I said and sighed. I hesitated to add: *Virtanen case.* Or: *I've got a witness to interview,* decided against it. Never say more than you need to: all successful liars know that. "Awful weather," I said instead.

The guard nodded but didn't look up as I picked up the keys to the white Studebaker parked near the exit. It was the car I took whenever I could, my pale horse. It was fitting: *and his name that sat on him was Death, and Hell followed with him.* Some things stay with you, however much you want to shed them. Maybe people were right when they said there was no escaping your childhood.

The fresh snow crunched under the studded tyres. The streets were empty but I drove just below the speed limit, glancing repeatedly in my rear-view mirror. Twenty minutes to get out of the city. Another hour to the countryside, to Ranta's pathetic little cabin where I had hidden Anita's body. Twenty minutes to the lake, then an hour to get back.

I knew Sofia might be a problem. The bump bothered her, it pressed on her bladder, she got up three, four, five times every night. My wife would know I wasn't in bed next to her. Whether she'd tell anyone was a different matter.

I stretched and yawned. I knew I should probably be scared, but I seldom felt fear or apprehension. Besides, the situation was under control. I was only going to Ranta's cabin because I was a professional; loose ends made my skin crawl. It was not enough to be good, to be credible: perfect was better. And the safety net I had taken such trouble to build *was* perfect. A masterpiece, really, all actions explained, all intentions noble.

By the time Nellie's body had been found, everyone on the squad knew I was on the lookout for a case to share with Interpol. This one had seemed as good as any – indeed, better than most, the port representing a possible international connection. And it was good for my image: I was a man who believed a prostitute's death merited as much attention as any other. No one had been surprised when I had taken the case. And I had started working on it seriously, carefully, like I would have done for any other file. Some days I surprised myself by actually looking for suspects or wondering if it really had been murder, if Nellie could have accidentally drowned. I could no longer distinguish my own lies from the truth.

When Jokela called me into his office and told me he'd recommended that Klara Nylund contact Mauzer, I wasn't worried. Amused, yes. I knew that Mauzer was good, but I also knew her weakness: Steve Collins. A perfect scapegoat. I had heard his name in connection with the Matilda Reims case, I knew that might come in useful – and it did.

And then, the next day, even better: I had found myself sitting in front of Ahti Virtanen's father as he sipped coffee, offering me his son on a plate. Two brilliant suspects, a steady source of revenue – Mauzer's boyfriend never missed a payment once he grasped what the risks were – and the chance to get rid of my corrupt boss, all in one go. Of course, there had been minor setbacks. Maria had been one, and the madam: they knew me, both of them, they could have talked. I stopped them just in time, bludgeoned the madam to death before going for a drink with Jokela, put the fear of God into Maria so she wouldn't talk. There was nothing to link me to the murders, I made sure of that, while for Ahti there was plenty: I had taken the tie and scarf from the wrecked car as I inspected it and had kept both on hand. For a final touch of perfection, I had added Steve Collins' name to the little black book while the madam was letting out her last breath in that dark back yard. It had been child's play – and Mauzer's imagination had taken care of the rest.

When Mauzer had written to tell me Ranta might be a suspect too, I had almost laughed out loud. So much for feminine intuition! Sofia was happy, my father-in-law was happy, the jeweller was labouring away on the brooch made from the dead girl's pathetic trinkets.

And suddenly: Anita.

Who would have thought? Certainly not me, who had filed her under the "stupid blonde" category, a decorative presence not worth giving a second thought. When the girl had started asking the first awkward questions about Ahti Virtanen or Matilda Reims, I thought she would never guess. Even when she saw Nellie's earrings in the jewellers – I had spotted her through the store window – and the drawing of the brooch on my desk, the ruby in the centre like a drop of blood, I still thought she wouldn't make the connection. Or, if she did, that her attention could be diverted. Interpol came in handy, once again. A trip to Paris. No woman in her right mind would have refused, certainly not a woman like Anita.

But she did.

And she had kept asking to see the file, with the groomed picture of Nellie, her earrings plain and visible and damning.

Jesus Christ. If Anita hadn't refused to go to Paris, all would have been well. Why had she? I'd never know now; it was just bad luck. I had laid the groundwork so well. I was ready. Ready to become that good person everyone imagined me to be. I didn't even know any more where the real Erik ended and the fake me, the better version, began. And that stupid blonde had to walk in and spoil everything.

How excited she'd been when she had unwrapped the flowers and pulled out the note. It was lunchtime; I had just come back into my office, leaving the door ajar, ostensibly working, Anita's desk in my line of vision. The girl had put her coat on as she ran down to the reception area to collect her flowers. She was still wearing it as she unwrapped the bouquet and froze, staring at the note, reading it once, twice, a dark crimson glow spreading over her high cheekbones. Her coat was cheap but pretending to be the real thing: only when you touched it could you feel the coarseness of the fabric, see that the buttons were plastic and not horn. Slowly, holding her breath, Anita had refolded the note and slid it into her pocket. Then, she took the coat off and hung it lovingly on a wire hanger, sneaking a glance in my direction. I made a show of frowning, of holding a page to the light. I thought of Virtanen's call the previous evening, the angry breathing down the line: "You must be out of your mind, Mustonen, to send your girl to spy on us. What did you think? That she could come back under false pretences and try to establish a rapport with my son?" I knew then that I had to act before Anita realized Ahti was not the real murderer and started looking elsewhere.

Deep in thought, I didn't notice I had left the city behind me; now my car's headlights were sweeping across the dark countryside. The road ahead of me was empty, as was the road behind. No moon, no stars, but the snow provided its own light, a sickening, bluish white. Soon it would be over and done with. Another case solved. A success to recount to Interpol. Jokela's office, Jokela's driver, the new house, another baby. I drove past the solitary pine tree and switched off my headlights. I parked the car in the shadow of a birch grove, next to Ranta's summer cabin. This is the last time, I thought. The risks were too high, it was not worth it. From now on, I would be faithful to Sofia. She wasn't a beauty, but she was a good spouse and she had class. In my new position, that was going to make all the difference.

63

Chief Inspector Mustonen

Twenty minutes later, having stowed Anita's body in the car, I parked next to the lake in Tuusula. It had stopped snowing and the moon was peeking out of its cloudy blanket, pouring blue light on the tall pine trees and the white expanse of the lake. For a short but blissful moment, I sat with my hands on the steering wheel, humming "Silent Night". My mother's favourite song. I was five when she had slipped out of the house one night, abandoning her husband and six children for a new life with a travelling circus. Had my father been unhinged before she ran away? Had my mother discovered something about him she couldn't bear? Now it was Sofia who sang the song to Arne before bed and sometimes, when I was home early, I joined in. But enough of that: it was too soon to relax just yet; now that I had picked up Anita's body from Ranta's summer cabin, I needed to finish the job. I turned off the ignition and got out of the car.

The air was cold and still and sweet, and for one surreal moment I was tempted to shed my clothes and slide under the ice with Anita in my arms. Cradle her as I swam, just as

I had cradled Lara's body. But the risks were too high – I had parked the car close to the lake, and passers-by might see it – so I gave myself a talking-to and pulled out the sack. The red pumps were sticking out; I pushed them down out of sight.

I was glad I had put Anita in the sack. I didn't want her blank fishy eyes staring back at me, and there was less risk of getting her hair and bodily fluids on my clothes, not that anyone would think to check. Now I carried the body towards the edge of the frozen lake. This was not the harbour in Helsinki, where the ice was forever thin because of the currents. To my practised eye, the ice at the edge of the lake was almost three feet deep. Still, finding a hole was not difficult. The Finns are a nation of ice-fishermen: there were dozens of holes on the lake. I looked carefully where I stepped. As I walked, Anita's body nestled on my shoulder, I decided that searching for it until spring came and the ice melted would represent an inefficient use of police resources; besides, the situation would lack closure. No, I needed to find a way to subtly direct the search to this very place. Should I ask Ahti's parents if the boy was on the lake often? If he liked skating? Ice-fishing?

Ten yards towards the centre of the lake, I found a nice large hole.

"Goodbye, Anita," I said softly. I crossed myself. Contrary to my father, who had never said a prayer for the ladies of pleasure, not even as he killed them in the name of his terrible God, I was not a monster. I had only killed Anita because I had to protect my family. There had been no pleasure in it. The least I could do was say a prayer for her. "*Eternal rest grant unto them, O Lord, and let perpetual light shine upon them.*" The words were familiar but something seemed off, though I couldn't quite place it at first. "*May they rest in peace...*" Suddenly, I became conscious of shadows moving on the shore, sliding up to my car in the darkness.

And then, worse, other shadows began to advance across the ice.

64

Chief Inspector Mustonen

I froze. Looked down at the red shoes spiked with dirt, glanced again towards the shore. In the moonlight I could just make out one of the shadows crouching next to my car, pointing a gun at me. Whoever they were, they were good. They had followed me to the lake, and I hadn't noticed. They must have called for backup, too.

I only had two options, and not much time to make a decision.

Option one was to surrender.

Unless the jeweller came forward, there was nothing to link me to Nellie's drowning, nor to the madam's murder. I could say that Jokela had forced me to get rid of Anita because the girl had discovered the cover-up. True, I'd exposed the cover-up already and Jokela was at that moment sitting in an interview room, waiting for his impending arrest, but I could be very convincing. I almost convinced myself.

I glanced at the hole at my feet, at the thin skin of ice that had formed on its surface. At the shadows drawing closer to me. One of them was Mauzer. The other one was hunchbacked and bow-legged. Ranta.

Option two was to get even.

I didn't know what would happen to me if I did. If one of my pursuers would open fire; if I'd be shot while trying to flee to the other side of the lake. The men on the shore hadn't brought dogs, I noticed, so unless I was shot, I had a good chance of getting away. A very good chance.

"It's over, Erik." Mauzer, stopping a few feet from me, an old pistol in hand. Ranta was to her left, taking aim.

I grinned. "Who *are* these people on the shore? Wilderness protection officers? Do they even know how to shoot?"

"I do," Mauzer said, "and I will."

I grinned again. "And lose your only chance to discover what happened to your family?"

"Put Anita's body on the ice, and your hands up."

I did as I was told, shifting so Ranta stood between me and the men on the shore. "Aren't you even interested? We can chat about that while you drive me back to Helsinki."

"My family was killed in a car accident." Mauzer pulled handcuffs out of her pocket. "On your knees, slowly, your hands behind your back."

Again, I did as I was told. But I kept speaking. "There's a file at Headquarters with your name on it. Classified Top Secret. I had a look."

Still pointing the gun at my head, Mauzer leaned closer. Ranta, like all sentimental people, could easily be stopped. If my plan worked out, he wouldn't go after me. And the wilderness protection officers? Them, I could manage. I turned ever so slightly, braced myself. A cuff clicked around my left wrist.

"And in that file, it says the truck that killed your family was driven by —"

I whipped round, knocking the pistol out of Mauzer's hand.

And then I pushed her into the hole.

65

Hella

It felt like falling into fire.

I clamped my mouth shut, fighting hard not to gasp. Through the roaring noise in my ears, I heard Tom's voice: *Whatever you do, don't gasp. Your only chance.*

My boots were dragging me down. I kicked them off. Tried to orient myself. Milky twilight all around me, like being lost in a dream; I could see no way out. And then, at the edge of my vision, a darker spot.

Could be a hallucination.

Could be a sign I was losing consciousness.

The pain in my limbs was unbearable, millions of tiny needles sticking into my flesh. I lunged for the dark spot and prayed it was the hole through which I had fallen. I couldn't hold my breath any longer. My body craved oxygen; it was refusing to take orders from my brain.

When I saw my nephew's face smiling at me from the darkness, I knew that it was over. I hoped it was. I couldn't take the pain any longer.

With one last, spasmodic movement, I propelled myself under the water. My focus was on Matti's face. I took a deep breath. Icy water rushed into my nose, my throat, my lungs. I wanted to say goodbye, but my lips refused to move.

After that, nothing.

Darkness.

EPILOGUE

Chief Inspector Jokela

"I'm sure you all understand," Chief Inspector Jokela said, "that this was not your run-of-the-mill investigation. What that means is two things. One, the identities of those involved need to be protected. Two, only some of your questions can be answered."

He observed the motley crew of reporters sitting before him. The police were in luck; on the other side of the border, in the Soviet Union, Comrade Joseph Stalin had finally kicked the bucket. Speculation ran wild as to who would be chosen as his successor – Stalin's deputy Georgy Malenkov, the genial Nikita Khrushchev or the terrifying secret police executioner Lavrentiy Beria. That was good. The Harbour Murders would not make the front pages, and the reporters attending the conference were not the cream of the crop either. Still, all the major dailies were present, their representatives alert and dapper, whispering to each other like excited schoolchildren. A stern-looking man from the BBC, sitting front row with his arms folded. An unkempt woman – a woman! – from some left-wing rag Jokela had never even heard of. A tall blonde man in the corner, looking a sickly shade of pale, hands deep in his pockets. So, Mr Collins had come as well. No big surprise. Even though only a small amount of information had been released to the press, this was still a major event.

Jokela smiled a measured smile. "You can start with your questions."

The man from the BBC lifted his hand, but the representative of *Helsingin Sanomat* was quicker. "Chief Inspector," he said in a high falsetto voice, "let me see if I've got this straight." He glanced at his notes. "Over the course of the last week, the Helsinki homicide squad conducted a covert operation to identify the notorious criminal known as the Harbour Killer. The victims were three prostitutes and a young man interviewed as a witness. In the course of the operation, a member of the homicide squad lost his life."

"Her life," corrected Jokela. A glance at the BBC representative. "You must know that the Helsinki police force is among the most progressive in the world. We have been employing women since the 1920s. And in 1948, I personally hired our first ever female detective."

"Was she the one who was murdered?" chipped in the unkempt radical in the flowered skirt, her eyes round like saucers.

"No, madam," Jokela responded gravely. "We have more than one female murder detective. So no, she wasn't the victim."

The *Helsingin Sanomat* representative coughed politely to remind them he was still there, waiting to go on with his summary of events. Jokela nodded. "Yes?"

"You also mentioned that the Harbour Killer has been apprehended. Is the man behind bars?"

"No," Jokela said. "The perpetrator of these horrible crimes refused to surrender and was shot by police officers."

"Dead?" the reporter insisted, pen poised above his notebook.

Jokela chewed on his lip. Dr Palmu had been vague about it. *The less they know, the better*, he had said. *But make sure they leave convinced we are on top of the situation.* Easier said than done. Would they swallow his lie? He said in a firm voice: "The suspect was gravely wounded. He fell through the ice. You don't expect anyone to survive an ice dip with a bullet in his body, do you?"

The reporter opened his mouth to ask another question, but Jokela was already pointing at his neighbour, a large man in his fifties. "Your turn, I believe."

The reporter smiled gratefully, but what flowed from his mouth was pure poison. "There's talk," he said, "that the suspect your people shot was himself a member of the police force."

"Utter nonsense," Jokela snapped. He wanted to wipe the sweat that was trickling down his forehead but didn't dare. "Next question!"

The BBC representative said stiffly: "It has come to my attention that a young woman who was not a member of the police force was also involved in the investigation" – he paused for dramatic effect – "as bait."

"That's conjecture," Jokela said, frowning to show that he had expected better from such a reputable news source. "Any other questions?"

The left-wing radical opened her big, sagging mouth. "I just arrived from the tiny village of Väinölä," she started, and Jokela felt his bowels loosen. "A number of people there report having seen a wounded man stumbling through the streets at dawn. Does this have anything to do with the investigation?"

"That," Jokela said, "is one of the questions I cannot answer." The left-wing radical wrote it down. "I can take one last question," Jokela called.

Steve Collins, who had remained silent and still throughout the interview, detached himself from the wall. "I have heard rumours," he said, as the murmurs died down, "that Dr Palmu will be retiring at the end of the month. Could you please tell us who will be replacing him?"

Jokela had the good grace to blush. "I am," he said. "I have this honour. Thanks, in large part, to the success of the operation we have just discussed." He lay his palms flat on the desk in front of him to stop them from trembling. God, he needed a drink. "Ladies and gentlemen, the press conference is now over. Thank you for your time." The reporters stirred and started shuffling towards the exit; only Collins remained standing there, an eyebrow arched, a cryptic smile on his handsome face. Jokela pulled a handkerchief out of his pocket and wiped his brow. "Thank you to all of you. Have a good day."

Hella

They said that when I first learned of my family's death, I fainted. I couldn't remember that at all. What I remembered, though, was the week that followed. The doctors injected me with sedatives, and I spent the time drifting in and out of heavy, empty sleep, waking up to a soaked pillow with no memory of having cried. That's what I felt like when I came to in the hospital. The dark was pulling me in and under and away. Then, when I least expected it, it would spit me out. An ice-tide.

Some days when I woke, Steve was sitting next to my bed. I wanted to tell him to go away, but I knew that if he realized I was conscious, he would insist on talking to me, and I wouldn't be able to stand that. Some days it was Tom, or Ranta, his face pale and pinched, his eyes hollow. He was the one who fished me out, they've told me. On other days, Elsbeth was there beside me, holding my hand. Her I was happy to see. She made me think of Anita, with her milky skin and her snub nose and her dimples. Once – but maybe it was only a dream – there was a girl sitting next to her, a tall awkward child who had her mother's smile. And then a day came when I opened my eyes and saw Irja leaning over me. There was a tiny baby in her arms. My god-daughter, Margarita. "As soon as you're well enough to travel," Irja said, "I'll be taking you home. To Käärmelä."

ACKNOWLEDGEMENTS

I owe thanks to so many.

My agent, Marilia Savvides, who had faith in me long before I had faith in myself.

My editor, François von Hurter, for working tirelessly (and tactfully) to make the book stronger. I feel so lucky to have found you. My deep gratitude also goes to Laurence Colchester and the team at Bitter Lemon Press.

The amazing international rights team at Peters Fraser + Dunlop: Rebecca Wearmouth, Laura Otal and Silvia Molteni.

Sarah Terry, for taking a poorly formatted Word document and turning it into a book, and for being such fun to work with.

To Eleanor Rose for the cover design.

To my first readers, Tamrin Ann Lever, Lisa Marie Knoll and Gabrielle Kremers; to Erin Ruth Carter for spotting the gloves issue, and so much more.

To Leo Kostiainen from Statistics Finland for his invaluable help in figuring out what a police sergeant was paid in the 1950s, and for providing myriad other details that supported my quest for authenticity.

To Maritta Jokiniemi, curator of the National Police Museum, Tampere, Finland, for the Browning.

And finally, heartfelt thanks to my wonderful family, for all their encouragement and for giving me space to write. This book wouldn't exist without your support.